CHILDREN OF THE LOCOMOTIVE

MITCHELL TIERNEY

CHILDREN OF THE LOCOMOTIVE

MITCHELL TIERNEY

Children of the Locomotive

Published by Ouroborus Book Services
www.ouroborusbooks.com

Cover Design by Sabrina RG Raven
www.sabrinargraven.com

Birthing of a dark figure
Bold and dripping with blood
A red hand reaches outwards
Death is coming

THE MAN WITH THE RAM'S HEAD

'Jesus, when he appeared to me, he wasn't a man. He had a ram's head and wings on his back. The tips of his feathers where dripping with blood and he told me who had done it and then he pointed west.'

'When did this happen?'

'One month ago. I was out shooting. I had my shotgun and a bottle in my belt. I had slept across from the old bridge, down by Cicada Mountain. I'd caught a rabbit and ate it that night. I watched other shooters come by. They didn't see me.'

'You didn't make yourself known to them? They could have shot you by mistake.'

'No, they wouldn't have. I can hide good. Ain't no one gonna see me. I've been out in the woods most of my life. Ain't no one can find me.'

'The shooters went past you?'

'Hmm mmm, yes. I tracked them for half a day. Watching them hunt deer, no good. They didn't know their ass from their elbow. They didn't know what they were doin'.'

'Did you continue to follow them?'

'Not for long. I was far behind them and stopped when they stopped. They set up camp and a fire. Animals will hear and smell that and won't come in close. I didn't care though. I was more interested in what they were doing.'

'And what were they doing?'

'They cooked in a pot. Threw the cans out into the

woods. They drank nearly half a case of beer and waved their guns around like they were cowboys. I sat on top of this rocky outcrop and leaned on a tree and listened to them.'

'Did they talk about killing the boy?'

'They talked about killing a lot of people.'

'But did they talk about the boy?'

'Yes, the boy. He was slow and easy, and he bled a lot. That's what they said.'

'Did they say when they did it? Or where?'

'In the woods. They didn't say when. They spoke of the sound he made when he died. A gurgling; like some beast was trying to escape through his mouth.'

'What else did they say?'

'The knife they used on the boy is the same one they used to kill the deer and the rabbits. They said his blood was still on it.'

'Now, tell me about the man with the ram's head.'

'It was no man. It was the first man and he will be the last man. Jesus reincarnated.'

'Where did you see him?'

'I see him in my dreams and sometimes I see him walking in the darkness. Sometimes at the truck stop parking lot, hiding between the carriages. He walks into the forest and comes back; his hands bleed and he points.'

'You said he pointed west? What is the significance of west?'

'The sun sets in the west, the animals come out at sunset. He shows me where things are.'

'And you follow him?'

'Yes, Sir.'

'Are you on medication?'

'I used to be. When I lived near the old service road, across from the fire station.'

'Fenwick house?'

'What?'

'Did you live at Fenwick house?'

'Yes.'

'How long ago?'

'Until it closed. I was there three years, maybe four.'

'Then where did you go?'

'I went to my aunt's in Fountain. She has two trailers there. She let me stay in one for free until I got a job at the saw mill.'

'How long was that.'

'I left… say, three months ago? I couldn't stand it there no more.'

'Why not?'

'A lot of drugs there. Dealings and stolen cars. Cops were always there, looking at my guns. Went to jail once.'

'Possession?'

'Unlicensed firearms. They took them all.'

'If I look this up at the station and you're lying to me, I'll have you arrested… Now, if I took you to the woods, could you show me where they buried him?'

'Well, I don't know. I heard them talking about the trees that had fallen, the big one they buried him under. I could show you where I think he is buried. But, I don't wanna see no dead body. I've seen enough of them in my life.'

—

The cabin was dark and cold, and the radio came on briefly,

searching for a signal. Static and hissing, then it was turned off.

—

'Here.'

'Under this tree here?'

'Yeah, that's where they said.'

'Show me.'

'I can't show you, I don't know where they buried him!'

'Start digging... over there, move those sticks and dig up that dirt.'

'I ain't digging up no dirt... What's this shit?'

'Do it. *Now.*'

'You gonna shoot me? You bring me out here and make me dig up some retard kid's grave and pull a gun on me, dammit. If I had my guns on me...'

'What? You would shoot a police officer?'

'I'll dig. You think you're a big man now. You know that? A big man with a gun, tricking people.'

'I think you killed the kid.'

'Me? I don't know a damn thing about no fucking kid. I ain't ever spoken to him in my damn life. I seen him around now and then, seen him buy records. I don't care about that, so why would I shoot him?'

'Dig faster, it'll be getting too dark to see soon.'

'Already too damn dark to see... Here, what's this shit?'

'What is it? Turn it over. Use your hands, not the shovel.'

'I ain't touching it.'

'Unless you want to join him by his side, you'll turn it over.'

'Shit! God damn shit! Is that him?'

'You tell me? Is that the kid you saw buying records?'

'I'm gonna be sick... It looks like him... Face is all fucked. I can't tell, I think so. I'm gonna be damn sick.'

'Cover it back up.'

'Ain't you gonna get someone out here to dig him up proper?'

'Who?'

'I don't know? Another sheriff? Someone from the morgue?'

'They ain't coming up here for some kid been dead this long'.

'I ain't covering him back up. That's fucked up man. I ain't doing it.'

'Lay down beside him.'

'What?'

'You heard. Lay down beside him.'

'What? I ain't getting down there. I'll do whatever, but I ain't getting down there.'

'I'll put a bullet through your skull, and you'll fall down beside him, or... you can choose where you lay. Wouldn't that be better? Wouldn't you want to choose where you lay?'

'I don't want to lay down. Why are you gonna kill me? I did what I was told.'

'Crying ain't gonna get you outta here, so choose the spot.'

'I don't wanna die, man. I just... I just... I showed you where they said! I didn't do this, man. I didn't do this.'

'You may as well have.'

'No. Why?'

'How many months now? You could have come and told

me about this. Instead, you wait til I hear about it and have to come find you?'

'I didn't wanna get in trouble.'

'Well you're in trouble now, so lay down!'

'Don't...'

—

There is a man who hides in the trees, naked and perverse. He is a tall man and his eyes gleam yellow and his flesh has the sour smell of rotting meat. His nails are long, and he looks for the train. A longing and burning, something he's been searching for his entire life. He is a man of concern and the authorities do not know of him. They don't know his name or where he lives. He travels by night, like a shadow in the blackness, a dark stranger; The Rider of the Woods. A figure who watches and searches and people know about him and know not to enter the woods at night because he may follow you.

Death lays here. It is where it sleeps and festers. Nothing comes out of the woods.

This soil, it burns
Blackened and in turmoil
The land, untold
Cursed

BOY WOKE

When Boy woke, it was dark. It was always dark. The line between night and darkness is the solitude.

He moves his leg and a shaft of light spills into the tiny space. His eyes sting and he looks away. He can smell the dust and the dampness of the clothing he is sitting on, it reeks, and he wants to puke. His stomach rumbles. Boy looks at the light and watches the dust particles dance and spin like falling stars. His right leg is numb, and he can't move it. Slowly, he reaches up and places his hand on the side wall, palm flat. With one leg, he tries to stand, but his back cramps and spasms. He slumps back down and cries out in agony. He tries to stretch his small leg outwards, but the space isn't big enough. He lifts it into the air, to the wall opposite him. All his muscles strain and pull. Tingles of sharp needles etch up his leg and into his backside. He starts to cry.

From outside the door comes the muffled noise of his father, beastly and annoyed. He grumbles like a wounded animal, lost in the forest and starving for meat. Each step he takes, the floor bends and screeches. The dust in the beams settles, also scared. A beer can is tossed somewhere beyond the door. Its familiar metallic sound – rattling and clunking. Then, the door swings open, light streams in, a flood of yellow and white. Boy covers his face, his pupils restricting. A thousand knives piercing his brain. He tries to struggle free from his encasement.

'Dad?' Boy asks, shielding his face.

His father eclipses the light. Heat steams off the man.

He sways and gurgles and scratches his stomach. A hot stream of urine splashes over Boy. The aroma, so strong it made Boy gag. His throat jerks, and his stomach heaves, but nothing comes out. Not even water. Not even stomach fluid. His father's piss is hot and soaked his hair and clothes. It runs over the floor, seeping into the joins of the walls and the clothes he had pulled down to make his bed. Boy hears his father's fly zip up.

'Get up,' he grunts.

Boy tries to stand, his spine protests, but eventually he stands like an elderly man, bent forwards and in pain. His father grabs him and yanks him forward.

'You didn't shit, did you?'

Boy shakes his head.

'No. But I need to.'

'Better not have.'

He lets go of him and he almost falls to the floor. His legs have gotten skinny and his muscles weak. His calves are as small as golf balls. His father snorts and looks over his shoulder. He slams the door shut again and the darkness returns.

Where does Boy go when his father locks him in the cupboard? Where do you go Boy?

It's so dark. He can't see anything. If he could see he would count the wood panels on the walls. He would count the nails or try and... and...

Why does he lock you in there?

Sleep. Unconsciousness.

A deep darkness. Thick and pliable. It has been raining. Boy hears the rain on the roof, he wakes, but not here. It is like music. He listens to it for hours and closes his eyes and imagines himself outside in the rain. Fat drops pelting on his skin, wet and dripping off his nose. It would wash the dirt off him. The cigarette-burn scabs would fall away and there would be no mark, no scar. Boy opens his eyes and sees the rain falling on his face. He smiles as the water cascades down over his cheeks and off his chin. The water catches in his eyelashes and he blinks them away, but every time he closes his eyes, he glimpses the inside of the cupboard. He starts to cry, 'No, I don't want to go back there, please. No. Not now. I want to stay out.'

Boy wakes, here. He is standing in his Toy House. He is still wet and dripping water on the floor.

Do you mind?

Boy looks up and sees the Torso.

'I'm sorry, I...' Boy looks down, he is dry.

Better, the Torso says. *What brings you here? Weren't you having a wonderful dream?*

'A dream? Yes. I thought I was really out. But that's okay. I got to feel the rain.'

The Torso walks around the counter top and stands in front of a row of finely carved puppets. Their strings limp and their smiles painted on and fake. Their hands open, as if grasping something, a bottle or... another hand.

The Torso speaks from somewhere around it's crotch. Someone called him that long ago, he has no torso, he has only a waist. The top, where the rest of the body should have been, is bloodied and gaping. Boy can only see the round, fleshy, white bone-discs of the spinal cord. An open sore of guts and intestines. The white pulp of the hips. The denim jeans it wears buzz with flies and maggots. Boy looks away. Behind him is a new shelf.

'What are these?' he asks, walking over to them.

Army soldiers, Boy. Like your daddy was.

'My dad?' Boy says, glancing instinctively over his shoulder. The Torso was walking behind him.

Yeah, your dad used to be in the army. He told you once about it… remember?

Boy couldn't remember. Since he had been hit with a block of wood when he wet the bed and went to hospital, it was hard to remember things. Along the shelf are plastic toy soldiers, all holding an array of weapons – rifles, blades, handguns, grenades. Boy picks one up and studies it… it is brilliant. He picks another one up and faces them towards each other.

You wanna play?

'Can I?'

Torso moves with slow, ambling footsteps. His shoes are worn and there are holes on either side of the toes. They are caked in dry mud. There are oil stains and scuff marks on his pants.

You can play for a bit, but… Boy moves another soldier *…you have to go back sometime. You will wake up.*

'I don't want to wake up… I like it here.'

The toy store drifts and wavers, made of false images and memories. Far in the corner of the store something moves. Its awkward gallop and twisted body makes Boy frightened, but he doesn't show it.

They've come already, Torso says, backing away slowly to the counter top.

Boy picks up an army man and slides it in his pocket, stepping into the middle of the room. Through the window near the door he can see only the wicked blackness of thought. The shadow-man, with backwards elbows and knees, jerks and grins. Walking haphazardly, he steps one foot in the dim light and Boy sees him for all his grotesque and cancerous glory. His stomach sinks, and he feels his guts push and cramp.

He wakes in the cupboard, no light. He has defecated in his pants. His father will know, and he will burn him again.

When will he come to check you again? Boy? Are you listening? He will come to check you and when he smells what you have done, there will be trouble. Do you know that? Yes, you do. You should not have done that.

Several hours pass and Boy is dragged from the cupboard by his hair. His skin burned raw against the wooden floorboards. He had been asleep, but not. The house is dark, the windows covered up. It smells like decaying waste and dust, of sun starved clothing and rotting food and burnt aluminium foil.

'I'm leaving for the afternoon, don't go anywhere.'

A cigarette butt lands by his head and his father's work boot stomps down on it, sending flecks of ash and small burning embers into the air. He smells his father's body heat and sweat. He can smell the beer on his breath.

'Clean yourself up.'

He hears the front door slam shut and the house is quiet. Boy lays still, too scared to move. He hears crickets chirping outside. Free from the cupboard and naked except underwear that are dry but caked with shit, flaky and stinking pungently. He tries to stand but all his muscles cramp and sting loudly. On hands and knees, he crawls into the kitchen and drinks water from the faucet, in great big gulps. His cracked lips thank him. Flies buzz around his body, but Boy doesn't care. He sees the setting sun coming through the window and he drags himself over to it and lays on the floor, bathing and basking. His skin is hot, but it feels good. He thinks of the toy house and his friend – Torso. He wants to crawl back into the cupboard and sleep, but he is dirty, and it stinks. He takes his pants off and puts them in the bin. He finds something to wear, a shirt. It isn't clean, but it will do. The sun sets, as if it was eager to disappear, as if it was horrified by the sight of him.

Boy shuffles and drags himself back into the cupboard and shuts the door. The house is quiet.

The darkness grows
Tender and forever
Reaching and secluded
Taken

MOAN

When the camera flashes, Cassie feels a piece of her soul die.

'Stand still,' her mother says. 'Stand like this. No, this way, look at me.'

Cassie copies her mother's pose. Her mother's boyfriend walks into the room, his eyes bulging and his hands jittering. He wears a filthy, brown shirt, the collar stretched out and hanging down low to the middle of his chest. A tan line is visible where his watch had been only a few months earlier, but that was long pawned and sold on again because he never went back for it. He wears shoes with no socks and has a faded Viking tattoo on his left leg. His stubble has roots of grey and tips of brown. Glancing up at his girlfriend's daughter, he catches her staring back at him and he looks down to his shoes. He digs something out of his pocket and places it on the table. His long, dirty fingers dig out a glass pipe from his pocket and it is held between his cracked, thin, lips. The lighter is flicked until it catches, and the fire lights the ball at the end, and he breathes deep. A rattle emanates from his lungs, deep and rhythmic.

'Do you have to do that in here?' she says, looking at her boyfriend. She turns back to her daughter. 'Enough, Cassie. Go play.'

Cassie pulls her dress back on and leaves the room. She hears him yell at her mother and they began to fight. A skin on skin slap echoes throughout the house. Cassie runs to her room. Her blanket is on the ground and her pillows lay strewn oddly. She can smell men. The stink of foul body odour. Large men, full of grease and hot meat. She can feel their hands on her, touching, grabbing. Cassie has seen the pictures her mother takes, like sports cards. The edges tea-stain yellow and her skin looks feverish white, her eyes bulging, her shirt hanging loose or open, showing her chest. She hides them in the cupboard in her room and takes them with her when she goes out.

Men then come to the house and stand in the doorway and look at her. They talk in whispers and grin with many teeth. They never caress like mother tells them to – no, never. They would fondle and pinch, hard. She feels her stomach squeeze tight and something – liquid – rise up into her throat. She ran back through the hallway and went to the door, pushing the fly screen open. Clear fluid comes out of her mouth.

Outside is loud with insects. The tapping and chirping drives Cassie insane. She can't be near the house after those photos. Along the cracked footpath she runs barefoot. The jutted concrete plateaus hurt her skin. Roy…

Call him Dad.

…Dad would come home, stinking of aged booze, his breath steaming hot and his hands black with dirt and smelling of gasoline. The fumes stayed in the house, lingering like an old ghost, punch-drunk and obscene. He would stumble over things, go crashing into the walls and knock holes in the plasterboard. Once, Roy (…Dad), lit a fire inside and the smoke bellowed out the windows and into the night, escaping. Cassie remembers the fire, its starlit grin and scarlet, diluted eyes, hissing and moaning, coming after her; the gentle crackle of wood planks, dusted with age and beer. She remembers wanting to run to the fire, letting it eat her. If only to be taken away from this place. Even for a moment.

Cassie stands beside the fence, no older then twelve and not yet developed. No signs of womanhood displayed, nor any intention to. The fence leans inwards, the wire twisted and the white paint all but gone. The once well-groomed hedgerow, now a bundle of sticks and brown leaves nestled in a bird's nest. Cassie has not been to school in nearly a year and her sister, Pi, is going to school because she wants to leave this town, and she's promised to take Cass with her.

('Don't leave me here… not with them.')

('I won't.')

('Promise?')

('There's no need to promise, Cass. I'm not leaving you behind.')

('I…')

('Does a promise mean that much to you?')

('Yes.')

('Okay. I promise. When I go… you're coming too.')

Cassie doesn't want to wait for her sister so close to the house, so she starts the long walk into town, to the high school. Her bare feet are blackened underneath from not wearing shoes, her white dress fingerprinted with dirt and yellowed with waste and food. The road is unforgiving, and the sun is hot, yet she walks uncaring and unsettled. She thinks of what her mother makes her do and wonders if this is normal, if other girls must go through the same. She knows her sister Pi did, and what happened to her, to her face. She remembers the blood and skin, the horror and the gore. She doesn't want that to happen to her, but she feels it's getting closer, maybe not the disfigurement, but death.

One day a man will arrive – she believes, she has already seen him in her dreams – he will wear a suit and smell of cologne. His skin will be pure white, and his nails will be trim. His hair will be as black as coal and he'll smile and have a lot of money. This is the man who will kill her. She has seen it in her dreams.

Her feet sting and blister and she stops in the shade of an overpass to rest. Along the ground is trash, stray coffee cups and wrappers, syringes and lengths of rubber and cloth. She hears movement behind her and turns suddenly. A man is lying against cardboard boxes and piles of newspaper. He waves his arms around, freeing the waste for him to see. His eyes are stark blue, watery and clear. His hair is long and dreaded like tangles of wasps' nests. The skin under his eyes are bruised and he yelps and claps his feet together. The school is too far to walk. She runs up to the road and looks down the length of the abandoned highway. No cars, no people. She begins to walk, but on the grass. The soil is soft and damp, it had rained, but she didn't know when. She doesn't want to go back home, but she must. Pi will not like her coming to see her at school. Although she promises to take her with her, Cassie knows she might just disappear one day, and why wouldn't you? This place is cancerous. The smell of this town is pungent. The forest encircling the boundaries is like a ring of purification, keeping the ghosts in.

Cassie, wandering like so many lost souls. Clueless and lost. All roads lead back home, and she stands near her fence. The sickness and neglect oozes off her house like spongey clouds. Her stomach cramps begin, and she spits on the ground, vile and putrid.

Cassie sits back on her bed, waiting for her sister. She sleeps and wakes. Unsure of the time, or for how long. A long, bleached, strip of light shines through her bedroom, across her bed and onto the floor. This room smells. Smells of men and sweat and blood, still and probably forever. The metallic aroma is sour and hangs at the back of her throat. A car goes past the house and she stands and looks out of the curtains, red like the blood she bleeds. Not her, not Pi.

She sits back down. She isn't coming. She goes to her door and opens it, seeing the silver locks on the outside sparkle like fireworks when it hits the sun's rays. She walks into the hallway, the carpet filthy, and feels dirt and trash under her feet. There is no noise coming from the lounge room, but she can tell her mother and Roy are there, somewhere. Sometimes, they seem to appear in two places at once, or blink in and out of existence. The very stench of their souls is aromatic, like a decaying animal on the side of the road with its guts split open and its intestines spilled out for the world to see. The air around them tastes like a compost of drugs, burning syringes and unwashed skin. She stands under the archway that separates the kitchen from the lounge and she can see them in each other's embrace. Half-naked and passed out.

Mother; with her top sliding to one side, like the hundreds of poses she makes her do. Now her own victim, now her own photograph. Her nipples still erect, and her jeans torn off in whatever drug fuelled love rampage that started and never ended. Their brains reaching orgasm before their bodies and then passing out, in each other's flesh.

Roy; his jeans still on, stained with grass and ripped

around the knees and hem. His shirt is off, ribs etched down each side like corrugated iron sheeting. A small hair patch in the middle of his chest, brown nubby fur, matted down with sweat. His mouth is open with yellow teeth, like tombstones kicked over or smashed. His chest rises and falls in a drug induced coma, the next breath staggers and his long fingers twitch, covered in scars from his chainsaw. He has one shoe off and one on.

Cassie steps over old brown paper bags and small plastic bags, microwave meal packets and fast food containers. She sees a mouse and instead of screaming tells it to get out of here – *you don't want to live here if you don't have to. I have to live here, and I hate it.*

The mouse sniffs the waste packets and eats a small piece of mummified food stuck to polystyrene. It looks up at Cassie with beady, pearled eyes and scuttles under the small, broken coffee table. Cassie turns to leave and notices the camera on the table. The very one her mother uses on her. More hurtful than any man could be, more hurtful than any object Roy has ever hit her with. She picks it up and looks through the small window. Her mother's body wrapped in Roy's; unconscious, like a demented snake eating its own tail. A drugged ouroboros. She snaps a photo and the flash ignites, bright like an exploding star in the small, dank lounge room. The mechanics of the camera printing is loud and for a moment Cassie is scared she woke up the beast that lays entangled in front of her. Roy moans, as if his nightmares had become momentarily highlighted by the flash. The camera spits out the photo and Cassie takes it and puts the camera down. Still no sound of Pi. She tucks the photo, still a bluey hue, slowly changing colour, slowly etching her addicted parents, into her pocket. To the back door, Cassie walks out into the coldness of March and the streets are empty of life and sympathy.

She had men before, whispering in her ear – *come with me. I'll give you a good home, food, clothes, schooling.* But she knows what it would be in return for.

This life is wasted on sex and drugs and poverty. Cassie wants to leave her body, float over this town and its inhabitants and travel away, start new, start fresh. But there is no escape... but there is...

This is secret, where Cassie goes. She hardly lets her own mind picture it. She will only dare dream of going to this place when everything else is nil. The Train.

She bolts across the road, as if being chased; the asphalt under her naked feet is hot, but welcoming. Into the vacant lot across the street where graffiti covers the walls like ancient dialects, unreadable but still full of meaning.

The Train – 'I am coming.'

She slips through a gap in the fence. This is the same route Roy takes to Kenner's house, if his car is broken. On the other side is another house, abandoned and left to die like everything else in this town. The windows are smashed in and the glass long ago used by homeless men to cut intruders or get stuck into people's feet when looking through the windows. The grass is long and brown. It was told, by her sister Pi, that the house is full of black Komodo dragons. Their mouths full of bacteria and their serrated teeth. She doesn't stop to look in. What if it's true? What if the house was full of dragons that have feasted on the homeless people or the drug riddled who wander in there for either a place out of the rain, or somewhere to shoot their drugs?

She moves quickly past the windows and onto the opposite street. The walk is long and tiresome. When she hears a car come, she hides and watches it drive by. After a half hour she leaves the road and travels west under the greying sky. She knows it's close, she can feel the iron tracks radiating like a beacon. Through the rough shrubbery and pines, she sees the mound of dirt, high off the ground and climbs it. She stands between the two iron rails and lets the heat warm her legs and thighs. She looks behind her and sees the tracks snake out of sight and looks back. Mountains far ahead where the sun hides at night. She walks. Chirping from crickets or insects keep her company, the far-off cry of a dog echoes through the trees and shivers her spine. She imagines Roy turning into a wolf and coming after her. His scarred hands and dreadful breath, his leathery skin and unwashed, scraggly hair. She moves faster, thinking he most likely isn't her father. Maybe it's one of the men that see her. The one with the hat and black cloak, the one she sees in her dreams killing her.

Travelling to The Train is a dreamscape of memories, both real and unreal. She remembers ghosts who haunt the woods and pray on their hands and knees, their eyes hollow and black, staring. When they walk, they're crumpled and stagger like drunken men. Their fingers are long, and they are the woodland spooks. She remembers running away from home when she was eight and being lost for two days in the woods running from the spooks and finding The Train.

Cassie, her feet bleeding, enters the forest. The

woodland ghouls perch on trees and watch. They know she is running and needs respite. They let her in, only this once and they disappear down their warrens and into the tree trunks to sleep. Cassie walks a track not yet worn, no one will follow her path as it changes every time, just like the trees. A crow, somewhere, hears her and flies overhead, its wings are red, but its body is black as ink. It doesn't call, as it too senses her need. The girl lifts her dress and steps over an entanglement of vines and fallen branches, the wood rotten and eaten by ants.

A leafy womb, the insides a still birth of metal and power. A man-made monster, built for strength, now lays idle and asleep. But is it? The train she comes to see is here. Nesting or hibernating, its limbs rusted and seized. It hides in an abandoned warehouse; the doors ripped from its maw, laying buckled like wet cardboard on either side. The train is grand and night-black in colour. The chimney along its snout caked in charcoal and ash, a grey washy hue. Cassie stands before it, like a worshipper to a deity. The God of Metal, the Saviour – the escape method. She walks in (she's only done this once before) and strokes the slumbering giant. The forest is so quiet. They watch and wonder what will happen. Even the animals dare not enter the lair. The train is still, its flesh is cold, and Cassie sees it's chained to the ground. The path leading out of its home is covered in vines and foliage, a stranglehold of grass and weeds.

Free me, and I will free you.

Cassie's eyes bulge open and she runs, nearly tripping over a pile of unused track railings. She yanks her dress up and bolts through the forest. There is no one to stop her. The trees let her out and she splits from the tree line, her breath laboured and her hands sweating.

STILL THE MONSTER

Pi, a woman, yet disguised as a girl still. The flash of her mother's camera still livid in her mind, still a reminder, still the monster. Her old sneakers are worn to frayed cloth. The soles are gripless and allow small stones to enter through the holes. She pulls one off and shakes it and slips it back on. Her jeans are faded around the knees and her jacket is moth eaten and the stitching is coming loose.

When she enters her house, she balls her hands up into fists, ready and waiting. Her heart beats faster and if she could live elsewhere, she would. She did once, moved in with someone, in their trailer. The trailer park isn't for people like her, she thought it would have been. A camouflaged moth, cocooned and safe; yet she wasn't. People, men, came into her trailer, at night. People would wander in and out, staring, looking. One climbed into bed and tried to touch her. They fought, and it kept happening. It is worse than here, if that is possible.

Inside the house; she smells the kitchen, rotten and tragic. A kingdom of poverty.

'Who's there?'

'It's me, Mum.'

'Where have you been?'

'It doesn't matter. Where's Cassie?'

Her mother – the word doesn't seem quite right. Pi looks down the hallway, she fears to go down there still, but for her sister, she does. Cassie's room is empty. The lamp is still on, burning white hot. On the bed is the red blanket, the one Pi is so familiar with. How many times has she lay on it? How many pictures has she posed for? It brings sickening bile to her throat and she turns back to her mother.

'What did you do?'

'Go away, Pi.' She lights a cigarette and narrows her eyes through the smoke.

Something is thrown, a plate, it shatters, morphing in with the other debris on the floor. The rats scatter.

'What is fucking wrong with you?'

'Get the fuck out, Pi. You don't live here anymore. Just leave.'

'I'm not leaving… not without Cassie.'

'I heard you two whispering… promises to stay. No one leaves here, Pi. Get used to it.'

'Just because you didn't leave, doesn't mean I can't. You fucking cunt.'

A slap. Cold. Stinging. Pi steps back, her hand goes to her face, it's hot. Another slap, from Pi to her mother. The wrestling of junky arms, malnutritioned bones and weak, drug filled muscles. They push and wane.

'Fuck you.'

'One call to the police and you're in jail… with Dad.'

'*Ha-ha.* Do you think they don't know about what goes on here? You've got to be fucking dumb. They are involved. Call them, see if I give a shit.'

'You're fucked. You truly are a fucking monster. How could you do this to your own daughters.'

'Come near me again, and I'll fucking make you sorry.'

'You don't scare me, Mum. No one in this town scares me. Do you think I give a shit? Look at me. This place did this to me.'

'No, you did that to yourself. You fucked your own face up.'

'You're a junky whore.'

'You're no daughter of mine, now fuck off.'

'Cassie!' Pi yells, staring at her mother. There's no answer. Pi turns and heads back for the door.

'She wandered off hours ago. She'll be back. You don't take her anywhere. She'll always come back to me.'

'You're wrong.'

Pi runs down the decrepit stairs that leads out to the overgrown front yard. Small insects take flight. The flies buzz around the bins that have not been collected for months. The trash and poverty of this town gets under your skin, the dirt and the bubbling of boiling blood. The stains of youth and the wasted adulthood. This is where people come when they have no purpose. If you want to waste your life – welcome to Hope Valley.

'What is the significance of a promise? It's as easy to break, as it is said. It means the same to a child as it does to an adult. The crushing feeling of a broken promise can be nearly as bad as anything? Don't you think, Cassie?'

Cassie is nowhere. Not here.

'I don't promise anything.'

Vines entangled
A nest of black spiders
The earth has its own aroma
Seductive and sweet

THE SAME REASON

A knock – strong and aggressive. Father stands up and looks to the cupboard. Boy is in there, locked away and suffering, as he should be. He walks, his mind dazed by drugs and booze. The air around the floor is cold and he can now hear the rain. Was he asleep? He looks through the curtains, unwashed and yellowing from the sun and dirt. A police officer, looking at him. Someone he went to school with. A man who left to go to the academy instead of the army. He came back and here he is, standing on father's front porch.

'What do you want?'

No answer. Father unlocks the door.

'I'm Officer Neadly. I've been sent over by the state warden for child welfare. Can I ask where your son is?'

'He ain't here.'

Boy shivers in the cupboard. Fresh piss covers the floor, it has blood in it, smelling of iron and vinegar.

'We need to ask him a few questions.'

'About what?'

'There's been a murder in the woods.'

'So? Wouldn't be the first. My boy wouldn't have done that, I can assure you.'

'Where was he in the afternoon of –'

'I just said it. He wouldn't have done it. He is always with me. He never leaves my sight, ever.'

'You said he's not with you now.'

'You playing smart? Don't play that with me. He's gone

to the store to get dinner. I know the path he takes, the roads and where he's at. If he's longer than I want, I'll fix him.'

'You'll fix him?'

'He's my boy. He'll do what he's told. He doesn't have a mother.'

'I know what happened to his mother and I'm sorry.'

'You're sorry? Why?'

'It's a way of saying condolences, that's all.'

'Well say it elsewhere. You can go now.'

'Look,' Neadly adjusts his belt, pushing the gun holster to the front, making sure the man sees it. 'I have to come back. I need to establish whereabouts and let the detectives build their case. I can't leave this be.'

'You can come back all you want, I ain't gonna answer the door to you again.'

'If you know your boy didn't do it, what's the harm?'

'No harm. He didn't do it, and that's the end of that. You don't need no questions answered. That's all you need.'

'The new detective wanted to come out, but I talked him out of it. I'll come back next Wednesday. We'll chat more then.'

The door slams in the officers' face. Dust and dirt are shaken loose and fall to the rotting porch. Jock, the father, the man who sees only in red, moves fast towards the cupboard door, but halts. His fists are tangled clumps of ham, ready to strike. He stares at the door, then places one hand on it and thumps it hard. The child inside starts to cry and Jock smiles, then laughs. He goes to his room: the bed, never made since his wife left, beer bottles strewn across the floor, clothes piled up and the stinking of sweat and blood and puke. A small standing fan is in the corner of the room, moving slowly, the blades gather dust and cobwebs around the base. He picks a shirt, doesn't matter if it's the cleanest, whichever one is closest. He wrangles it on and slips into his boots, peering out the window to watch the man get into his patrol car. He sits in the car for some time and Jock watches him, mumbling under his breath for him to leave.

The drive out of the suburbs is fast and he runs every red light. Once Jock gets there, the music is loud, and the smoke is thick; it sits along the ceiling. The harder it is to breathe, the more you drink. The barman is the owner's son. Two whiskeys – straight – followed by beer and he's already forgotten about the intruder at the door.

How long's it been since I fed the boy? Don't matter anyway, he thinks. The thought slips away. He's unsure why he even thought it. Another beer and he hears something. *Did someone say something? Who said that?*

'What did you say?'

A man walks past, he looks in his direction, then away. The music gets louder.

'Say it again, motherfucker.'

The man looks at him. He didn't say a word, but he's here for the same reason. Jock nearly falls off his chair getting up and the man cocks his hand back and punches him in the jaw. The clicking of jaw and skull is heard over the music. The bartender knew it was going to happen. The fleshy slap and the man falls back. It is unexpected that Jock would get up from his hit, but Jock is ex-marine. They scuffle and fall and land on a table, breaking it in half. Most the patrons move back but keep drinking. Another hard smack and the man is out cold, his head wobbling to the side. Jock is escorted out and he sleeps in the alley beside the bar.

Listen, but never to be heard
The sky that looms
Let it sing
Covered and devoured

MEND

A scar ran down her left elbow from a man named Chris she knew a long time ago. He broke her arm and it never mended well. A bruise above her left breast; it never went away, this was done by a man named Davis. That was four years ago. She remembered that when grandma drinks, it's with her right hand, never her left as it shakes from the medication.

Slippery hands make it hard for the devil, grandma used to say. Keep yourself perverted and drunk. Her swollen, purple eggplant lips quiver and curl words, smouldering dark thoughts into language. Her skin is shallow, waxy powder, set hard by age and sun. With sunken blue eyes, the shade of chemicals, she sees the town of Hope Valley as little more than a cess pool of the dying and decaying fragments of people that once were here but aren't really anymore. The thick blackness of cancer and disease, she can see it all. Witch or shaman – she is neither – she simply engorges herself on the town like a creature from another land or another era, sinking its teeth into the cruel, yellow underbelly. Listen to her stories and laugh as she laughs, as they are of misery and sorrow. No one can escape, or can they? No one has.

But her son, the oldest one, Gus, he had a fit in his room and Mother watched from the doorway. His hands reached out to her, grovelling and helpless. His fingers curled and quivering. His bright white eyeballs rolling into his head and his jaw clenching shut. She watched from the doorway and wondered why God had given her a son like this.

'Miss?'

Gus's mother, Pearl, looks at the strapping young man behind the counter. His white pharmaceutical uniform starched and itching around his neck.

'Yes?'

'$145.95 please.'

'Say that again?' the old, black woman's wrinkled fingers swab and uncrease a twenty-dollar bill.

'Ma'am, it's one-forty-five-ninety-five.'

'For medicine?'

'Yes ma'am.'

A terrible demon lives in *you*, boy. His name is epilepsy and he feeds on your very soul. Can you save your soul before Jesus takes it from you? Can you redeem thyself?

Mother's lips are cracked and rotten from the outside in. Her breath smells of liquor and potent chemicals from corner-brought meth. Her eyes widen and shut. She feels bubbles in her heart. Her mind wanes and feels like a lacquered piece of wood. She turns from the counter and leaves. Gus follows her. His jaw hurts and his fingers feel like they are nearly broke. His chest is tired and his whole body aches.

A BURNT SCAR

Pi let her long, sun bleached, hair fall over her face. She could smell the shampoo she had used that morning. It hung like curtains of silk, spun by golden spiders. The boys knew better than to tease her about her nose. What had happened had burnt a scar into the subconscious of everyone living in that small town of Hope Valley. Piano wire scraped down Pi's face in a fit of rape and anger, carving her nose off, like peeling the skin from fruit. The cartilage was torn away and now healed with rippled skin, bumpy and abnormal. Pi licked her lips, they were naturally pink. The top: an archer bow – perfect and defined. The bottom: an apron – puffy and moistened to a glistening shine.

Pi takes a cigarette out of her pocket and lights it. She breathes it out her nose and it comes out in two long streams. She stands with one hip popped outwards, one hand resting on it. From somewhere out of sight comes the car she's been waiting for. She had to get home to Cassie, but here the car is. Plans change, life sucks.

TEETH

The air is cold and chills her bones and makes her teeth rattle. Her gums ache, and she is sore all over. The man had hurt her, his weight too much to bear. Her mother had heard her whimpering and had come in and told him to stop. He yelled and said he had paid good money. This made Cassie believe there was *bad* money, and she thought she had seen that Roy kept bad money in his pockets when he came home every few weeks. It was crumpled and sometimes torn and dirty.

After the men leave, her mother would count the money in the lounge room. Cassie had to stay on her bed and pretend it didn't hurt.

She sits on her bed, sore and praying for the bleeding to stop. She hadn't cried the whole time, she had done that before and it just made them more excited. She stands up, but sits back down again. *Not yet*, she thinks. Her bed still smells like Him and she hates it.

The fog is blind
Watch for it!
The never-ending knot of snakes
Travelling through the dead wood
Unguided

GREY WATER

Pi waits outside the liquor store. There is a single street light and several cars parked underneath it. Trash lines the footpath surrounding the building; the lights strobe on and off and small black insects circle around, crazed and hungry. A bar across the street is loud and she's heard glass smash several times in the last twenty minutes. She slaps her arms and looks; a mosquito is pressed into her flesh. A small streak of blood is smeared from the bite to the dying creatures pulsing wings. She hears gravel crunching and looks up; a man is coming. He's smoking a cigarette and the smoke is hiding his face. He's wearing a navy-blue shirt, the logo reads "Joe's Radiator Service" and a phone number. Pi steps out of the dark, she already has money in her hand.

'Can you buy me a bottle?' she says.

At first the man acts as if he doesn't hear her. Then he stops, the light flushes down on his face and she sees he is handsome. A fine chin curving up to a solid jaw and ears hidden in short, curly, brown hair. His right hand is yanked from his jean pocket and he pulls the smoke from his mouth.

'Buy you what?'

'Whiskey.'

The man looks at the shop door. He can see the clerk behind the counter reading a porno magazine. His skin looks yellow and his hair greasy and combed back.

'I don't know,' the man says. 'What are you gonna do

for me?' His eyes widen.

Pi knows he just saw her face. The vacant fleshy hole where her nose once was.

'Never mind,' she says, and steps back into the darkness.

The man steps towards her. 'What happened to your face?' He puts the cigarette to his lips and takes the tobacco into his lungs. The smoke pours out like grey water down a waterfall. He tries to eye Pi, to see her face.

'Don't worry about it,' she says, pushing her money back into her pocket.

'I just wanna know how your –'

'Just fuck off.'

'You're a rude bitch, you know that?'

He throws the cigarette down on the ground and stomps on it hard. He twists his foot and small embers spit out the side of his boot. He stares at the figure in the dark and looks over to the bar, people are milling around outside, laughing and smoking. He turns back to her and sneers before heading into the store. Pi moves when he's inside, to the other end of the car park. When he comes back out, he's unwrapping a cigarette pack. He pauses and tosses the plastic onto the ground. He's looking for her. A single smoke is pulled from the pack, he smells it first and then lights it as he walks back across the street. Pi watches him from the darkness. She waits until he has crossed the road. He glances back over his shoulder and shakes his head before entering the bar again.

Pi looks at her phone. It's getting late. She steps into the fluorescent light of the store again and waits; no one else is coming. She pushes the door and goes inside. The sudden flood of lights blinds her. The clerk looks up, throws his magazine under the counter and stands up straight. He licks the palm of his hand and runs it over his hair. Streaks of light shine off the saliva now sticking his hair down. He nods to her and Pi nods back. She walks slowly to the end of the store and looks over the shelves of booze. The bottles dusty and their labels peeling off. A spider nest is camped in the corner of the shelving unit. Pi looks behind her and sees the clerk watching her. She reaches for a bottle of whiskey and takes it to the front. He eyes her carefully and scans the bottle.

'$24.05,' he says, staring at her nose, then down to her breasts.

She pays him and snatches the bottle from the counter top. The clerk grins, his face slippery with sweat. He licks his hands and runs it through his hair again.

'You should stay and keep me company. I'll help you drink it.'

Pi doesn't look back. The door chimes on her way out and she runs to the darkness.

Cancerous caverns
A darkened weed
Blistered oil wounds
Taken to the end

TREES

When school has finished, Gus walks instead of taking the bus. He goes across the oval and jumps the fence into the neighbour's paddock and skims the tree line until he reaches the road. The outside world is alien to him. He knows the roads and the street signs; he knows the buildings and the police station, but it is so foreign. Each morning the town changes; staggeringly small changes, yet still visible. It became a maze of soap-box preachers, street hookers and violence.

The trees finished, and Gus ran across the road. Putting his back to the trees makes his skin shiver. He walks with unabandoned shame, with no rush to get home and enjoys the sweet air. There's a fire somewhere, its tastes like charcoal on his tongue; there is no fire in the sky. A car drives past, fast, and there is hollering. Something is thrown, and it lands at his feet. The car continues until it rounds the bend in the road and is out of sight. Gus looks down, it's an empty beer can. He picks it up and examines it. It still smells fresh, the inside croaks from the bubbles and the sun makes the tin glisten. There's something wrong with leaving this in the forest, even though it would be on the edge. The trees gnash and sway; Gus finds a soft area of earth and buries the can. The trees are happy again.

He walks and lets the sun warm his back. His dark skin radiates and feels the burn but doesn't show it. The road dips down and there is a sign – *Area Prone to Flooding* – and there is a measurement down the side of it. Gus looks at the small trickle of water coming from somewhere inside the forest. From behind him he hears a car. He steps off the road and bends down to look at the tadpoles at the water's edge. The car slows, and Gus looks over. It's the same car that drove past before. Kids stare at him from the inside, the windows smoggy and dirty. The car rattles and coughs. Gus stands up and takes a step to the side. One foot is in the forest.

We cannot save you, the trees say.

Gus isn't sure. He watches the car. Maybe they knew he buried their beer can, maybe it was a marker, or a bread crumb, a totem to be left, untouched; a sacrifice. The car speeds away, screeching tires and the trees move after them, their long branch-limbs reach outwards to confiscate them, to crush them, but they are gone. Gus follows the stream up though the large trees. The water is fresh and drinkable. He splashes it up his arms and onto the nape of his neck. It's cool and relieving. Something catches his eyes and he runs to it, half buried in the soft, black dirt. He stands for a moment, looking down, an unusual object, out of place and far from the road. He falls to his knees and digs his hands in, the earth opens up and welcomes his touch. He holds his fingers wide open and the loose dirt falls through and back into the ground. In his hands, what is left, is a small necklace. The chain is rusted and the pendent is a butterfly with a wing missing. Gus holds it up to catch it in the light, but it is too dirty. He takes it to the stream and washes it. The dirt comes off and he holds it up, into the sun's beam. The butterfly shines with a dull sparkle. Gus smiles and places it in his pocket. He will show his brother when he gets home. He will like it.

The streams go into a thicket, and then underground. Above him is a rocky lip, where moss and vines hang down and two dead trees above it look like lopsided eyes. Gus moves away quickly and back towards the road. He comes out at the bend and he can hear noises. He stands on the loose rocks and looks left. The car from before is parked in a small clearing. There are two boys wrestling. The other boys are drinking beer and throwing the empty cans at them, hollering and laughing. Suddenly, one of them stops and turns towards him.

'Hey, that's him,' the boy says and the rest of them stop and turn their heads.

Gus is struck by fear, unprovoked, unaware. The terror rises in him and his legs tell him to run. He bolts back the way he came, running as fast as he can. His skinny legs heave and thrust. The kids give chase. His heart pounds faster than it ever has. Long strides, leaping and bounding through the thicket and into the forest again.

We cannot save you, the trees repeat.

Gus feels a meaty hand smack him across the back of the head and he falls, tumbling and crawling into the small stream of water. His sweat drips into the water and he sees his own reflection, then that of the boys behind him. One picks him up and speaks, but the words are backwards. The tall boy upper-cuts Gus hard and he hears his jaw clamp shut, his teeth chomping together. It makes a clacking noise which one of the other boys laughs at. Another one kicks him in the chest, and he rolls onto the ground, his intestines squirming like freshly earthed worms. He knows it was bad to be on the ground, but he knew if he lay still, acted dead and didn't react, and waited for them to finish spitting on him, they would go away. He learned death from his mother. He learned to wait. The plaything is boring, and they would leave.

A sudden flash and a white light appears; a sparkle and a soft fade, like fireworks. He feels his eye swell and another kick comes, swift and to the groin. The pain is immense and the mind leaves…

Gus remembers he had been fishing once, with his grandfather he now no longer knew. It was a long time ago and somewhere he didn't remember. There is a big tree there, it spoke to him as well. He remembers the day was very sunny. He remembers the cool air coming off the river. They sit on an outcropping of rocks and his grandfather shows him how to bait a hook. He has hooked his finger, piercing the skin and a blood dollop appeared. His grandfather winces, shakes his hand and sucks the blood. Gus wonders if this man looked like his father, who he can never recall seeing.

'It's okay, Gus,' he says in a smoky voice. 'That happens sometimes. Now, look how I've pushed the bait around the hook, like this. See?'

Gus tries pushing the bait around, being overly careful of the point. He pushes, and the bait snags. He applies more pressure and it slides over, cutting through the meat and into his finger. He holds it up to his grandfather who smiles. He pushes his finger against his.

'See, Gus, we're more than just grandfather and grandson, we're blood brothers.'

He casts the line out into the running water, and it sinks and pulls more of the fishing line. He lets it sink to the bottom and hands it to Gus.

'Now, we wait.'

Wait, yes, Gus thinks. Just wait til it's over. A flashing light and Gus arches forward, his stomach cramping and his nose beginning to bleed.

'If we catch a fish, we can eat it for dinner. Sound good?'

Gus tries to open his eyes. The water smells sweet and the trees are aromatic. There is no sound of traffic or people. Gus's foot is reefed outwards, yanked and twisted. He drops the fishing line and is dragged down the rocks, towards the water. His grandfather looked up at the sun and squinted.

'God invented days like this, so you could go fishing, Gus.' He reaches into his pocket and pulled out a tobacco pouch.

Gus's head snaps to the side and his cheeks pucker up as an invisible fist pounded on his flesh. Gus groans and waves his arms, pushing the kids off him.

His grandfather takes out a cigarette paper and places a hearty amount of tobacco in the middle. He licks the edge and starts rolling it between his thumbs and index fingers.

'You can keep your city life, hey, Gus. They can keep their cars and fax machines and emails and all that rubbish. Give me the country, a sunny day and a fishing pole, and I'm a happy man.'

Gus spits up blood and turns to his grandfather.

You need to do something. They are looking to kill you, the trees say.

A gust of wind and the large willow tree thrashes from side to side. Grandfather places the cigarette between his lips and looks at the tree with his head cocked to the side.

Gus's head is pushed into the water and he sucks it into

his lungs, coughing and gaging. For an instant, through puffy, bruised eyes he sees the kids holding him under the water. They are drinking beer and laughing.

'By the grace of God,' his grandfather says, and lights his cigarette.

Gus kicks his leg out, hitting the nearest one in the shin. He drops his beer bottle and it smashes on the rocks beside his head. It's a sound like crackling thunder.

'You'll pay for that,' he screams, kicking Gus in the stomach again and again.

His head is pulled from the water and he gasps for air. His lungs squeezed tight, and he feels them pop and refill. His grandfather watches momentarily, then picks up the fishing line and holds it between his fingers, feeling a little bite.

'I think we may have something here, Gus.'

Gus stares through half-closed eyes. His vision is blurred.

'Come on, fishy.'

Gus reaches over to the rocks and picks up the broken beer bottle. It is just the neck, with three, sharp points. He swivels on his knees as the three kids surround him and laugh. One takes out his dick to piss on him and Gus launches forward and stabs him in the side of the ribcage. The boy screams and falls backwards. The other boys run to him and see the gushing of blood.

'Shit. Shit. Shit.'

They pick him up and his face drains of blood. None of them look at Gus. They drag him back to the car and Gus watches the blood trail. The car roars to life and reverses, without care, back onto the road. With screeching tires, it speeds away, leaving the smell of rubber and burning brake pads.

What have you done?

'What was needed to be done.'

They know you. They've marked you. They've sworn an oath to one another, in the car. Now they will find you again and kill you.

'They would have killed me.'

Gus's grandfather yanks on the line and laughs heartedly.

It doesn't matter. This has started a reaction, you need to leave. It is no longer safe for you here.

'It was never safe for me here. Where should I go? There is nowhere to go.'

Go home. Stay for a day or two and get out. Come back here, to the TREES. There is a path beyond the old rusted stove, just there, look.

Gus turns, his sore neck cracking as bones slide over one another. An ancient iron stove sits like a glorified tombstone, just metres off the stream. A crow sits on it, beating a snail shell against the metal, desperately trying to open it. Gus stares at its eyes, he had seen them somewhere before. His mother perhaps.

Once you come back, go in there. Walk until your legs give way and you will find your way out.

His grandfather yelps with glee, pulling a fish from the water. It sparkles silver in the sun.

'Looks at this, Gus! We'll fry him up good. Right from the water.'

Gus smiles. 'It's time to go.'

'Yes, you're right, Gus. It is time to go.'

TEENAGE WASTELAND

A soft warmth rises like vapour from the wet ground in long ribbons. It smells of rich soil and decomposed leaves, fresh and upturned. The trunks of the trees sit long and stern, their gravestone stillness divides the forest up into columns. Enough places for people and animals alike, to take refuge.

An abundance of bones can be found exposed and rotting in the woods. There is a calm about them. At night you can hear them howl.

Encrypted messages and the moaning of the dead; these bones carry endlessly to the edge of the forest where a man of seventeen urinates against a fallen fence. His face red from booze, he stares up at the sky. The number of stars he sees makes him blink and focus and refocus. He looks down and he's pissed on his shoes and fingers. He zips up prematurely and a small stain grows around his crotch. He shakes his leg, feeling the drips go down his shins. He rubs his hands on his denim jeans and then runs his long fingers through his jaw length hair. It's brown, but in the dark, it appears caramel. He takes two steps and halts, something is behind him. He turns. The forest speaks, soft at first, in hushed tones. Then nothing. The kid feels his heart inside his ribcage, pounding faster and faster. He turns back to the house and wants to run but doesn't.

The house is a rotten tooth amongst the vastness of the forest. Every window removed, or smashed in. The glass long gone, picked up by curious birds or eaten by foxes.

The paint long ago peeled from the wooden planks; now blistered from the sun and pocked with holes. Graffiti covers the external walls, and internal. Cryptic messages of love and hate. The teenager wanders back through the rear door where music is playing loudly. Obnoxious guitars with heavy bass and chaotic drums, vocals – undecipherable. There are more people, lounging in near darkness. They smoke weed and fill the room with white smog. It lingers up near the ceiling. A girl shouts and no one hears it or ignores it. She stands up, her nose is gone completely, and she walks over to the teenager pouring himself another drink on the kitchen counter top. A hole where a fridge once sat, a hole where the microwave should have been. The oven still there, rusted and the door torn off and tossed into one of the bedrooms.

'Where did you go?'

'To take a piss.'

'Pour me one.'

The teenager does and hands it to her.

'What's your friends name?'

'Which one?

Pi points to the boy in the corner, his jeans torn and his face dirty with soot. His arms are long, and he has broad shoulders, unlike the other boys.

'Jakob.'

Pi chews the boy's name in her mind like gum – *Jakob. Jakob.*

'You wouldn't know him.'

'Why?'

'He doesn't go to school here, or anywhere. His dad makes him work.'

She keeps her eyes locked on him – *Jakob*. Another girl walks over to him and whispers in his ear. The music gets louder, it skips as another teenager walks past the stereo and kicks at it.

'He's not from here?'

'No.'

The piss-pants teenager brings his drink up to his lips and sculls it in two gulps. He starts refilling it again. He stares at Pi's breasts as she is looking away. Her lips full, her hips wide enough to pull her jeans tight. He can smell her amongst the house's rotten, sour aromas.

'Where is he from.' She turns back and sees his eyes avert away.

'Crowne.'

'So? That's not far.'

'He used to go here, til final grade. Anyway, who cares.'

The teenager pours another, this one stronger. The music gets louder, and the house starts to shake. The foundation, full of black rats and shredded snake skins, quivers and stutters. On the ground near the door are egg shells from a bird's nest above the door bell, perched haphazardly on a light fixture, the bulb long blown, its coils vibrating with the movement. The teenager, full of lust and need, extends his hand and takes the girls slender fingers. At first, she resists, then is interested. They go through the house. They see dust and ash falling from the ceiling. The paint on the ground is curled and rotten. It smells of damp plaster and decaying food waste. In the first room, there is a boy and girl, they fuck on the floor, entwined and heaving. The boy is moaning, and the girl has her eyes shut, her back rubbed red raw from the splintered wood. She is bleeding.

The boy watches for mere seconds and the girl opens her eyes and sees them standing. She reaches for something to throw, but only finds her lovers shoe. It hits the door with a loud smack, but the kid on top of her doesn't stop. They walk down the corridor and find an empty room, the master bedroom. There is an old mattress, covered in cobwebs and yellowing stains from past lovers. They stand in silence and listen to the house thrust and wane. The door is missing to the ensuite and Pi looks in, curious of the decay. The sink is broken in two, but stays attached to the wall. The pipe underneath it is cracked and broken. Long strands of hair hang from the fissure, past lovers – past occupants before the rot. The bathtub is covered in dust and specks of blood, above it, the shower head is missing, and the pipe is bent and facing upwards. The window is smashed out and the breeze comes in, hesitant. The boy, he slips his hands around Pi's waist and kisses her on the neck. She allows it, but not for long. She pulls away and looks at the toilet bowl, it is full of used condoms, stacked on top of one another, clogging the drain. It makes her sick to her stomach. Her gaze shifts to the outside and she wants to climb through the window and run into the darkness and vomit. She drinks her drink, it's strong. She places it down on the counter top and turns to the boy, he looks handsome in the dull light, but his movements are eager, and she doesn't like that. He leans into her and grabs at her breasts and she pushes his hands away, so he kisses her. His lips are soft, and he isn't rushed or pornographic. She gently slips her tongue into his mouth and he does the same. Fleshy and wet, they push closer to one another and he tries for her breasts again. She allows it. He's soft, gentler. He begins to walk away and slips his shirt off. He has a tattoo on his right shoulder. He looks over to her.

'Come on.' He waves to the bed.

Pi stays in the ensuite. She looks to the window again. The kid sits on the bed and slips his shoes off. They're muddy and plonk on the ground with a heavy thud. The house reacts; another pair of lovers. He sits with his knees brought up high into his chest and he lights a cigarette. He uses the palm on his hands to wipe a clean space beside him. He knows she's not coming. He holds the cigarette out in front of him, as if to lure her.

'Are you going to join me?'

Pi moves towards the window.

'Everyone else here is fucking but us.'

She steps into the bathtub and cockroaches scuttle and run down the plug hole.

'You shouldn't have kissed me and got me excited, you know. That's really not cool.'

He stands up, the skin under his feet feels the brittle floorboards and pieces of broken glass. He undoes his belt and takes the zipper down.

'I fucking hate when girls do that, it's fucking…'

He looks, and Pi has gone through the window and is walking out into the dark forest. He thinks about chasing her, grabbing her, but the forest is on her side, and he knows it.

GUS AND THE BOTTLE DUMP

The transformers rattle on rusted hinges, humming as the sun peaks over grey-water clouds. The powerlines hang loose and careless, like tendrils of soaked intestines. Black crows sit along the beam and on the wire, random and fat on field mice and insects. Their wings large and leathery, hanging on either side of their dark bellies like carved black wood.

The streets are cracked concrete, and wet from the rain. A sun shower perhaps. Not proper rain. Trash lines the curbs and stinks a pungent stench. A desolate silence from the streets and then the screeching of crows and cranking of an engine somewhere, turning over. The trees, dead from the cold, shake when the wind comes and shivers when it leaves.

Gus stops and looks at the house. He turns and walks down the long, pebbled path that leads past the dilapidated fence and onto the dirt road. Away from the weeds and stale metal, the air is thin and icy on his skin. The sun is blaring and cooks everything under it. Ahead of him, Gus can see the path shimmering in a mirage. Waves of illusion, snaking the path beyond it. He wobbles his head to shake the flies free and walks with his hands by his side. He wishes he had kept the stick he had found before; he didn't remember dropping it. He walks through the small, forest corridor, listening to the insects telling each other that he is approaching, but it was some time until he reached the road. Its asphalt laid over twenty years ago, now cracked and broken, pieces disjointed like the remaining pieces of a puzzle. He wanders down the road like a hitchhiker.

For an hour it felt like an apocalyptic playground. He doesn't hear or see another soul. The world is his and his alone. His mouth becomes dry and he needs water. Far in the distance, the simple rumbling of a car carries to his ears.

Gus walks down the train tracks, old and abandoned. The metal is hot and the colour of scotch. Up until yesterday it had rained, so there are still fresh puddles of water down by the banks. Small insects float, motionless, their wings transparent and fragile. He picks up a stick and swings it around. Pieces of bark peel away and splatter like dough against the pebbles. He leans on the stick and feels it like it's an old bone and looks down the tracks. Nothing there.

He tosses the stick high into the woodland and it falls amongst the shrubs, now tangled in vines and foliage. An animal is startled and scuttles away. He stands, staring at the sun; it's warm on his hands and feet. It heats the ground, and the earth breathes when no one is looking, its breath a rich fragrance of dirt and still water. The pines bring in delicate scent and there is the noise of birds.

Gus looks through the tracks of pine trees, thick set and unsettling and he sees something shiny glittering in the sun. He stands and looks at it from a distance. What could it be? It's emerald green and appears like a diamond, winking in the rays of yellow coming through the lush canopy. Gus shuffles down from the embanked tracks, finding the earth loose and it slides underfoot. He rushes over the water and in through the tree line. In here, the air is thick and heavy with tart smells, sweet, sour and rotten.

Eclectic shapes move in and out of the trees, shadows dancing. At first, he's afraid, his heart pumps and his palms sweat, but he sees the diamond again, reflecting. He walks on dead leaves and twisted, rotting branches. He sees a bird skeleton, nothing but bleached white bones. He steps over it. The ground is uneven and misshapen, like scar tissue or acne. He hears something through the trees, and he sees a deer, large. Its ears twitch and it watches him.

Run, little one. Run.

Gus stops and waits to see what it does. There is no fear in the animal, none at all. Its almond eyes read him, and it knows. It sniffs the air and walks away, morphing into the trees and shimmering out of existence. Gus waits. Is the animal here for him? He tries to look for it, his eyes startled and frantic. It was like it never existed. A warning perhaps? He moves forward through the dead undergrowth, feeling the heat rise up from the ground, a molten, wet stench, piquant. He looks up and thinks the trees have moved. He is lost. From the corner of his eye he sees the gleaming again; the star blazes, as if on fire. He leaps over the debris and falls to his knees, staring down at the trapped light.

'What is it?'

No words have been spoken in this wooded area for years. The birds now quiet. Gus digs his hands in the deep black soil and pulls it out. The reflection is like a supernova and he wipes the dirt from it. A bottle. Empty and green. It's old and misshapen, but otherwise the most perfect thing Gus has ever seen. He holds it up to a beam of light running down from above. He holds it like a sacrificial element, up to the gods. Take this. *Have this.*

He digs again, more. Another one. A third. He wipes

them clean of mother's soil and lays them out before him. A trident of perfectly kept glass. This ground has held them for years, preserving them like diamonds now cut from the rough and admired. There is movement far in the forest, darkness. He has disrupted the ebb and flow of this place, the peaceful calm, the balance, the current. He collects the bottles, wraps his thin, young arms around them and runs.

Run, boy. Run.

He escapes the last line of trees and the branches snap and heave, licking at his boots. With a yawn and mash of wild wind, the forest returns to normal. The haunted playfield is quiet again and it leaves Gus unscarred. He stumbles over wet and loose rocks and makes his way up the hill to the train tracks, almost dropping his treasure. He stands with the iron rail between his legs and feels its vibrations. He walks again, a wanderer with gold. The sun beams and makes the glass sing and strike brilliantly. The tracks end and there is a fence. He crawls under it, pushing the bottles through first and then he slides under. His belly rubs against the ground, caressing his skin. He collects them once again and walks through the first scatter of houses. An old man sits on a chair on his front lawn and watches him go by with weary, dead eyes. His shirt torn and shredded at the cuffs and waist. The holes in his belt faded and puckered. Gus ignores him. A girl rides past him on a bike and stares at his bottles.

He walks through the town and out the other side. It takes some time, but he reaches the warehouse where the flea market is on. People are scattered and few. They linger like moths, filthy and ravaging. They finger change in their pockets and look for TVs or radios that work. They stare, anonymously, curious and bored. The kid walks past them with something new, grand and creative. Old men with false teeth and sunken cheeks turn and stare. There is a man at a table at the far end. He extinguishes his smoke and licks his cracked and peeling lips. They are stained brown and yellow at the join. The man sits hunched forward, his left hand is missing, and his stubble is random and light toffee-brown. Considering his age, they should be silver. Gus stands in front of him, nursing his glass bottles like triplet babies born from a watery, diamond cervix.

'What boy? Don't stand there. What you got?'

Gus gently places them down on the man's table. They stand apart from his junk – broken engine parts, tea pots, gun parts and assorted other glassware. The old codger looks at the bottles like he had stared directly into the face of God.

'Where did you get these?'

'Around.'

'Around where?'

'Not far from here.'

'Can you show me?'

'No.'

The man shifts uncomfortably, played for a fool by a child. He rubs the nub of his left wrist against his temple and smiles.

'These are nice. You sellin' em?'

'Yeah.'

'How much you want for them?'

Gus shrugs and looks around. The surrounding shop owners are curious like crows to road kill. The man leans forward, his yellow teeth poke out from his lips.

'I'll tell you what, I'll give you five dollars for all of 'em.'

Gus nods and holds his hand out for the money. The vendor looks at him curiously, feeling as if he had been tricked. One eye shuts and the man squints. He leans under his table of cluttered junk and unlocks his small metal container. He rummages through coins and some notes, nothing bigger than a ten and gives the small, black boy the money in change. Gus examines the coins; he can't count but it looks right.

'Thank you,' he says and turns to leave.

The vendor takes a glance to his left and the others are sitting back in their seats or returning to their bargaining. He glows in the spoils of his new-found riches. He collects the bottles in his arms like sacrificial lambs and smells the rich earth still encrusting them. He puts them under the table, out of view.

Gus walks to the convenience store and buys sweets. He buys soda and liquorice and goes to the alley beside the store and eats it. He feels sick, but full. He throws the wrappers in the bin and goes back to the store and buys more. He's down to his last few pennies and is struck with guilt. He walks the isles, looking for anything. Not sweets. Not bread. He stops and looks at the frozen food inside the fridge. The clerk watches him, jotting down the colour of his clothes and his approximate height and age. He buys several tins of tuna and a sweet bun and pays with the last of his coins, now there is nothing left, not enough to buy anything. He wanders the streets, heading in the direction of home. The cloudless sky is painted with an unsteady hand. The faces of those wandering as well are clueless and aimless, much like Gus. A general purpose but lacking the connection to this world. A soft skinned corpse, with blinking eyes and moving mouths, with words that seem incoherent and baffled.

Gus moves off the streets, sick of the unforgiven. They breed to comply. He feels like a wolf in wolves clothing, however, a different sort of wolf. He stops by a park and rests. He needs water and drinks from a fountain. He sits out of the sun, on a bench and listens to his own heart. It steadies his breathing. In amongst the trees, near the carpark he spots a familiar shape. A deranged stride; a hovering movement, back and forth to cars. Gus stands up and walks towards the car park. A car pulls in and drives slowly past three women; one is a man with long blonde hair, wearing a skirt. Gus stands beside the tree, eating liquorice, watching. The man in the car talks to the women. He laughs, checks his rear vision mirror, speaks to them more and checks the mirror again. The woman leans into his car window and they talk. The other women soak back into the pavement, like patient crows waiting for the vulture to finish eating. The car door opens, and the man in the skirt gets in and the car swerves fast out of the parking lot, leaving the smell of burning rubber to sicken the nostrils.

Gus was curious of the woman to the left, her body shape familiar. She leaves the shade of the trees and ventures to the sidewalk closer to the road and flashes a car that had slowed. The car hollers and drives away. She walks up the street, then back again. She lights a cigarette and turns around. Gus sees it's his mother and leans on the tree, still eating his liquorice. He turns and walks the other way, out of the park. There's a stream that runs out of a drain and he stops and watches the tadpoles gather. He steps over the rancid water and up a small embankment. Beyond the sewer is the forest again. The trees wave and motion, back and forth, as if on the sea, but there is no wind. Something tells him the forest is dangerous right now. He avoids it; avoids looking at it. He skims the forest line, taking a long way back to his house.

Inside the front door he can already hear his brother crying. The smell is of shit. He walks into the kitchen, hearing his brother's fumbled words, calling out to him.

'Ga! Ga!'

'I'm coming. I'm getting you water.'

The sink is full of dishes, maggots flip and flop on the counter bench, birthed in filth and food for the rats. Gus cleans a glass and feels the need to puke from the smell. He fills the glass and goes to the toilet for a bucket and paper. He walks into Joel's room, and he's half off the bed. His legs limp and crooked, skinny and covered in blisters and sores. His malformed hand outreached and desperate.

'Ga! Ga!'

'I know. I know. I'm here.'

He reaches into his pocket and pulls out a strand of red liquorice rope. Joel eats it with furore. Red juice squirts from his lips. Gus feeds him more. His brother, smelling like faeces is hot to touch, his skin sweaty and his hair damp and strewn over his forehead and cheeks. Gus moves his hair away and opens the can of tuna and Joel eats it, quickly and without chewing.

'Ga. Ga.'

'I know. You're hungry. Mum isn't here.'

'Ga.'

Gus pulls the sheet off and wipes down his brother who isn't wearing clothes other than a shirt. He takes the soiled sheet to the back yard and places it in the bucket, filling it with water and detergent. He returns to the room and wipes his brother clean and settles him back into bed. He sits on the edge and cries and feels sick. Joel moans and ambles his legs and hands, restless and unable to leave.

'I saw the forest today,' Gus says to him. 'It was so big I thought I was going to get lost.'

Joel calms, and listens.

'Ga.'

'On the way back, I felt something pulling me, like a magnet towards it. I have to go back. I found bottles and someone who will buy them. They aren't nice people out there, Joel. You're better off in here.'

'Ma. Ma.'

'She's not nice either.'

He lay down next to his brother, and together, they slept.

FLIES

Faint movement. A blur. Pi wakes in a room. It is dank and stuffy. The window is shut. She moves her hair from her face. She isn't wearing a shirt and her bra is off. Her breasts hang low, milky white with pink-button nipples. She looks to her right and sees Jakob. His face is turned away from hers and he is snoring. On his back are long scratch marks. Pi remembers what happened. She gets up from the bed and finds a shirt. There is noise coming through the closed door. TV noise. She walks to the door, softly, stinking of sex. She places her hand on the handle; it's cold, and she hesitates. She opens it an inch and lets the cool breeze from the house caress her body. Her bladder is to bursting point and she can't wait any longer. Jakob stirs, but doesn't open his eyes or make a sound. Pi leaves the door open and heads down the corridor. She can sense someone in the lounge room. They move and moan like a hibernating giant. She goes to the bathroom and shuts the door softly. Tearing off two sheets of paper she tries to push her urine out, squeezing her insides until she cramps. It comes in loud splashes, sending droplets up onto her buttocks. She sighs with relief. She wipes and closes the lid, ready to flush and run back to the room. She opens the door and steps into the hallway where an elderly woman with a glass of water waits. She looked at Pi's face. The twin nasal holes covered in a fleshy curtain. The woman opens her mouth to speak, or scream, but nothing comes out.

'Jakob,' she mutters, moving her eyes from Pi to her son's door.

'I'm Pi, a friend of your son.'

'Jakob?'

A rush of movement behind her and suddenly her son is at the door. He is only wearing boxer shorts.

'Mum, you're up?'

'Who's this? Why is she in our house?'

Jakob pushes past Pi. 'It's okay, she's my friend.'

'I don't allow anyone in the house. The flies Jakob... the flies.'

'Yes, Mum, I know. The flies will get in.'

Pi walks backwards until the door frame hits her back. Jakob's mother looks at her face but doesn't turn away in disgust. She mutters and tells him to make sure there are no flies in the house. Jakob walks her back to the lounge room. She can hear them talking. They talk about a TV show and he offers to make her tea. She can't have anyone in the house. The flies get in. She mutters and screams and babbles and Pi puts her own clothes on and waits in the dark room. Jakob returns and looks restless. He paces up and down and runs his fingers through his hair.

'You should probably go.'

'Is your mum okay?'

'Yeah, she's fine. She just doesn't like anyone else in the house.'

Jakob walks her to the back door. The sun is up, and the land is hot. The soil bakes.

'I'll see you tomorrow, okay?' he says.

Pi nods and leaves through the path and runs through the overgrown backyard and climbs over a tilted, broken fence.

INSECTS

When the insects speak in May, it's loud enough to shake the glassware in Mama's cabinet. They hum and buzz, igniting the black fog that creeps over the fields to suffocate the inhabitants. Clouds that seem otherwise pregnant with rain, slink away to another town, for another time, leaving whispers of seasons and leaving their trials unheard. When morning came, there is stillness and quiet. Trees that dare move are stripped of their leaves by the winds. The grass cracks and bends; their blades frozen through the night and then thawed to leave them brown and lacklustre-green. A town that otherwise cares not for its occupants and more about the lies that runs through its veins, sees a boy, no older than twelve; Gus, drifting like a soul lost in the breeze, gazing at the trees curiously, as if he had laid eyes on them for the first time in his life.

When the Train speaks to him it's in heavy words, distinctive and monotone.

Come to me, boy, come to me.

Gus follows the ghoul of the night, hypnotised by the dark vehicles invisible thread. It's not for everybody, only a few. The great magnet has attracted him.

Gus walks. The mosquitoes bite his arm and his skin welts. On black skin, it turns purple. He slaps at them, sprinkling blood over his body in patches. The boy is familiar with the infamy of the tracks; the iron spine of the town, thick and humming, indestructible and undisturbed. He has often run his fingers along it and been stung by the cold iron – but behold, it leads to a beast!

The boy, away from home, traverses the countryside. The land is dark, and the moon is far away, hiding its light for something else, hunters perhaps. He follows the call of the beast and marches along the path of the pine trees. Some cut down, the forest gutted of its wood. The stumps are cut haphazardly and without care and Gus hears the forest moaning in agony. He lifts his hands up to his ears to stop it, but he still hears them. The call is louder than the forest, and he must find it.

Find the end of the tracks and the thing that dwells there. Find where it lives and look upon it with his virgin eyes. See it in all its glory – the very thing that has been calling out to him. Sometimes soundless, the feeling can be of fish hooks in the flesh, gently tugging him closer… away from Ma and away from Joel. Gus finds the tracks dip down off the raised ground and onto a long patch of dirt running deep into the woods, past the rusted stove, just as the Trees had told him. He stares at the entrance of a cavernous, overgrown mouth. Slabs of concrete are chipped and lay in clumps around its bottom lip, bleeding green and hanging with viny tendons. It has teeth of long, spiralled metal, the poles once used to hold the concrete, now exposed and demented.

You've found me, now come… look!

Gus doesn't hesitate, he knows too well the metallic creature isn't wanting to kill him or hurt him, but to show him a way out. Into the grotto of wildlife and through the barbaric undergrowth there is the brick and mortar cave, inside, like a lying serpent, lying dormant and hibernating – The Train. Many have found this. Gus feels their shock and awe still in the air, lingering like gentle rain, but none of them proceeded forward, except, yes, a few. Those who dare view inside the sleeping giant dares knowing how to leave this town. Gus steps inside. Instantly the air is different, cool, maybe freezing. The air is coming up from the ground, somewhere, travelling through tunnels and air pockets in the rock, caressing the quartz. The steel and iron serpent sleeps. The Train, a deep raven black, its snout, a long, triangle grate at the front. A long chimney, matte to look at, and prickly like gooseflesh to touch.

Bare me! Look upon me!

It has been found by another. The triangle almost complete.

Gus walks along the cavern floor, underfoot is rotten leaves, unable to float away and turn to dust, trapped in the void of this giant's chamber. The Train is monstrous and opaque. It sits undisturbed, yet restless. Gus steps onto a metal, grated, foot hold. He heaves himself up and clutches onto the railing. The Train accepts his touch. He peers into the driver's seat. There are rat droppings and a curled up, semi-translucent snake skin. No other animals are on the Train. Gus is hesitant but pulls himself up and into the cabin. He has a clear, unobstructed view of the rails in front of him. They are covered in vines and dirt and mud and plant roots.

You know what you must do.

'I can't do this on my own.'

There are others. They will find me in time.

Gus climbs down, his lungs full of new air. His mind has opened a new door, one that lay dormant at the rear hallway of his mind. He starts clearing the tracks of detritus.

THE OTHER CROWS

Sometimes the darkness screams. The tears that roll down his cheeks, he laps up with his tongue. Now his lips are dried, and the inside of cupboard was getting hotter. He reaches up, his arm never fully extending, and he tries the door handle. It was unlocked and swings open. Boy falls out of the cupboard and lays half out of the doorway. His eyes roll up at the ceiling, expecting any moment that his father would come from his room at the back of the house, charging and stampeding and kick him in the ribs and drag him by his hair again, back into the cupboard, but there is nothing. No movement, no sound.

He grips the wall and stands up. His back protests and pops, the discs compressed and twisted. He hobbles to the kitchen, still thinking his father would be here. He drinks from the faucet as quickly as possible, swallowing large gulps of water until his throat hurts and his stomach is bloated. He feels sick and vomits instantly into the basin. It is as clear as the water he had drunk. He stands, unsure what to do and walks into the hallway and stares down into his father's room. He could see a blanket haphazardly tossed onto the floor near the entrance. He was too afraid to go down there. Boy didn't want to say his name, so he grunted and there was no answer or movement. There was no snoring or gasping for air, the normal sounds his father would make when he fell asleep on the couch.

Boy takes slow steps to the front door. He can't find his socks, so he doesn't wear any. His body smells of decay. He doesn't know where his father is, and it terrifies him. He opens the door and steps onto the balcony. A car drives past, slowly, and keeps going. He shuts the door behind him and inches his way to the path. He remembers where school was, it was all right turns. He starts walking.

A woman taking garbage out stops and stares at him. Boy's cigarette burns were blistered and peeling off. He takes no notice of her and keeps walking. The sun is hot this day, but Boy liked the heat on his skin. He feels the sweat under his arms and tries to laugh but had forgotten how.

By the hours end he has found his school and walks into an empty classroom and sat down. This isn't right. It has been too long. He feels nervous and suddenly very fearful. Boy feels the urge to wet himself but holds it. There is a knock on the door behind him and he jumps, startled and leaps to his feet and almost falls. His legs aren't used to reacting this way.

'Um,' a man stammers, staring, popeyed with his mouth agape. 'What are you doing in here?'

Boy stares.

'Can you speak?'

'Yes?' Boy says.

'What's your name?'

'I don't know.'

'You don't know your name?'

'No.'

The man shuts the door behind him and looks to see if any other students were in the room. A shaft of morning light comes through the window, flickers of dust drift around aimlessly. Lost. Boy stares at the man, he doesn't recognise him.

'Do you go to this school?' The man is worried, his brow furrowed and curious.

A small gathering of students stand outside the door, looking in through frosted glass.

'I used to. Maybe. Yes.'

'You used to go here? But not anymore?'

'I don't know.'

'Where are your shoes?'

Boy doesn't answer.

'Who's your teacher?'

'I don't know.'

Boy is filthy, and his shirt ripped at the back. His pants smell of dried piss and one foot is bleeding. The teacher looks him up and down and turns to the glass panel, waving the kids away. They are laughing, mocking and shouting.

'Can you... come with me?'

'Where?' Boy asks.

The teacher watches him. He folds his tie against his stomach nervously and watches as Boy moves slowly away from the desk. He runs his fingers over the wood, as if remembering. The teacher goes to the door and opens it. There is no one in the halls. They have left for class, much to his relief. He holds the door open for Boy, but he doesn't move past him. The teacher walks out into the cold corridor. Boy stands in the vacant room and listens to his own heart beating in his ears. He follows the man.

For a long time, he waits in a room. The teacher had brought him into this room and left him. He had fetched him a polystyrene cup of water and he sips it slowly. Boy looks at the desk in front of him and sees a picture in a frame. A woman with short cut, brown hair, smiling with a statue of a little boy peeing behind her. He sees a coffee cup, the rim stained with old, cracked lipstick and where spilt coffee had run down the side and dried. The floor his bare feet are on, is sticky, but smells of cleaner, strong. It stings his eyes and burns his lungs. The books stacked on a shelf to his right are left haphazardly on the shelves, Boy can't read the titles, but he looks at them curiously. There is movement behind him, and he turns to look. The lady from the picture frame is standing in the doorway looking back over her shoulder, nodding.

'Yes, yes. Okay. Yes, fine.' Talking to someone else, or no one. Boy can't tell.

She finally turns back and is startled at the sight of Boy. His cigarette burns are the first things she sees. She sees a purple bruise on his neck, bulging and fresh. He doesn't sit right in a chair, his legs pulled up and crooked.

'Hello, I'm Susan. I'm the counsellor for the school.'

Boy looks at her and turns back around. He wants to go back to the classroom and sit and look at the board, or at the books. Susan walks around him and sits in front of him. Dirty, brown curls of hair hang over his ears. His chin is covered in sores.

'You told Mr Hilary that you used to go to this school? Is that right?'

'Yes.'

'Do you go to school anymore?' she asks, pulling out a notepad.

'No. Dad wants me at home.'

She looks at him as if he is dissected and under a

microscope with his guts pinned to a foam board.

'Does he get you to work?'

'No.'

'Do you eat? Does he give you water?'

Boy is stammering before he speaks. He can hear a faint voice, far away like an echo, or words coming down a long pipe. Torso is speaking;

I look after him.

'Does he?' the woman pushes.

Boy isn't used to being talked to like this. He has a sudden fear and wants to leave. He regrets ever leaving his house. Whatever his father does to him, he tells himself he deserves it.

'I dream.'

There was silence. A shift in thought and need. The woman knows this is not a case of an attention seeking teenager, but of neglect and abuse.

'You dream? When you dream, where do you go?'

Boy looks to his feet, then out the window. He sees a crow land on the power lines, and it eats something from it claws. He watches and thinks of how it must have caught it, and took it high to eat, away from the other crows.

'I created a place. I like to close my eyes and go there.'

'What is this place?' She pushes her glasses up the bridge of her nose.

'At first, it was an empty room. It had wood floors and the windows were blacked out.'

'Is this place based on somewhere you've been? With your father?'

Boy shivered at the word *father.* He felt his bladder tighten. The burn marks under his shirt itch and he scratches them.

'No.'

The counsellor, Susan, writes something down and looks back at him. 'So, it was an empty room. What's in it now?'

'Toys.'

'Toys? That's fantastic.' Her words are flat and false and edging on true fear.

Boy looks away, unimpressed by her forced enthusiasm.

'Every time I would go up there, there would be more things, more toys, more shelves. Like someone was working on it when I wasn't there.'

'Did you ever see who it was? Who was working on the room?'

Boy thinks of Torso; his dried blood and maggots, the stench of his rotting skin. His mouth opens to speak, but he closes it and thinks. His eyes shut and open, and he looks over to her.

'In the beginning, I would see these... shadows. They were hunched over and moving around the room in the dark corners. They didn't like me seeing them. If I got too close to one, they would leave.'

'You weren't afraid of them?' She taps her pen on her bottom lip.

'I was...' *but nothing was scarier than being in that closet*, '...but, I got used to seeing them.'

'Are they still there?'

'Sometimes. If I stay too long. They built the room into a toy house. I think they bring things for me to play with when I'm not there, because every time I go back there, there is something new.'

'You have quite an imagination.'

Boy looks back out the window, the crow is gone.

'Have you told many people about this toy house you go to?'

Boy shakes his head.

'Does it upset you to talk about it? Because we can stop.'

'No, it's fine. I don't want Dad to know I go there. He would be mad. No one else knows.'

Susan looks down at her notes. 'I won't tell anyone. It's just between you and me... Tell me more about these shadow people.'

'Boys,' Boy replies. 'The shadows are only boys, not girls.'

He watches the counsellor write frantically. He knows he has made a mistake.

'As the toy shop grew, they started to stand upright. Their arms got longer, so did their fingers. Before, they didn't have faces, but eventually they got eyes.' Boy points to his eyes and flares his hands out. 'Some had yellow eyes, some had red. They were like fire.'

Susan looks at the small boy sitting in the oversized chair opposite her. There is a small glimmer inside her mind that this is real. No child she has ever met or interviewed has this much of a vivid imagination.

'Tell me about your home life. What's your family like?'

'My mum's not around anymore. She used to go out to Mackie's. She used to come home and...' *Fights. Don't say fight, don't say fight.*

'What do they do? When she got home? Do they do things in front of you?' Her pen rests millimetres from the writing pad, ready to write.

'They argue. It's okay. Mum was drunk, and Dad

normally was too. They don't remember much in the morning.'

'Is that when you go to the toy shop?'

No. I go there when they lock me in the cupboard. 'Sometimes.'

There is a knock on the door and the teacher sticks his head in. His eyes are narrowed, and he looks worried.

'Sorry to interrupt. Lane is on the phone.'

The woman stands up in an instant, almost startling Boy.

'Excuse me a minute, this shouldn't take long.'

She moves around the table and Boy could smell her strong perfume. He hasn't smelled anything like that before. It catches in his sinuses and he blinks it away. The door closes behind him and Boy sits in the quiet office. His eyes close for mere seconds and he can see his father, enraged. In his memory, his skin is blue, and his teeth and eyes are red as blood. His finger nails are long and white as bone. He is coming after him in great long strides, like a spider with broken legs. Boy yelps, and sits up in the hard, uncomfortable chair. His head spins wildly. He rushes to the office window and grips his fingers under it. His small arms hardly have the strength, but he manages to lift the window open. He can hear voices coming through the walls. He scrambles, punch-drunk out of the window, falling to the grass below. He lands hard and hears the thud as air is pushed from his lungs. He gets to his feet and runs. The sun is hot and hurts his eyes. Behind him he can hear the cries of the woman yelling a name he doesn't recognise. Not his name – surely not. Disorientated and confused he runs onto the road and cars swerve around him, honking loud horns and screeching their tires. Boy is crying, and his feet are stinging.

This way.

Torso! Boy sees him in the bushes and runs towards him. Together they run, and Boy is happy. Away from the school and the teacher and the woman. He should never have left. Torso runs ahead and down several streets, and Boy follows. He stops, out of breath and feeling his heart nearly beating out of his chest.

Why did you leave?

'He left the door unlocked.'

You can't just leave. You know what he'll do to you if he knows you've been out.

Boy feels his head spin and the black circles come down on him like iron. He crumbles to the ground, a soft landing and is relieved to be off his feet, temporarily. His brain can't fathom which way is up and which way is down.

Get up. We must get back. Father will be home soon. He'll know!

'I can't move.'

Yes, you can. Rest for only a few seconds, then we must go. It isn't too far.

Boy rolls around on the ground. A car drives past and stops, watching him for several seconds, then continues. The sun warms his bones and exposes his bruises and sores. He likes the feel of the grass, lying outside in the open air, no walls. All the sounds make him smile a little, the birds especially. He hears a frog and wants to go explore and find it.

He will beat you to death. He will have no remorse. Now get up!

Boy rolls to his knees and tries to make his spine

straight, but it hurts. He pushes off with his hands and stands on shaking knees.

Down there, to the left and we're almost home.

Boy shakes as he walks. He hears the school bell far in the distance, like a warning. Maybe they are looking for him, maybe they aren't.

Boy stumbles on uneven ground and falls. He gets back up and reaches the end of the block. The sun is too hot now, he can barely keep his eyes open. He strains and squints and tries to blink the bright light away but can't. He falters, and Torso moves to catch him, but only stammers himself.

Quick! You must move. We can't waste any more time.

'I'm tired. So tired.'

You can sleep in the cupboard. Remember the burns. Remember how much they hurt. He will do it worse if he catches you out. Now, please...

Boy moves with awkward grace. He reaches almost a slow run and turns off the main streets into his suburb. Down another two streets, half blind and chaotic. He sees his street; the decayed houses, kept alive by welfare and drugs. His house, at the end, like a beacon, not one to go to, but to avoid. He goes up the front stairs and inside. He wants to collapse, but Torso is behind him, close, making sure he gets in the cupboard and slams the door behind him.

Inside the cramped space, Boy cries. His feet ache and his eyes sting. His skin feels burnt and now he wishes he had never left. He knows better. Like a voice, soft and sounding of charcoal, the Train whispers to him. He will have to leave again, for the Train. Boy sleeps.

Emerged in water
Choking and floating
Binge on the swamp
A fare on the banks
Pay the toll

SMOKING GODS

The teenage boy wakes. It is still dark. He gets up and goes to the bathroom. In the darkness he pisses, not bothered when he pisses on the floor. He goes to the kitchen and drinks milk from the container. He cuts a piece of cheese from a large block unwrapped on the second shelf. He sees his mother passed out on the couch. She has a cigarette in her hand, and it is still smoking red. It's burnt all the way down to the filter where her fingers rest casually. He takes it from her and snubs it out in the metal ashtray beside her. It is full of filters, all standing erect, a phallic monument to the smoking gods. The ash has dropped onto the floor and the teenage boy rubs it in with his foot. He returns to the hall and back to his room where he sees the girl sleeping.

His dirty boxer shorts button still undone and his cock shows. It gets hard as he watches her. Her perfect hair and skin. Silky and smooth to touch. Her hair is tucked behind her ear and he can see her corneas move through her eyelids. If she's dreaming, she doesn't make a sound. He traces her arms under the sheets, all the way down to her hips, then legs. He slowly moves the sheet to see her breasts and he is fully erect. Her nipples are pink and small. On her side, her left breast is resting on the other, cleavage almost up to her collarbone. He starts to rub his dick. The skin is red and dry, and he moves quickly, his moans are soft and quick, like a gasp of air. He leans over to her and aims his cock at her hair. The foreskin bunches up around the base of the head; the skin flaky and beginning to show specks of blood. He ejaculates on her hair and pushes his fingers together, from the bottom, near his balls, all the way up. Squeezing the last pump of cum onto her. She doesn't move or wake.

THE WHISTLING

Cassie finds the town library. The smell is of decaying paper, rotting glue and paper lice, the formidable stench of old books rotting on shelves, untouched and unread for years. The shelves themselves are rusted and put together with bent metal tags and screws. The carpet has been wet and then dried, leaving it warped like sandpaper and it cracks and pops when it is walked on. The desk near the front is abandoned. A small computer sits beeping to itself, waiting for someone to come. A stamp dries.

The rack near the front desk has magazines dating back four years. The edges are dog-eared or torn. A sticker is placed on the bottom corner with a barcode from the old library where they came from. They were going to throw them out but gave them to this place instead.

A man wanders through the aisles of books, running his fingers up and down the spines, gently whistling to himself. He stops and pulls a book out, opening to a random page and he starts to read. The whistling stops. He turns the page, nods and places the book back. He continues down the aisle until he reaches the end and enters a new row of books.

Cassie sits in the corner; she has four books about trains. She reads, but her eyes blur. The man sees her and watches. He's never seen her here before and he comes here every day. He doesn't read, just looks at the books and wanders. This small girl, sitting on her own. She is like something lost at sea, maybe something that had washed up on the shore. Curious, he moves to the other side of the magazine racks and stares until the librarian asks him if she can help him. He responds 'no' and leaves.

A BLACK MARQUEE

A bloodshot eye. The twitching movement of muscle and sinew. Flies buzz on parade, a black marquee of noise and cloud. Grey sink water and three dirty coffee cups. The stains days old, forever drying into a hard crust. One has lipstick; rose red with remnants of cracked and peeled skin. The phone rings loudly and it echoes through the small room. The holder shakes, and it stops. Something moves in the rear of the office, a man. He's large and rubs his hands together, dry with an indentation where a wedding ring should be. He can't stop fingering it, trying to turn it around and around, but it's not there. He stands up, his body moans and cracks, his hair tough and short. He goes to the phone and picks it up. Only a dial tone. He leaves it rest on the desk near several folders. He urinates and changes his shirt. A black shadow moves across the front door and he reaches for his gun. It isn't there.

'Drake?'

'Yeah. Back here.'

He sits on his chair and swivels. His computer is off. The phone rings again and stops. The room is full of cigarette smoke. The window is closed.

'Jakob's father is missing. You hear that come through?'

'Yeah, I heard. Not from this town, not our problem.'

'There was mention of searching the woods.'

'No. Nobody is to go in there. Understood?'

Several feet in front of Drake, the shadow lurks behind the door. Skinny and pacing nervously. The shadow runs its fingers through its hair. Nods to itself and nods again and goes to open the door but decides not to. Drake watches the puppet show through the frosted glass.

'If the chief calls again?'

Drake turns to the window and pops open the slats in the blinds. They make a disturbing snapping sound. He looks out the window onto the street. A boy goes past, nearly naked, covered in grass. Drake watches him run out of view.

'Put him through to me.'

The shadow puppet dances, as if lit on fire. His limbs free and limber. He disappears. A lost boy, nothing. Gone.

WAX AND WICK

Gus counts his money again in the car park. $16 and not a cent more. He has returned to the bottle dump and found another flea market, further away. They give him more money for the bottles and ask less questions. The money feels weak in his hands, soft and delicate. Some of the edges are torn and missing, others are folded over, flat and smudged with ink. He's never had money before, never had money of his own anyway. He looks up at the tool store and waits in the sun for a moment longer.

Inside the air-conditioning makes the store smell of fake air. The damp forced air of the deep swampland. People mill around, staring and looking at equipment, whispering, but not to one another.

'Can I help you?'

Gus is taken by the man's voice. It booms and is loud in his head, eager like a wolf and dies quickly. He grips his money.

'I need a shovel.' His voice meek, soft and at a whisper, like a whimper.

'A shovel?'

Gus nods, the lights above are too bright and scorch his eyes, white tidal waves circumference his vision.

'Yeah, we got shovels, this way.' The man walks, and Gus follows. No one here is like his mother. No one here is black or large, reeking of booze and men and drugs.

'Down aisle six we have heaps of shovels. All shapes, sizes and prices. After any in particular?'

'I need something to cut chains too.'

'Cut chains?' The man is now interested, judgmental and his head cocks to one side. 'Like a bolt cutter?'

Gus wanders the store and the man follows. He asks him again why he needs them, Gus doesn't answer. The man is preoccupied by another customer and Gus finds the things himself and heads to the check out. He sees large tins of processed meat and tubs of water, but he doesn't have enough money. He pays for what he came for and is glad to be out of there.

The day eclipses and surges forward, soon it is dusk, and Gus is walking with a shovel in one hand and bolt cutters in the other. He has two dollars fifty left in his pocket. He was going to stop for food, but his appetite left when the store clerk asked him why he needed bolt cutters and was questioned further.

The tracks run for miles through this naked city, like the only flame left that continues to burn, even though the wax is gone, and it is only a wick. The moon is to the west, sitting patiently, praying to a god that never shows its face.

Gus stops and looks over his shoulder, something large lands on a distant tree. The branch shakes. An owl. Snow white with speckles of brown and black. It has a field mouse in is talons. Its intestines hang out of a tear in its flesh like ropey worms from a bag. The owl eats it first, the mouse still partially alive, then it dies. Gus walks in the dark, over the tracks and through the forest. He can hear *them* talking, *them* he knows by now and they scream and jitter to themselves, some who don't know him want him to leave – *don't come in here!* But the others know and let him through.

He gets to the end of the rail line and the coal-black barn

that houses the Train is larger than he remembers. Its maw, darker than any darkness he has ever seen, even the blackness of his dreams. He places the shovel down on the ground and hears the crackling of twigs behind him. He doesn't turn. Something has followed him. Be it human or animal, it watches him. The bolt cutters are heavy and coated with red, plastic paint. Gus walks into the strange lodge, covered and shaggy with vines and pushed apart by tree roots and bent by wind and animals.

Untie me.

'Yes, I am.'

Several long, thick chains course through the monster-machine, holding it to the ground. The binding spells of the trees keep it afoot, keep it close, but the chains keep it physically bound. They are rusted but serve their purpose. They are tight and nearly unbreakable. Man-made bonds only break by man-made machines. Gus approaches the first chain. It runs through the cabin, through the steering mechanism, over cogs and levers, to the other side where it is attached to the wall. He leans the cutter's blade on the dull grey metal and feels the Train lurch and take a breath. It sinks in as Gus applies pressure and the first of many metal rings snaps.

Yes.

'I am being careful.'

He pulls the chain through and piles it on the ground outside the cavern. He goes to the next and cuts it. His arms hurt. He is barely strong enough. He goes to the other side and cuts the last two. The chains snag as he tries to pull them off the machine, so he climbs up. Clambers. Spider webs hang from everywhere. The dust is thick; the dirt is caked unevenly and is an inch laid in some areas. Gus runs his hands over it and underneath is its brilliant, matte black metal. He reaches his long, skinny arms down into the beast's ribcage and yanks the chain free, tossing it on to the ground. He hears something: a heartbeat, a sigh, a breath? Freedom.

I still cannot move.

'You aren't tied down by anything,' Gus replies, wiping more filth from its body.

I cannot move. The fire needs to be lit.

'Yes, we will.'

Gus climbs down. His hands are dirty, and the spider webs are smudged against his pants and shirt. He notices more chains, underneath. Someone did not want this beast to leave.

'I have to go home, but I will be back.'

I am not freed.

'It will take time, but you will be.'

Gus leaves the cavern and hears the Train breathing uneasy. It wants to drive, fast and never look back, just like everything else born here. Gus knows Joel needs to eat and his brother is his priority over leaving this place. He finds his way through the forest, now knowing the landscape and continues down the road, to home.

Tumble recklessly and without abandon
Target the growth
Long grass in the sun
Sky is clear and uneventful

THE HOPELESS WITCH

Pi waits on the corner for Taylor. He lives with his grandma near Fountain and he only just got out of juvenile detention. He didn't care if he went back. He once told Pi he preferred it to the trailer park. The food, he said, it wasn't great, but still, you know when you're gonna get it. He learnt to make crystal in there but forgot most of it when he got out and went back to stealing cars. He has a tattoo on his right arm. It runs the length of his upper arm, down to his elbow. It's a fish or a dragon; Pi never looked properly. He said, once he's legal age he'll be sent to normal prison. He didn't want to go there. His uncle was in there once and he saw three people die.

She waits for ten more minutes and lights a cigarette. She has a bad feeling in her guts. She watches the clouds move overhead in large fists of cotton.

Pi looks at her small bag. Everything she owns is in it. She never looked back when she left, although she thought Cassie would know what she is doing. She had made a promise, long ago, but what's a promise worth these days? Was it ever worth anything? To anyone? She feels bad, in the pit of her stomach, like a knot made from rope found in the sea. Taylor isn't coming, she thinks and stands up. A car horn honks, and she looks around. A small brown car with black exhaust smog trailing behind it pulls up onto the curb. He waves her over.

'Wait,' he says. 'I had to steal money to get fuel.'

'I don't know if I can leave.'

Taylor looks at her. 'I knew you wouldn't.'

She gets in the car and they drive, without knowing where they are headed.

They drive til they were hungry and stop at a small burger place on the outskirts of town. It's a small, white brick kitchen with a single window. Outside are bench seats with large red umbrellas. They're torn and covered in green mould.

'Who did you steal money from?'

'My grandma.'

'You'll have to give it back.'

'Nah. She won't know. It's okay. Mum takes it all the time. She doesn't need it.'

'Your grandma doesn't need her money?'

'No. It's okay. Just eat. Don't worry about it.'

Pi eats and watches Taylor barely touch his food. He picks at the fries and looks around, down the street and watches people stopping and going into the burger joint.

'Where do you wanna go?' he says.

'I don't want to go home, not yet.'

'We can drive to the Lowville?'

'There's nothing there.'

'Exactly.'

They get in the car, Pi sipping her drink through the straw she had been chewing on. She wears sunglasses as Taylor drives. He drives with one hand on the steering wheel and the other out the window. He makes running motions with two fingers and every now and again looks at Pi and smiles. The music is loud but is carried away by the wind and noise coming through all the open windows.

When the forest ends, nobody notices. The Town, a

being in itself, let's them leave, knowing too well they will return. The trees still watch from a distance. The car bumps and hobbles over pot holes in the highway. A dead fox lays on the side of the road, its guts eaten out and its stomach cavity emptied. Pi wanted to stop and take a picture of it, but was too afraid, in case the city behind them beckoned them back early. Several large farms pass by, large red barns and old tractors. Wheat and corn fields to the left, empty fields to the right. A farmer sits on a harvester and waves as they speed by, neither of them waves back.

Taylor sees a small dirt road coming off the main highway. He slips the car off the road and onto the unmarked track.

'What are you doing?'

'We've gone far enough. We'll never get back in time.'

'Back in time for what?'

Taylor looks at her. He doesn't know, but he smiles and sees his reflection in her large sunglasses. It's warped and makes his eyes pop out. His mouth is small, and he wonders if that is how the world saw him.

'Besides,' he says, looking around at the rocky landscape in front of them. 'I gotta piss, bad.'

The road seems to suddenly end and in front of them is nothing but flat land. The ground is sandy but peters off into dirt and small knots of shrubbery and desert plants. The sun is setting, giving an indication that they have now been gone too long. Taylor goes behind the car and pisses. His urine puddles yellow, then soaks quickly into the dry ground. Pi gets out and goes to the front of the car.

'We gotta head back soon,' Taylor yells, shaking his

dick and flipping it back into his pants.

Pi stands and looks at the desert landscape. Her eyes fill with tears and she lets it fall down her cheeks.

'It's gonna rain,' Pi says, and holds her arms up. Rain comes, soft and sparse. The hopeless witch instructed the gods and they agreed – allowing the sand to feel the rain.

'Pi, get back in the car, we gotta go.'

Pi slides her shirt off and lets it fall from her fingers, landing on the ground. Taylor gets in the car and watches her through the windscreen. He can smell the piss inside. He leans forward and turns the headlights on. They splash over Pi, her back lighting up in yellow. Her bra is pink, and she unclips it and lets it fall to the ground also. She turns around and stares at Taylor through the glass. Taylor leans back. He knows she has finally given up on leaving. He can see her heartbeat from where he sits. Her gorgeous breasts and perfect nipples. Her waist and the gentle showing of her ribcage. She isn't made for Hope Valley. She is made for somewhere else but was shoved here and told to die. She could be anyone, anywhere else, but whatever curse was put on her, she was born here, and she will die here. She unclips her jeans button and takes the zip down. Taylor holds his breath. He runs his fingers through his hair and can smell the rain in the air now. His hands are shivering, and he doesn't know why.

Pi slips her jeans off and they drop around her ankles and she steps out of them. Her underwear is black, small leg-shorts. The rain becomes heavy and pounds her. The droplets hurt at first on her bare skin, but she holds her arms up, knowing perfectly well nothing can hurt her more than this town. The lights illuminate the rain like falling crystals. Her body is soaked and dripping, her hair matted down. The water slinking in her nose cavity, the folded and moulded scar tissue, healed and pink. Her arms fall to her sides and she takes her underpants off. Naked in the rain, she accepts she will never leave and enjoys the one single moment she is away from it all.

The night is darker than black in the desert. Pi stands shivering until Taylor gets out of the car and fetches her. She is delicate in his hands and he isn't aroused. He is curious and afraid, like she is. The town beckons them back, and they both know it. She dresses in only her underpants and shirt only and sits on the passenger seat, her skin gooseflesh and ice cold to touch.

'Are you ready to go back?'

'No. I want to leave.'

'No one leaves.'

The car reverses, and the desert watches. It knows the forest and everything it owned. The headlights spill out across the highway once again and they return home.

OLD SALT

Boy sits weakened. His arms are thin and the skin near his armpit sags, yellowed. Flies buzz around his face. His bottom lip is swollen. He sits on a chair and stares at the wall. The closet door is open. The front door is also open. He can hear a car screeching its tires far away, people cheer. He smiles and sits.

Darkness comes, and the front door remains open. The air is cold, and he shivers, shirtless and only in his underpants. He sits on his father's chair and can feel the indentations of his body in the cushions. He wonders how long it will take for the chair to mould into his shape. That thought went as quickly as it came, and he stares continuously at the wall, the peeling, white paint now hidden in darkness. He gets up to turn the light on and to find food. The fridge smells of old oil and rotten milk. There is a plate with crumbs on it and Boy collects the crumbs up in the palm of his hand and inspects them closer. He tosses them in his mouth and swallows. There is a jar with nothing in it, some cans of beer and box of old Chinese food. He lifts the lid and maggots spew out from the sides, landing on the clear-view shelf. Boy shuts the door and goes to the pantry. He wonders if his mother had ever kept food in the house. He can't remember so it doesn't matter. The pantry is equally empty. One shelf has several dead cockroaches, their legs detached from their bodies, laid out close beside them. A small spiders web lays at the back of the space, unused and starving. There is a container of rice, which Boy doesn't know how to cook and a cereal box, several years old and empty. He shuts the door and Torso is near the sink.

'I'm starving. I think I'm dying.'

You're not dying yet, but you are getting closer.

'There is nothing here.'

Get back in the cupboard, he will be home soon.

'I'm hungry.'

In doesn't matter. Would you rather be thrashed with electrical cord, or eat?

'I need to eat.'

Boy opens the cupboards above the oven. Old salt, nothing more. He goes to the next and the next, the shelves empty and dusty. Dead bugs lay upside down, their antennae twitching. Rat droppings scatter the floor and Boy stands on them. Torso moves with angular, distorted motions, its bloody, circular hip bones gleaming as if they are fresh teeth coming through rotten gums. Torso follows the boy as he opens every cupboard until he gets back to the fridge, looks up and sees the freezer. He opens it, as if it is his last will and wish. It isn't cold inside, only stale, rotting smells of spilt liquid and malignant ice. Boy walks back into the lounge. He starts upturning chair cushions and looking under them. He looks under the table, near where his father sat. He looks near the door and under magazines of women and old utility bills.

I sense him closer, boy. Get back in the cupboard. The voice panicked and quick.

Boy didn't answer.

You have felt the sting of this man. You have felt it across your flesh! You have tasted your own blood in your mouth! You will taste more than that if he catches you out. Shut the doors and be in the darkness again.

'If I'm in there any longer, I will die.'

Death is better than this.

'I don't know what death is like.'

Death is like dreaming. Forever and ever. A vacuum of endless imagery and feelings that are twisted and unreal. Yours, but not yours.

'I don't dream. I only have nightmares.'

The toy house is your safe place. If you die, you cannot go there.

Boy stops.

'There is nothing there for me.'

There is. Everything is there. But you can't live there forever.

'If I die, I'll be free.'

The pain in getting there, will not set you free.

'How do you mean?'

Listen Boy! Get in the cupboard. The voice devilish, demonic.

'I can't move.'

The toy haven only exists because you are alive.

'It is filled with demons.'

They are there, only because you are dying. They are closing in. You must get back into the cupboard.

'I'll lie here and let him find me – the man I call Father.'

Boy lays on the ground between the kitchen and the lounge. The floor is cold, and a stream of clear liquid and blood drips from his anus. His skin lays on his ribs like melted wax. Round sores seep and flake pieces of dried blood. He convulses, and again. He moans, an inhuman noise. The house rattles and tries to keep him warm.

Darkness comes like fog; blurred visions and static noise. One eye opens and his father is standing over him. He is in his work clothes and smells like beer. He grunts and steps over him. Boy can hear him pissing, then a door slamming. Boy is picked up off the ground and carried. He feels like he is floating. Maybe death has come and taken him away, finally.

Boy opens his eyes and doesn't know where he is. He knows he is on a bed. It is large and comfortable. The blanket under him is warm and delicate. Near the end of the bed are clothes and he can smell shoes and socks; his father's. He sits up and his stomach hurts. There is a window, but it has newspaper stuck to it, tape criss-crossed around the frame, but there are holes in the paper and wind is getting through. To the left is a small cupboard, the drawers pulled out and clothes laying limp and dirty over the edges. Boy moves slowly to the edge of the bed. He wants to stay and sleep, but is afraid he has put himself here, in his father's bed, and he will find out. The floor is scattered with magazines, like the ones in the lounge room, food containers and clothes. Several boots, all the same, line one wall. They all smell with sweat and mud. Boy walks to the door and can smell something else. It isn't rotten or sour like the other smells in the house.

'Come out here, Boy,' his father's voice thumps through the house like dull lightning.

Boy walks towards the kitchen. It feels weird for Boy walking this way down the hallway. As long as he can remember, he had never walked away from his father's room. He gets to the kitchen and his father sits at the dining room table. He is eating something. There is a plate opposite him.

'Sit down there and eat.'

Boy does as he is told, quickly. In front of him is two slices of bread, unbuttered, with sandwich meat between them. He looks at it and then looks at his father, who nodded. Boy picks it up in a hurry and starts to eat. His teeth hurt, and his throat is restricted when the food slides down his gullet. His stomach rumbles, and he feels sick.

'Eat slower,' his father demands. 'I don't want you throwing it back up.'

Boy eats slower, even though every conscious thought is to heave it into his mouth and swallow it. He finishes it and stares at the plate.

'Go back to your cupboard,' his father says, sipping a beer.

Boy stands up and heads towards the cupboard. It feels too familiar, too homely. He knows he belongs there and now it scares him.

'If I ever catch you out of there again, I will whoop you. You understand?'

Boy nods and shuts the door.

CRIPPLE JOEL

His mother wipes warm water and vinegar over his infected eye. It has become swollen from the eggs that the flies had laid there. Joel knows if he swats them away, they will come back, again and again. Their tiny feet tickling his eye lids. His hands are so deformed that every movement is painful, every finger twitch is protested against, by his bones and unformed muscles. Now, his eye is completely shut. It stings and seeps clear liquid down his cheek. The flies still buzz over his face.

The room is small; too small for anything but a single bed, the sheets filthy and stained. There is a bedside table with empty bottles with Joel's name printed on them. Once they held his medication, to take the pain away, but his mother had taken them and either swallowed them with gin or sold them. When it rains, water slides down two of the walls and soaks into the carpet. It smells of rotting waste. Along one wall is a clothes cupboard, the wood chipping off and flaking onto the ground in small bundles. In the far corner, where the left wall meets the ceiling, a spider has built its web. It sits to the left. Joel eyes it curiously as the days pass. For two days it doesn't move, nor does Joel. He can hear his mother in the far lounge watching TV, coughing from her cigarettes and screaming when she's drunk. She comes to his room; she is hardly able to stand. She drops the empty bottle of vodka at her feet, her eyes clumsy and her motions staggered and unpredictable.

'You're a waste,' she slurs, her teeth clattering and her tongue rolling around in her mouth.

She stumbles and falls, hitting her head hard on the flooring. She cries and spits and lays there cursing. Joel doesn't have the strength to move, if he wasn't in so much pain, he would have gotten on his rolling board and left the house. Instead, he watches the spider in the corner as his mother crawls on her hands and knees, laughing in hysterics.

'Like you,' she bawls with laughter. 'I'm like you Joel, look at me!' Her lips are cracked and bloated from booze.

She climbs on top of him and sits her weight on his torso, crushing the air out of his lungs. Joel never takes his eyes off the spider as his mother slaps him repeatedly across the face.

'Like you, Joely. Just like you.' Spit hangs from her lips, dripping down to her massive breasts, dangling large and spilling out from her night gown.

Her breath is heavy with alcohol, stinking. It drives Joel to near sickness. His cheeks sting, and he moans for air, for her to get off him. She has fallen asleep there, on top of him. Joel watches the spider and gasps for air. He moves his hands, but he is too weak. His wrists and fingers don't work properly. He's too afraid to wake her, so he watches the spider.

The night is long, and he stays awake. She becomes seemingly heavier and her arms press on his bladder until he pisses and hopes she doesn't wake to find him pissing on her and started slapping him again. He passes the time by counting the links in the spider's web.

We are the same, me and you.

Joel stares at the spider. *Why do you think that?*

You cast a web, like I do, and you've caught something.

It is my mother. I never caught her. She has stumbled in here and passed out.

That's where you are wrong. A trap is set, and then you wait. All you do is wait. You catch your brother, but you let him go.

You have nothing in your web?

Patience, Joel. I do not eat as often as you do, so I have time.

I know time well. I can pass the days and nights and not have a single thought in my head.

You don't think of escaping?

Do you?

I came from the outside. Through your window when your mother left it open and you almost froze to death, during the winter. Do you remember?

Yes. But you've not been in my room the whole time.

No, I was in other parts of the house, but I sensed stillness in here. There are many flies in here, as you well know.

I hate them, but I can't do anything to stop them.

The spider moves from its web and down the wall. Its motion is quick and erratic, then it stops and become dead still.

If I could entice them into my web, I would.

I know. Thank you.

You are not like the others.

It moves down the wall and across to the window frame. Joel's one open eye tracks it. It is much bigger when exposed to the light.

I was born wrong. That's what mother said.

She thinks you were born wrong?

Yes.

I've seen what she does to you.

Joel closes his eye and tries to shift his shoulder. Her weight has made his chest feel numb.

It upsets you?

I can't move or go outside on my own. Gus made me the roller, so I could go out into the backyard and look at the birds, but I can't do it on my own.

I think you can.

The spider crawls across Joel's pillow and stops, facing him.

My arms and legs don't work like Gus's. They are fused this way and I have no control over them.

The spider climbs onto Joel's face and the flies scatter. Joel feels its prickly legs on his skin. They are soft and tender. He isn't afraid.

Thank you, Joel says.

Gus wakes and goes to the lounge where his mother should have been passed out with the TV on, but she isn't there. He was hoping she would have left for the day, to go God knows where. He knows she doesn't work as they never have money. She leaves all day and sometimes all night. There are times where they don't see her for a week, and she would return and leave again straight away. He goes to the fridge and fetches an old container of fried rice he had bought a few days earlier. He puts it in a bowl and microwaves it to heat it slightly. He heads to Joel's room and walks straight in to find his mother laying on top him, Joel's face going blue. He drops the bowl of food and rushes towards her. He tries to drag her off, but she is too heavy.

'Wake up!' he cries, seeing Joel's eye open, staring at

nothing. 'Wake up!'

The spider skitters back to the window frame, scurrying up the wall and back to its web.

He shakes her, and she moans. He grabs her arm, chubby and engraved in tattoos, all pinched through the skin and raised. He yanks and pulls and eventually her weight is distributed to one side and she loses balance and falls on to the floor – heavy, with a thud. Joel gasps for air and starts to moan, tears falling from his face. Gus goes to him, cradles him in his arms.

'It's okay, Joel. She's off you now.'

Joel moans, his words forced and undecipherable. He cries and gasps for air and then suddenly stops. His brother still holds him. Joel eyes the spider in the corner of the room. There is a fly in its web. Joel smiles.

FRAGMENT

Cassie is sore and tired. Her thoughts are fragmented and her soul crippled. She stands up from the bed, it hurts. She sits back down. A stabbing pain winds itself through her hips and spine like a coiled snake. She smells the man's sweat on her sheets and she starts to cry. He hurt her, and her mother left them in the house alone, so she could get cigarettes with the money he gave her. Cassie, poor Cassie. Her vision is blurry out of one eye and she feels sickened. The pit of her stomach rumbles and turns, it's queasy and suddenly it clenches hard and rushes bile up through her throat. The taste in her mouth is foul and acidic. She lets it dribble out of her mouth, over her lips and down her gown. It splatters on the floor. She stands up again and her mind blinks complete blackness. She goes to the door of her room and leans on the frame. Someone is in the house. She steps out into the hallway; the floor is cold on her bare feet. It hurts to walk or move. The snake in her spine delves into her mind and turns everything black. She sees only darkness. She sees only death – it is a snake's head with golden eyes staring at the forefront of her mind.

She wants to die, anyway. Right now, she wants to. If there was a way, she would take it. Now. Give herself to death, no more pain, no more rape. The snake will never uncoil. The snake will never die.

THE WEATHERED MAN AND THE MICE

Kenner stumbles outside and lights a cigarette. He looks upwards and shades his eyes with his hands. When he went inside it was near the middle of the night. The streets look dirtier in the daylight. There's more garbage, more homeless people and the smell of disillusionment is intensified. He walks over to his truck, one of three still in the parking lot. He turns the key and it hisses from under the hood. The rust is coming through the paint work in large patches; a large hole has opened on the roof and it whistles. He pulls the steering hard to the left and the car moves like a dead weight.

Through traffic he swerves and brakes hard. He runs a red light, and no one honks at him. Kenner's arms are thin, and his ribs push through his olive-oil skin. He pushes his hair back and stops and lights a cigarette. No smoking near the kitchen, he knows this, but instinct tells him to make sure he's in the clear. One naked flame and the whole lab goes up like fireworks. He purses his lips around the rolled cigarette and sucks the smoke into his lungs. He feels the sacs widening and he holds it, letting it roll out of his mouth and nostrils like frosted smog from a waterfall. There's hubbub to his left and he turns and sees a kid setting up a table in front of a house. He pops the table legs out and flips it over. He wipes the dirt off it with his shirt and places a box gently on the surface. The kid runs inside and then comes out moments later with a folded piece of paper. Kenner looks back down to his cigarette and taps the ash out the window. His phone vibrates. He digs it from his denim jeans pocket and eyes the kid in the front lawn; Mice for sale, $2 each. It's from Tucker.

TUCKER: TOMORROW IS GOOD. BE HERE EARLY.

Kenner yanks the truck over to the side and opens the door and steps out. The sun scorches his back and he finishes his cigarette in two long hauls. The smoke sits in his throat and he lets the butt drop from his fingers. His boot puts it out and he wanders over to the kid.

'You selling these?'

'Yes.' The boy looks up.

'Where did you get them from?'

'I caught some in my backyard. They just kept having babies. Mum doesn't want any more.'

Kenner looks in the box. 'How many you got there?'

The boy shrugs. 'About six.'

Kenner digs around in his back pocket. The money he pulls out is filthy and folded. Some are torn, and dog eared. He holds out a five-dollar note. The boy looks at it.

'I'll give you this for all of them.'

The boy doesn't consider it for long. He takes the money and hands the weathered man the box. Kenner nods his thank you and takes it back to the car. The car seat is hot, and his phone vibrates again.

ROY: YOU AND TUCKER ARE DOING IT. TALK TO HIM ABOUT A TIME. I WON'T BE THERE.

Kenner doesn't respond. He tucks it back in his pocket. The drive home is short, and he hopes Tucker isn't there.

His eyes droop and he fights back the need to sleep. He scratches his face, his stubble is long. Looking at his own fingers on the steering wheel, he worries about the veins bulging from his skin, deep purple and congealed with junk. The mice in the box beside him squeak and he turns, startled.

The sign for the trailer park, *Highway 88 Villas*, has long since been shot at, torn down and decayed. A few of the letters still light up at night, the fluorescent bulbs blink and stutter; the sign turns around and around, always showing "no vacancy". The entrance road has been pushed up from tree roots; exposed concrete, shattered and in pieces, juxtaposed over mud and contaminated soil. He drives slowly over the speed bump near the reception desk. No one sits at the counter, but a TV is on. The wallpaper is imitation wood panels, peeling and infested with cockroaches and mould. It hangs like loose skin, shedding and bubbled.

The mice beside him squeak in hysterics, as if they know their destiny.

The first road winds along the villas, there's music and dancing inside. Humans slink and slide between the curtains; watching who is coming and who is going. Kenner pulls up to his trailer and slams the door hard. He walks around to the passenger side and retrieves the box. There's a crash of metal from inside and he stops and looks at the door. He waits before going inside. The door creaks and the fly-screen hangs off the frame, useless. Missy is in the kitchen. She has a pot in one hand. She looks around the corner and sees Kenner with a box. She throws the pot across the room and swears.

'What are you doing?'

'I ran out of stuff.'

'I got more.'

Missy turns, her eyes red and her clothes hanging off her like a second skin.

'Where? Here?'

'Yeah, in my pocket.'

Her eyes dart to his jeans. Kenner pulls it out, knowing perfectly well she would have jumped him and knocked him back out the door to retrieve it.

'Tucker's gonna kill you.'

'Yeah, he will. If you don't shut up, he will. He'll kill you too.'

Missy doesn't speak another word. She disappears into the spare room. Kenner takes the box into his room and sits on the bed. Across from him is a fish tank. In it is a long, broken piece of branch, a few stones and a single bulb hanging from the ceiling. A snake is curled up on the ground. Kenner opens the box and looks inside. The mice are all in one corner. He picks the first one up by its tail and steps over to the enclosure. He looks down at the snake – Hank. He appreciates its bestial form. He lowers the mouse and drops it right in front of Hank's head. The mouse sits and sniffs, immediately knowing it is in danger. It scampers towards the rock and over the log and into the corner. All it can see is darkness.

'Eat it,' Kenner instructs.

He goes to the box and fetches another mouse. He holds it up to his eye level to inspect it. Its small legs are spread outwards. He lowers it closer to the snake's mouth. Its long tongue darts out, quivering and shaking. He drops it and the mouse runs in the opposite direction. It falls into the water basin and clambers up the other side. Sopping wet, it finds the far corner and pushes its head into the glass.

'What is wrong with you? Stupid fucking snake.'

Kenner puts his hand in and latches onto its body, the snake turns in an instant, small fangs bare and it slides them deep within his enlarged veins. Kenner jolts backwards, yanking it from his arm and throwing it back in the cage. He flips his hands back and forth and blood spatters on the walls. He looks at the damage. Twin bite marks. He holds it up to his mouth and sucks at the wound, spitting it onto the floor. He hears Missy in the other room moaning and calling for him.

'I'll be back… and those mice better be gone.'

He stampedes out of the room. The snake watches him.

A CONVERSATION OUTSIDE OF THE HOUSE

'Let it be known, that the officers attended your house, but you would not let them inside.'

'That's right. You can't just come into someone's house.'

'We had reason to suspect your son was being mistreated.'

'Why would you suspect that?'

'We were advised he went to school. His face and back were covered in sores.'

'He doesn't go to school.'

'He must go to school. It's the law.'

'I don't care for school. I never went.'

'Can I ask where his mother is?'

'I don't know. Look around the streets up town, you might find her there or maybe she's dead? She had talked about going back to Fountain, but I don't know if she went or not. Either way, she better not come back here.'

'Witnesses say your son was in a state of confusion. He didn't know his name. That, on top of you declining to let State Officials in to see him and the environment he lives in, I'm sorry but it's only a matter of time until he is taken from you. You need to let him go to school. How old is he now?'

'Eleven... twelve.'

'Mr Shepard, it's against the law. You must –'

'Enough. He's not going to school. He's not leaving

my house.'

'By the state law, I have to tell you that I'm within my jurisdiction to legally remove the child from your care and place him in a foster home.'

'And I'm in my jurisdiction to stop you.'

'You're getting aggressive... I'm trying to help you, Mr Shepard. He needs to eat regular meals. Go to class, go outside.'

'When I grew up, my pa beat me every day with his belt. Even if I deserved it or not. My mother left too, just like his mother left.'

'You're doing to him, what your father did to you.'

'You can't psyche me, lady. I know what's best for him. He doesn't need school. I'll teach him how to work and when he's old enough, I'll get him a job and he can start earning. That's what I did, and that's what he'll do.'

'State's rules, he needs to attend school. He needs to learn maths, how to read and write...'

'Let me tell you... one afternoon my pa picked me up from my job. I was moving boxes at the back of a liquor store. He came in one day drunk as he could be and told my boss I no longer worked there. He drove me straight to the naval recruitment agency and I was in basic training within a month. I served my duty on a boat for eight years. And now, I'm the furthest from the sea that you can get in this country. Nobody gave me nothing when I left. I was on my own. I know what it's like to be chewed up and spat out. Nobody cares.'

'We care about your son, Mr Shepard.'

'Get outta here before I call the police.'

'I would encourage the police to come here. I need to

know if your son is eating, if he's healthy and safe.'

'I said get outta here! Now!'

—

'You in there?'

'Yes.'

'...'

'Can I come out?'

'No. You have to stay in there. I told you.'

'Someone was at the door.'

'You never mind who that was.'

'They wanted to see me.'

'I said you never mind. Don't speak back to me again. If they come back while I'm not here, you don't open the door. You understand me, Boy?'

'Yes.'

'If I come home and find you missing, or that you let them in, I'll kill you.'

'Okay.'

CURL OF THE BURL

Roy paces back and forth in front of the trailer. Its body like a fallen tree, bloated and seemingly unconscious. On the left side, the roof has caved in from the weight of time and debris falling on it. It is covered in dark green moss and smells like a combination of human waste and decaying plant life. Leaves fill the crevasses, spilling out from murky water and running down the side of the trailer in spotted brown clumps. All the tires are flat, and it sits on the rims, sinking into the soft ground. The rainwater pools around the perimeter and mosquitoes vibrate their siren and land in the still puddles. Somewhere, several streets away, a man curses, and a dog barks aggressively.

Roy sits back down on an upturned crate, next to his chainsaw. Its teeth are nearly blunt, and the chain is already partially rusted. He picks up a stone and throws it at nothing. He stands up again.

'Tucker!'

Thin fingers grip a torn brown curtain inside the trailer and push it to one side. Beady black eyes stare out. Tucker looks and at first doesn't recognise who is calling him. He sees the chainsaw and moves the curtain back. The front door opens, only one hinge attached. He stands there staring, as if a million miles away. Eggplant-purple bags hang from under each eye. Roy walks up the steps and follows Tucker inside. The trailer is quiet and there is a familiar aroma lurking in the air. The carpet is ripped and folded over in one corner; a patch is missing, cut straight with a tool and lifted from the flooring and tossed against a far wall. The smell lingering in the air is chemical.

'We going?' Roy asks.

Tucker moves with a staggering motion. His left leg lifts from the ground, swerves and jitters and stomps down hard, this is followed by the right leg, in the same motion.

'Wait.'

Roy follows Tucker into the next room and there's a bare mattress on the floor and not much else. There is a woman, naked with a sheet covering only one leg. She's on her stomach, in a recovery position. One arm laid straight out. Her long, unwashed brown hair covers her eyes.

'Who's that?'

'Missy.'

Roy looks at the pipe on the ground next to the mattress and sees the hole burned black. He picks it up and smells it.

'Tucker, are you taking from Kenner?'

'No. I ain't,' Tucker says rifling through a dirty pile of clothes. He picks a shirt with a faded picture of a car on it and slips it on.

'Where'd you get this?'

'Missy bought it.'

Roy knows he is lying but doesn't want to get into a fight. He puts the pipe back down on the ground and the woman moans and reaches out for his hand. Roy pulls it away. Tucker looks at the woman as if seeing her for the first time. She says something neither Roy nor Tucker can understand. Tucker pulls work boots from under the clothes cupboard and walks out of the room. Roy lingers, looking at the woman. He has never seen such untainted, pure white skin. Tucker moans and walks around her and down the hallway. The trailer moves and speaks. Roy looks at the woman's breast that has peeked out under her arm. He looks back to see where Tucker went, then turns back to her. She moans and licks her lips. Roy shakes his head and leaves the room.

When Roy finds Tucker, he's in the kitchen looking at several keys.

'You have a car?'

'Yes.'

'Good.'

Roy sees the fridge door is open and water is pooled around the floor. There are a few beer cans in the fridge, a bag of rotten, brown carrots, a glass of water, and nothing else. He shuts the door and they head outside. Far in the distance the rain clouds are black. The air running from the storm is chilled and bittersweet. Both the men's arms have gooseflesh. Roy picks the chainsaw up and puts it in the back of his pick-up truck. Tucker sits in the passenger side and digs out his tobacco bag from his pocket. The engine doesn't turn over the first or second time. On the third it revs so high it sounds like it will tear away from its brackets.

'Got enough fuel?'

'Yes.'

'I ain't stoppin'.'

'I got enough.'

The roads through the trailer park snake around haphazardly placed trailers, and trees that look out of place. Graffiti carved into the trunks – trailer park love and inscriptions of successful places to fuck and the name and trailer number. One branch is burnt black. They pass a large mobile-home with hundreds of dream-catchers hanging from every available space on the camper porch. An old woman sits under them. The feathers hang low enough to cover half her face. She watches them drive past slowly. There's a cross roads and Roy stops, looking at which way he came in. Tucker points, left, go left. Roy doesn't want to argue. The car wobbles and bops over pot-holes and craters made from ill made roads where the waste water has eaten the banks away. The screeching of springs protests the path that leads to a gate on the far-left side of the park. On this side, the trailers are scarce, just a few randomly dropped from nowhere. One is covered in darkness. Over the fence is an abundance of pine trees, casting their long shadows over the home. A young boy comes out, his age undecipherable. Tucker gets out of the car and walks to the fence. There is a length of metal pole with wire wrapped around it. He yanks it hard and the fence opens. He drags it to one side and waves Roy through. He drives and waits on the other side.

'You're not meant to go out that way,' the boy says.

Kenner looks at him, up and down. No threat. He doesn't answer.

'Papa said not to.'

Kenner yanks the fence back behind him.

'Who's your papa?'

The boy hesitates. 'Elroy Hobbs. He works at the factory.'

Kenner leans on the fence and smiles. He weaves his fingers through the wire. It is his stance when he was in lock-up. Grip the fence and look out to nothingness.

'Your papa is Hobbs? I know him. He said I could use the gate. It's okay. Go back inside.'

The boy runs back inside.

Down along the highway, trees have fallen and have been pushed to the side by trucks or towed off the way by four-wheel drives. Roy slows and looks at them; there was nothing he found interesting. They stop along a creek bed. Tucker rolls a cigarette between two fingers and lights it. Coils of almost invisible smoke gently curl from the tip. Roy looks around the road and moves the car forward through the small running water bed and onto the other side. They drive further. Roy weaves between trees that were planted by hand, a long time ago. Each one is the exact same length apart and all the same height. They drive until they reach another dirt road. Tucker shakes his head wildly and spits out the window.

'Keep going. Ain't nothing here.'

Into thick forestry, the rumbling of their engine, the only noise for miles. Ahead they came to a small clearing, no bigger than a parking spot for a car to be able to turn around in. Roy pulls in and sits with the engine on, looking out the windscreen. Tucker is quiet. He stares out the window. They listen for other chainsaws, nothing. Roy gets out and walks to the rear of the pick-up and snatches the chainsaw, his knuckles white. Together they walk into the woods. The ground underfoot is soft and loose, the soil moist and potent like freshly brewed coffee. The smell of pine needles and mulch fills their nostrils. They are both looking up, gazing towards the sky, heads cranked back. An awkward stance. They walk, staring and looking. Roy points and Tucker shakes his head. They keep walking.

The ground is getting softer, harder to walk. Roy looks back, it's too far. He stops and trails back, looking up and around. Blinking and covering his eyes from the sun coming through the canopy.

'There,' he hears Tucker say. 'Over there. Look.'

Roy backtracks, and climbs over a fallen trunk, the guts hollowed out and black. Bugs and insects call its innards their home, buzzing and laying eggs, or eating it. He waves them off and finds Tucker standing at the base of the tree. He looks up. A great knot of burled wood. A tree cancer, all twisted and deformed, with black bubbling nodules hanging in the crux of the tree's fork.

'It's beautiful.'

'Should fetch good money.'

Roy places the chainsaw on the ground and checks the filter, the pull switch and the oil. He turns it upside down and checks underneath. He heaves it up on a rock and clutches the pull string, yanking it hard, his scrawny muscles tense and looking stringy and aberrant. Tucker doesn't take his eyes off the burled wood, as if looking away would give it a chance to disappear. Roy tries again, and again. The chainsaw doesn't make a whisper, too scared to be loud in the deathly quiet forest. He tries again and can hear Tucker walking over. He won't spare him any chances to get it started. Roy pumps the fuel button twice more and jerks the pull as hard as he possibly can. The chainsaw roars to life. The motor howling wildly and the teeth rattling, waiting for the trigger to be pressed.

'Here,' Tucker yells. 'Cut down here.' He draws an invisible line with his finger against the trunk.

Roy carries the chainsaw over and cuts the tree at the

base, where Tucker had pointed. Wood chips fly up into Roy's face. He cuts deep and pulls the chainsaw out before walking around the other side. He slides the blade into the wood, and it tears at it easily. The tree creaks and screams, lulling back and forth. Tucker is laughing. He runs up and pushes it. His junky body is also small, meek and weak. The tree concedes, and it topples over. The sound of it falling is catastrophic; a deafening boom of weight and age. It lands on the ground with a depth, sending birds flying into the air. The other trees around it scream in anger, lusting and rancorous. If they had arms, they would flog the men to death; if they had mouths, they would howl. But there is only deathly silence after the fall.

Tucker is invisibly laughing in slow motion; Roy walks with the chainsaw, his mouth open in awe.

He cuts the arms off, then the body. The burl is large, but not too heavy. They push and tug and swear and wrench it upwards, looking at it closely. Yes, it is good. The burl, an imperfect perfection. They drag it back to the car; over dead trunks and through the water. It's covered in mud and moss and vines. Torn grass and leaves stick to it, a death not respected. They lift it into the back of the truck and pull the entangled ropy vines off it. They sit in the car and catch their breath. Tucker rolls a cigarette, his hands shaking. It's bulky and fat, but he smokes it anyway. Roy drives them out of the forest. The nearest place that would buy the burl is the cabinet maker in Weaver's Peak. Neither of them feels like the drive, but the money is quick money. They drive out of town with the forest still screaming behind them.

Dead and decaying
Laughter amongst the rivers
Turning of the tides
The soil will bring darkness
Memories

TRUTH

Cassie has noticed her sister's breasts and the way her hips push through her jeans. She often catches herself looking, staring and wondering when it would happen to her. She doesn't want it to. The boys pay more attention to Pi; the boys look creepy and zombified by it. At thirteen and fourteen they are greasy and slender; their hands and feet are big, and she never likes the glint in their eyes. They often talk about masturbating and drinking at school. The truth is school is some place to be that isn't home. Cassie would prefer to be anywhere but home, but school is closed for break and home is the only place she can be.

That night she sees blood in the toilet. She stands outside Pi's room and can hear her crying. It is dark in the hallway and there is no noise. Her head tilts towards her mother's room and she can hear someone snoring, but it isn't her. She may not even be home. A heavy thud echoes through the house and the snoring stops. Cassie looks at the peeling door.

'Pi?'

There is no answer. She places her hand on the silver handle. The knob is loose.

'Pi?'

No answer still. She turns the handle and glances in through the gap. She can see Pi sitting on the window sill, staring out as rain started to tap on the glass. She turns quickly, startled and her long legs hit the ground, ready to run.

'Oh, it's you.'

'I couldn't sleep.'

'Come and sleep in my bed, with me.'

She puts the cigarette in her mouth and pushes the window down half way. She blows the smoke out through the gap and continues to stare out the window. The rain becomes heavier.

'You can see the school on the hill, if you look through the dark.'

Cassie sits on the bed and tries to see, but all she can see is constellations of streets and car lights.

'Do you go to school still?'

Pi shrugs. 'Not really. Sometimes.'

'I don't like Roy,' Cassie says, her words even surprise herself.

Pi looks to her briefly, then back to the darkness. 'I wish he would die.'

'Die?'

'I could get someone to kill him.' The smoke bellows. 'I know someone who would do it.'

Her stare stays. Cassie lies down and doesn't respond. Pi's pillow is softer than hers. She looks up at the ceiling and pulls the blanket over her. Pi, in her underwear, pushes her cigarette butt into a mug by her drawer and throws it out the window. She turns and sees her sister and her heart breaks. She looks safe in here, where no one can touch her. She smiles, but wants to cry, again. Another cigarette is pulled from the packet. Two are left.

'Roy's hardly here. It's mother.'

Pi holds the fresh cigarette in front of her, lights it and looks at the embers.

'We can't kill her. If she dies, we'll go into foster care. We would be separated.'

'I don't want to be separated. We made a promise.'

Pi remembers the promise. She knew she wouldn't keep it.

'Mother was passed out on the couch yesterday. I thought she was dead,' Pi says, watching the rain drops drip down the windowpane.

'There was another woman in the house. She walked past my bedroom and looked in. She laughed and smiled at me.'

Pi looks over to her sister. 'I don't remember anyone else being in the house?'

'She wore white. I saw her again at the library.'

Pi smokes her cigarette down to the filter and leaves it smouldering in the mug. She climbs down off the sill and slides into bed beside Cassie, pulling the blanket up to her neck. They hold hands under the sheet.

'When do you go to the library?'

'After the men leave.'

Pi turns her face away and tears roll down her cheek and onto the pillow case.

'Cassie, if I could stop them I would...'

'I know, Pi. It's okay.'

'It won't be like this forever, okay?'

'Yes. I know.'

They sleep off and on and listen to the rain. Pi gets up and makes warm milk and brings it back to bed. They sleep til day break, and it is still raining. Neither Roy nor their mother call for them or speak to them.

A kiss undistinguishable
Lavender and gauze
A structure built for two
The uncoiling of skin

ROY AND THE SERPENT

Kenner is alive with electricity. The drug running through his veins feels like a serpent. His eyes bulge open and he rushes to the toilet. Through his eyes, the bowl has teeth and it swirls, a black vortex ready to suck his nuts down the sewerage pipes. His stomach cramps and he runs to the bath tub. There's a ring of green algae running the circumference, three inches down, around the rim. He yanks his pants down and squats over the basin. His shit is watery and squirts up the porcelain and onto the faucet. He belches and feels stomach acid rise into his throat. He shits more, his anus puckering and pushing. It dribbles down the sink hole and when he finishes, he stands up and goes to the toilet and wipes and lets the tissue fall to the floor. His attention is drawn to conversation in the next room. He pulls his pants up and wanders. His feet feel like tubes of water. He walks and they slosh.

Roy has a small plastic bag that he is holding up to the light. Small crystals stare back at him. Their light blue hue is enticing and utterly familiar. He opens it and takes a small filament and smokes it through a glass pipe. His eyes instantly widen, and his skin stretches and tightens. His rotting teeth sting and ache, but he doesn't register the pain. Voices chatter in his head, indistinguishable to those around him. Missy squats in the corner of the room, where the carpet is torn up and pisses. Kenner can smell it and takes his shirt off. Tucker opens the front door and falls out onto the grass. His nose shifts to the side and the cartilage breaks, it sounds like crunching sticks. The door wobbles, as if liquid, and shuts behind him. He can no longer hear the music or the talking. The night has no time or pressure to disappear, and the air is crisp from fresh rain. He props himself up on his knees and touches his nose, trying to shift it back. The blood gushes out and he holds his hands in front of his face and stares. So bright, so red. The door behind him opens, Kenner and Roy stand there looking at him. Tucker twists and looks over his shoulder. The two men by the door don't look like men. They look like redneck lizards. A macabre breed of reptiles, peeling off their human shell in an attempt to be free, sick of the burden of fragile skin and teeth.

Tucker stands up, shirtless, his knees muddy, with blood pouring from his nose and he looks at his hands. They aren't his hands. The bones aren't his; the skin isn't his. He walks like a puppet, his body floating in a river of absurd consciousness.

'Tucker, damn it. Get back inside.'

They speak our tongue. But their tone is off. Liquorice drips from their eye sockets and they wave reptilian hands, motioning him to come back into their lair. Tucker stays outside. He wanders off, unaware and directionless. The park is spread out wide and far, acres of mobile homes and trees, abused and scarred. A trash pile of human waste and degradation. The flies are fat and buzz loudly, Tucker swipes at them. If he were to catch one, he would eat it.

He meanders with careless abandon; looking through the windows of trailers. Looking at the scenery inside and he wonders if it's real. A woman walks past him. His gait is stupid, ludicrous and unpredictable. His arms and legs try to weave their way through the fabric of narcotics, a steaming chemical rushing through his heart and brain, searing and playing havoc with his nerve endings. His small heart pounds and pumps like a second-hand lawn mower engine. The ventricles creak and widen, before closing momentarily and he bashes his chest with a closed fist. Sweat pours from his body and he tries to focus his eyes, and his mind. He has no clue where he is, but he knows this trailer park. There is a street in front of him and he is in the middle of it. To the left, and ahead, is a shower block. The light is on, it's yellow. Something loud buzzes around it. When he walks, he can't feel his feet taking the steps, but his mind shifts and he's standing at the precipice of the blinding light and the darkness. Tucker touches his nose and there is no pain. He straightens it and hears a choking, gurgling noise in the back of his throat. He looks at the hands in front of him, nervous at first, then realises they are his. Suddenly, the drug prince is startled by commotion above him. He waves his hands in defence and crouches down low to the ground. An albino bat flies over head and lands in the nearby fruit tree. It is mostly bare, but the soft apples that are there, are too sweet to eat and already mouth-bit by other creatures trying to eat them.

'What are you?' Tucker says.

The bat neither moves, nor speaks. He looks up at it and attempts to climb the tree, but the tree shakes him loose and he falls to the ground. His eyes roll up into his skull and then recede back down and in front of him is an abandoned amenities trailer. The windows are smashed out and the shell is covered in graffiti. He enters the trailer, while looking over his shoulder to see if the bat follows him. The sinks are cracked and dirty, caked in grime and mould. The urinals reek of piss and sweat. The light above flashes twice and goes out for a moment. He's thrust into darkness and is suddenly terrified. He's now floating and experiencing the ride to another consciousness, but suddenly he's lost in space.

The light comes on and he's facing the other direction; right at a cubicle. The door is missing, and the toilet seat is broken and lying by the side. He smiles and hears the choking again. This time it's louder, followed by skin-on-skin slapping. He looks everywhere in the washroom, touching every surface, running his cold fingers along the dirt. The noise, its origin is not within this bathroom. He walks out, backwards, staring down the side of the brick hut to see a trailer behind it. A red light is on. There are people through the window, bucking back and forth, writhing.

He walks down the corridor of bricks and overgrown vines and prickle-bushes. He sees a woman, naked with a mask on, a plastic device keeps her mouth permanently open. Her long, brown, hair is out and flows down to her tits like spider-silk. Her hips are wide, and she has a hairy bush. In one hand, she holds a paddle. The body of it has studded leather and she looks at him through the window, not curious or afraid. She waves him forward. As Tucker approaches, he sees a man on all fours. His dog position has his ass towards him, his cheeks are red and there are specks of blood dotting his skin. The man is wearing a blindfold and his hands are cuffed. His cock is flaccid and dangles; a useless appendage.

'Why did you stop?' the dog-man protests.

'Shut up,' the woman says. 'Someone has come to join us.' Her words are muffled and saliva drips from the mouth apparatus.

The man's head spins around, as if he can see through the blindfold.

'Should we invite them in?'

'Yes, I think we should.'

She waves him in, and points to the edge of the bed. There's a bottle of lubricant and a hairbrush. Tucker, his mind reeling and succumbing to bizarre madness, climbs through the window. His eyes bloodshot and his cock hard.

—

Roy stares at Missy. She dances in the lounge room to invisible music. He rubs his genitals and watches, as her eyes close and she dances slowly and seductively. Her joints are smooth, then wavy, as if she has turned to water. Roy rubs his eyes and looks around the room; the whole room is water. Everything flows in here and he feels it. He's done right. Yes. He reaches upwards, to nothing. Some prehistoric cave-man innate reflex. Look up for predators. He lies on the ground and moves his arms and legs involuntarily. He remembers the tree he cut down. It speaks from afar:

You will die for what you've done.

'No,' he replies. 'I won't. I take what I want.'

Is that so?

'Yessss,' he hisses. 'Whatever I want. I just take it.'

Come to the forest. We'll take your life from you. Our worms will eat your flesh and our dirt will crumble your bones.

Roy sits up. He feels sick and runs outside to vomit. His spew is clear, and the water puddles by his feet. He watches it writhe and swirl and soak into the dirt.

I told you. Come closer... come speak with us.

He looks up at the trees scattered through the park. They are all shaking from side to side, violently, wanting to grow legs and mouths, and destroy him.

'You have no mouths, yet you speak?'

I speak for them.

'Who are you?'

You know me.

'I do?'

Yes. You found me. When you were cutting down burl wood. You took me home.

Roy's head snaps around to the door. Spittle still on his lips, he runs inside. Missy is standing in the darkness of the kitchen. She blows out smoke and looks at Roy. She walks to him and lays her cold hands on his face.

'Who are you talking to?' Her words are far apart, different pitches and seem to make nearly no sense to him.

'The one who speaks for the trees... is in this house.'

Missy's head rocks back on her neck and she starts laughing. Roy pushes her away and runs into his bedroom. In the far corner is the fish tank. Empty of water and filled with a dead branch, rocks and grass. The singular bulb that hangs overhead by a chain, is off and black. He turns it on, and the small, brown snake stares up at him.

Return me to my home. The dirt is my bed and the grass is my blanket.

Roy stares, his eyes bulging and are about to burst from his eye sockets. The snake – Hank Williams – slithers over the rock, turning its diamond-head gaze away from its captor.

I hunger for the tunnels underground, the field mice and the free roaming grasslands of the forest and swamp. Free me or die.

Roy lifts the lid off the tank and stares down at the tiny snake.

'I found you, therefore you are mine.'

Not all that is found, is lost. The earth owns me.

Roy reaches in and the snake strikes at him. Its small fangs bury deep within his skin. He picks it up, its jaw wiggling and turning, pushing its venom into his blood stream. Their gaze meets. The golden nugget eyes of Hank Williams, a cyclonic typhoon of purple and yellows. Roys' are bloodshot white and green, maple-syrup coins for irises.

He carries the snake to the kitchen.

What you take from nature… it will come looking for.

He lays it out on the kitchen bench. Missy is holding her stomach, doubled over in guttural pain. She falters her steps and lands on the wall, sliding down it. She sees Roy in the kitchen, holding a knife.

A darkness is brewing on the horizon. Mankind should be afraid.

The wilder snake is wrapped around his hand, its constriction only built to strangle mice and other snakes. Roy unlatches the serpents jaw and lays it out longways. He straightens the tail, but it curls.

Evil that grows in the forest has succumbed to its surroundings, the children of the locomotive are close, and you will die.

Roy slices as its head, its jaw opens and shuts. The knife cuts through it and it disconnects the head from the body. The blood is little, and the body squirms in his hands. The eyes roll back, then look straight forward. He steps back and the snake, still alive, hisses. Its tongue darts out of its mouth and the head rolls, falling onto the kitchen floor. Roy looks at his hands and screams – bestial and gut-wrenching. Missy vomits from watching what Roy has done. Her hands shake uncontrollably, and she crawls on all fours to the bedroom where she collapses on the vacant, stained, mattress.

'Death is coming for me,' Roy says, staring at the snake's body as it writhes. 'The children are close, and I will die.'

He rushes to the pipe on the coffee table and packs the opening with more crystals. He lights it and the flame seems hotter than it did before. He waves his head backwards, as if being burnt. He sucks on the mouthpiece and breaths out. The windows shut with a darkened veil. The doors become a watery cesspool, bloodied and fragrant. Roy steps with backwards knees and a sense of motionless stupor. He gets to the bedroom and collapses next to Missy. He whispers in his sleep that death is coming.

Impregnated mountains
Jolting and full
A distant scream
The bitter smell of coal
Crows eyes are cunning
Let it out

TO MOVE

The Train – how it bellows. So significant yet restrained. A bronco will buck due to its innate defence against wild animals, as will machinery. The Train, it sits, unable to buck or move, tied by man. Caught and strung up for the trees to bare witness. *Behold!* The Great Train – now our captive. Unfed and uncared for, except by the three children. As it's told in the cards, so it shall be.

A pulp of metal and ingenuity. A cancerous polyp grown from Man to move and shift and bare weight and never die, lying here, so unnatural and so aching. It strives to be led away, to be free, to roam... to move.

THE CALLING

Jasper sits on a lawn chair looking up at the stars. He has been there since the afternoon, sipping whisky and watching the sun die away. The crickets have started their long night of noise and to him, it is the sound of the dark. Soft blues music comes from the house behind him. He has gotten up whenever the record runs out and turned it over, or to refresh his glass. He can hear the swamp through the trees, moaning, and he is suddenly afraid.

LICE

Douglas grips the brown paper bag so tight his fingernails gnarl and tear the paper. His palms are sweaty, and he stands, hot and stinking under a large, red oak. Its giant hands are raised up into the air, holding the sky from his face. He listens. He can hear a tractor, miles away. It stops, then starts again. The bag is heavy, and he is nervous.

He has a thin neck for a young boy, with long arms and fingers to match. Each knuckle like a ball bearing in a socket, greased with oil, and translucent. They bulge and buck, gripping and regripping his bag. The forest can never be quiet; the wind whispers and tells the trees, in turn they tell the animals. Douglas walks through the woods. Every time he walks a new path, so his tracks don't leave a trail. Douglas, a bug, eyeless and wandering. His treasure – drug money. His hair, full of lice and lose skin, flaking. He tracks on fallen branches and dead leaves. He steps over hollowed trunks, cut down and never taken away, silently screaming, without blood. Douglas has a demon on his back, black with red, watery eyes. It guides him.

'Where is it? Where are you?' he talks, asking the forest.

Have the trees moved? Have they swallowed what he is looking for? No, there it is! He has found it. The sheet of nervousness and apprehension slides off him.

From somewhere in the darkness of the forest a boy watches him. He hides, fox-like, but not hungry. Eager, but not willing. Douglas digs the ground like an excited dog.

His hands flail in the air and he yelps in joy. He reefs up a plastic bag. It's heavy and full. He opens the brown bag and adds to it. He rewraps it and buries it again. He stands and kicks dirt on top. He reaches into his back pocket and pulls out a knife. Carving into the tree the initials DE. He looks around, nervously, making sure only the forest is watching him. If it disappears, it falls on him. He is dead either way. He returns to the cabin.

Gus watches. Hidden.

THURSDAY

Kenner strolls out into the warm sun and the chills slip away. He raises his hands over his head, his fingers in balls of flesh, pink and wrinkled. He yawns and moans like a mountain bear. His singlet is the colour of piss or stale beer. He scratches his underbelly and takes long, bleached sheets off the line. He folds them and notices his track marks. Purple cobwebs. Blue cobwebs. They etch up his arm and spiral out in a labyrinth.

Inside, a man sits at the table, a beer bottle in front of him, another one, full, to the side. A small glass tray holds a cigarette. The smoke curls all the way up to the ceiling. He's reading the newspaper, now two days old. A cane chair is in the corner, folded white robes are stacked high. Somewhere in the rear room a radio crackles softly, no music. Voices, someone talking, barely audible. In the room to the right, a young man is sleeping, shirtless. His arms are heavily tattooed, and his head is shaven down to his skin, which is red raw. Patches of blood mark his knuckles. He snores and wakes himself up, turns and rolls over.

The man from outside yells.

'Stop reading and get that shit ready.'

'He ain't comin' til midday.'

'It's close enough.'

The man stands up, goes to take a swig of his beer but its empty. He eyes the emptiness through the hole and swears. He plonks it down hard and the boy in the next room wakes again. The man picks up the other beer, but it's warm. He gets a beer from the fridge, pops it open and takes three large swigs. He heads for the front room. The man from outside comes in, his fingers wrinkly and he stares at them.

'The sheets are ready. The wood needs to be chopped and loaded.'

'We'll get the kid to do it.'

The boy opens one eye, then closes it.

'Did you hear what's happening in Lowville?'

'They're armed and ready. The rally is on Thursday.'

'We're going, right?'

'That's not what Keiser says. He wants us to stay here.'

'Why?'

'The new officer, Drake something. He's watching us.'

'I saw him last night. Up near Cicada Mountain lookout. He drove by. He's watching everyone.'

'We can't afford to lose more people. We have to keep our heads down, stay quiet for a bit.'

'I hear that he's here to stay.'

'We'll see. People can't just come in here and dig their heels in. The town won't allow it.'

The boy swings his feet off the couch and rubs his head. There's a welt on the back of his skull and he winces.

'You have to go out and cut that wood. Use the drop saw, not the axe. Then load it in the car.'

The kid nods and stands up. His frame is small, and his ribs are corrugated through his skin.

'We have to stand up for what we believe in. Here, take that and pack it away. Put those in the bag. If he turns up and its fucking not ready to go, he'll shoot us both. And if I see you sleeping all day again, I'll shoot you myself.'

'I was reading and fell asleep. I'll wash up and go cut the wood.'

'We need you to go to the shop too. You can't take too long either.'

The boy nods. The man places his beer down and walks to the book shelf. His fingers run the length of the spines and he yanks one out from its resting place. He hands it to the kid.

'Leave this in your room. Before bed every night, read ten pages.'

The kid nods and takes the book.

'Would you rather be some dead-shit, white fuck-up who has spent half his life in jail, or an educated fool?'

'*Ha-ha.* An educated fool.'

'Listen, there's a man, right next to you. Are you better than him? You're at a bar, or on the street, are you better than him?'

'No.'

'You should be. I don't want no dumb shits waving these flags around. Understood?'

'Yes.'

'Read books. Every night. Know the law. If Drake comes up and asks you something, you should know your rights.'

'They read them to me enough.'

'But you don't understand them. We go to jail because we are stupid. Do you think the man on Wall Street goes to jail because he does cocaine? No. He might deal pot to all his yuppie friends and never get caught, why is that?'

'He's smarter.'

'That's right. He's smarter. We can be smarter. Shave

the rest of the boys' heads, do it tonight when Keiser comes by. He's around here. He'll be in at some point. He sees everyone's hair long, he'll be cut. I'll tell you. Shave them all now if you can. Stop sleeping so much, there's too much to do.'

FIT

The sun beats down hard, bright enough to burn Gus's eyes. He blinks and looks up at the sun, trying to see its sadistic eye. His skin is starting to peel; the flesh under it is pink and blistered. He looks down and can see spots circling around. He falls and lands on the grass. His body shakes wildly. His head flopping from side to side. He bites his tongue and blood washes his mouth.

When he comes to, it is dark. A soft howl of animals comes over the mountain.

FAR ENOUGH

Kenner stands in the field and watches the sun come up. It breaks over the forest like egg from its shell. The orange luminescence spreads like a tidal wave. It breaches and wanes, scoring the earth and bringing colour. The taste of fresh morning, out this far from town, is tender and succulent. The first bite as the sun rises is reserved for those who are willing to endure mother nature's true scent. The unwavering and unforgiving dew of the gods.

This miracle of pure selfishness is not reserved for those like Kenner. He is the stain smudged amongst an extraordinary picture. The artist's foul move that rendered the broth spoiled.

He fingers his front jeans pocket for his smokes and blinks wildly, as if waking up from a coma. The sun caresses the green spears of the treetops, giving them life and breath. He taps his back pocket and feels it. Slowly, as if too scared to look away from the bleaching sun unveiling its virgin day before him. He sneaks a look over his shoulder. The shack is drawn against the backdrop like a fingerprint.

He is far enough.

He pulls a cigarette from the pack. The plastic crackles against the cardboard. He straightens it out and smells tobacco, rich and full. The powdery brown guts spill out from a split in the paper and he licks over it, spitting out the small hairs of the smoke left in his mouth.

CONVERSATION IN THE FOREST

'I saw you watching from behind the trees.'

'I wanted to know what you were doing.'

'The Train, it needs to be freed.'

'I see it in my dreams, but I didn't know it existed.'

'I saw it too. Then, I found it.'

'It's tied up in chains.'

'Yes.'

'But we can remove them, eventually.'

'Does anyone else know you are here?'

'No.'

'I kept thinking someone is following me, but there is no one there.'

'The forest has eyes. The animals watch us.'

'No one else can get in here, but us. And now you.'

'I was afraid of the trees as first, they would hang down to touch me.'

'They needed to know you were here for the same reason.'

'Can the Train go? It looks old.'

'We're trying to get it going.'

'It wants to run free on the tracks and feel the wind against its body.'

'We are trying to make it work.'

'Do you go to school?'

'No, my father won't let me. When I'm old enough I will work, like him.'

'You're not old enough. Not for a while. Are you hurt?'

'No.'

'I can see sores on your arm and back.'

'Please don't look at them.'

'You can tell us. We aren't like the others.'

'The others?'

'The rest of the people here. We're different. They say you can't escape. That's what the others say. But we are going to.'

'I'm coming too.'

'Yes.'

'We need to free the Train.'

'I know the tracks. I've walked them.'

'It will take us far from here.'

'Yes.'

'But I can never come back. Not ever.'

'We know.'

'We don't want to come back either.'

Lies will come in two forms
Red like hell,
White like a thigh
Burning will cleanse

FIT (2)

I must be fitting. I'm in the car again. Through the windscreen I can see the small river snaking around those trees with the huge trunks. The roots are so big and round and curl into the ground. Inside the car it is hot. Sweat seeps down my neck and behind my knees. The dash is black and cracked and hot to touch. We must have just got here.

When I fit, I always come to this place. I don't know where it is or have any memory of it from my childhood. There is a man in the car with me, he's older. He looks like my father, but he isn't, but he has the same nose and large ears. He points to the river and talks, but I can't understand what he says. He puts his hand on my thigh and laughs. The laugh is loud, and the birds are scared and fly away. My muscles are sore; my body will be convulsing and writhing, uncontrollable. I hope I don't bite my tongue again.

The old man is talking about the Train. He would board it to get away from here, but all things that serve the forest, would bring him back. For one reason or another, he always came back to Hope Valley. His hand goes further up my leg and I start to black out. I can taste the blood in my mouth, copper like coins and I swallow it. I know the Train is holding me. Even though I am not, I feel safe.

LIFT

It has been almost a day since Boy was locked in the cupboard without food or water. His body is emaciated and yellowing. He grips the wall with a flat palm and shimmies himself to his feet. He tries to stretch upwards, but his elbows clank against the wall and the door. There is a coat hanger on the bar near his head. He reaches up and takes it. He holds it in his thin hands, looking at it; an alien artefact. It's cold. He lifts one leg and tries to balance. He puts the coat hanger back on the metal beam and holds onto it and lifts his leg again. His muscles ache and scream. Pain shoots up his spine and into his neck. He grimaces. He lifts the other leg and holds it. He sits back down and waits.

KNUCKLES

The day is black and purple like a fresh bruise. The ground craves wild dirt and holds puddles from the night before. The stench is sour and lingers like rotting fruit. A call goes up, sharp across the sky and splits open the clouds, sending bats into the air, wild and screeching. Their bodies are black like deranged tar, their wings morbid and web-like.

The blood spills out onto the freshly upturned soil. The heat sinks right down into your stomach. His knuckles are raw and sliced open, bleeding rose-red fluid down his forearms. The sweat is pungent and bitter, lights flashing somewhere on another plain of existence and Kenner rolls over. Jasper stands over him.

The clicking of bone, the jaw moving to the side and his skull touches the ground. Lights flicker inside his head and he momentarily lapses into unconsciousness. Douglas runs in, seemingly in slow motion and kneels before the King; the Purple King.

'Please,' he pleads. 'Please… the money was there and now it's gone.'

The Purple King (Jasper), shirtless and covered in sketchy tattoos, all black, rough and juxtaposed on his skin like crayon drawings, his fists balled. He punches the half unconscious man again, kicking him in the ribs.

'Don't, it was here.'

'Well, someone took it.' He takes out a gun and aims it at the breathing corpse. 'If you didn't take it, then he did.'

'No, no. No one took it. I'll count it again.'

'You are never wrong.'

'I might have been wrong this time.'

The Purple King looks at the scared black man before him, grovelling and on the verge of tears. He nods and tucks the gun back into his pants.

'All here tomorrow, or you both die.'

He walks to his car and stops to scan the house in the middle of the forest. The stained windows are getting thick with chemical dust. The wood is rotting and the grass around it is dead. He slides into the driver's seat and speeds out of the forest.

TOWN

Sand mixed with dirt and dried seaweed. A black tide. Nothingness (Hope Valley) in a place that will be nothing. A nowhere town, still breathing, with broken ribs. It chokes and coughs up cancerous lives, thriving and working and drinking and smoking. Loud country music coming from a bar two streets away. The sun is hot today. It might rain later.

FATHER

'Dad, where are we going?'
    'Shut up. Don't speak. Just follow me.'

TRACKS

An iron spine, running through the timberland. Enveloped in weeds and vines, strangled to death, the iron bends! A warping run of metal up and down, overgrown with roots, holding it still, a python with the victim in its jowls. Fangs of poison, long ago syphoned dry, no one escapes, not now, not ever. Maybe.

Gus follows it. He holds a stick and he hits it hard against the metal. Boy behind him. He has no shirt and the cigarette scorches are healed and the scabs hang off him like wings, translucent and shedding. Boy bends down and his aching back kills him, pain like a million razors shoots up his spine and he yelps like he is stung. Cassie runs to him. They don't speak and she sees water in his eyes. He nods, *I'm okay*. He bends down again, slower and picks something up from the ground, dug deep and hiding. A shell. He gives it to Cassie who looks at it against the sun. A small hole, pecked by a bird, lets the light through. She slides it into her pocket.

'Where does it go?'

'This way.'

They follow the tracks and see small trees growing between the two spinal cords of metal. The lumber used is split and seedlings grow from the crevasses. No flowers, just weeds. The dull rusted stench rises and is indifferent amongst the sweetness of the pine trees and animal scat. Boy places his hands along the base of the small shrivelled tree and yanks it. Lightning bolts of fiery agony shoot up his shoulder and into his neck. He yanks again, black dots swirl amongst the trees and he watches them. They watch him. He pulls again and the tree slips out of the softened ground. The soil fresh and bare. Worms wiggle and push themselves back into the blackened earth. Boy throws the tree into the undergrowth.

'It could go anywhere.'

'Anywhere is better than here.'

'We need to clear the way.'

Ahead, Gus stops and looks to his right. A makeshift camp. An old fire. Some plastic bags. He strays from the path and the Dark Rider sees him. Thirsty, yet patient. Gus moves the bags with his stick and looks in them. Condom boxes and empty cans of beer. A bottle of vodka lies in a sliver of sun, baking and fading. On the red cap sits a fly. Its lime green eyes dart left and right. Cassie stands in the circle, a clearing with the fire pit in the middle. Rope hangs from one tree to the next. An old shirt is over it, wrinkled and grey.

Boy says, 'We shouldn't be here.'

'Why?'

'It's too far from the tracks. They might come back.'

'Who?'

'Whoever was here.'

'They aren't coming back.'

'How do you know?'

'They're dead.'

Boy looks to Gus. His face smudged in soot, his hair dishevelled and tangled like sailing knots and pushed to one side. Cassie agrees and heads back to the tracks.

'Look.'

Boy sees a small shack made of wood and branches cut from trees not from around here. The branches are old and browning. The bark peels off, curling and indignant. Boy stumbles over rotting brushwood and slippery foliage, covered in moss and water waste. He peers in, but it is dark.

'Someone lived in here long ago.'

The ground within the shack is clear of grass or seedlings. No plants grew. It had been worn bare from feet, or bodies sleeping. Boy turns and his heart drops into his stomach, standing on the tracks is a dark silhouette of a man.

'I know he is there,' Cassie speaks.

'He's been following us.'

'What do we do?'

'We keep going. Leave here.'

'Will he hurt us?'

There is no answer. Gus and Cassie move quickly through the thicket. Brambles grow along the ground, sprouting tiny fruit. The smell is sweet, but rotten. Boy trailed them, his feet bare and cut from stones and twigs. He glances back. The figure is gone.

They clear the tracks for hours until the moon watches them from the sky directly above them. Cassie sees the street lights past the vacant, unused road ahead and decides to go home. Boy heads back to the train, to sleep on the cold metal.

Gus thinks of Joel and leaves quickly.

ANNOTATION

Roy hasn't slept for three days. His eye-sockets are blood red and purple veins are raised on both sides of his neck. His knuckles are bleeding from cracked skin and burnt by chemicals.

'Where the fuck is it?' he screams, the house awakens.

The woman they call Mother, wanders into the lounge room where Roy is turning over tables and pulling out drawers. He turns them upside down and tosses them across the room.

'Stop fucking throwing shit,' the woman screams back, her hair knotted and wet. 'What are you looking for?'

'Shut up, just shut up!'

Roy goes to the fridge and yanks the freezer door open, there is nothing in there.

'I had three hundred dollars, rolled up for Kenner. From last week… It's gone!'

'You gave it to him yesterday.' Mother sees a cigarette pack on the TV and shakes it, there are three left. She pulls one out and lights it.

Roy scratches his arms and hair; his frantic movements disrupt the quiet atmosphere of the house. In the backyard the dogs start to bark.

'That was two weeks ago, for fuck's sake!'

Roy slows down, his heart beats and beats, throbbing against his ribs. His legs turn to jelly and he grips the kitchen bench. The freezer door still open, the coolness circling around his head.

'Pi,' he whispers. 'Pi took it. I saw her two nights ago buying booze with it. That fucking bitch.'

Mother steps in front of him. 'No! Stop, she didn't take it, Roy, listen. No, stop, wait…' Her hands flailing. She tries to stop him, but he pushes past her. She hits the wall and slides down it. 'Where the fuck is she?' His words come out as one long, joined, word. His sweat is cold and his head swims and dances, relinquishing in the pounding blood coming from his heart.

Roy goes to Pi's room, it's empty. The bed is made. He grabs the sheets and tosses them aside, upending the mattress. He throws what little make up she has onto the floor. He looks at the perfume bottle, still nearly full. That bitch. Through the window he sees her long shadow cut across their unkempt lawn. He bolts for the hallway where Mother is standing. In her hand is a kitchen knife.

'Get out of the way.'

'I took it. For food.'

'There's no food in this house, you fucking bitch. You're covering for her.' Tears stream down from Roy's eyes. The silky, clear tears run clean tracks down his cheeks. 'You're covering for her, like you always do. You didn't take it, she did. She doesn't fucking work and fucks guys… They talk about her you know. The slut with no nose, the slut who'll fuck anyone because she's got no fucking nose!'

He lunges towards Mother and wrestles the knife from her hand. It falls to the carpet. Cassie appears at her door and looks at the knife on the ground. If she could, she would have snatched it up and plunged it into Roy's neck and watched him bleed to death. But her body is too weak. Roy steps over the quivering body of Mother and runs to the back screen-door, kicking it outwards.

Pi smokes. Her gentle lips full and gracefully nips at the butt of the cigarette. She's holding her phone, texting someone, anything. Organize something for tonight. She can't stay here, she doesn't want to.

PI: ALLEY BAR TONITE?

JP: THAT PLACE SUX. WAT ABOUT HANGMANS?

PI: THAT PLACE IS WORSE!! CAN I SLEEP AT URS. I DON'T CARE WHAT WE DO.

JP: EZRA WILL BE HERE. IF YOU DON'T MIND THAT.

PI: BETTER THAN STAYING AT MY HOUSE. I'LL GET RUM AND BE OVER AT 6.

JP: ☺ SEE U THEN.

She hears Roy's ranting before she sees him. She looks up. He's mad. Like always. Always in hysterics. It's the drugs – the come down. His fists are balled up and his face is red. His neck bulges and he's bolting towards her, pumped up on fiery vinegar.

'Don't you come near me, Roy,' Pi shouts as the punch rings in her ears.

Her phone flies from her hands and bounces along the long grass. Crickets take flight, like small, lime-green fire flies. She feels Roy's hands over her body, touching and feeling his way through her pockets. He swears and spits, the noise muffled and half muted.

'Nearly all gone, I see. You're a thieving little cunt. You know that? If you want money, you have to work for it.'

'Like you work for it, Roy? Selling drugs…'

Her hair is pulled and yanked, sliding across the grass. Her shoes dig into the soft ground. Slumped against a tree, sharp lightning bolts of pain, zigzag up her back. Her shoulder blades feel like crushed terracotta plates.

'The fuck are you doing, you psycho!' she screams.

Roy tosses her to the ground hard, then runs into the dilapidated shed leaning against the rear fence. He appears quickly, his steps are fast and meaningful. He pushes Pi with all his scrawny arms can muster and she falls back. He drags her by her hair to the nearest tree. Rope is tied around her legs and waist. The tree holds flat against her back. Roy knows his knots. Pi tries to pull her hands free, her legs kick outwards. Roy yanks hard and they tighten everywhere. Roy kicks at the grass and walks around the house instead of going through it. Mother rushes outside, with the knife in her hand and cuts at the rope. Pi's hands wrap around her.

'Why did you take his money, Pi?'

'He didn't earn it, that redneck asshole. It's not even his.'

Mother is upset and they hear the sound of his car starting and leaving.

'If he doesn't have it all, he could get into big trouble.'

Cassie watches through the window.

'I don't care!' Pi screams, making fists, but lowering them to her hips. 'Get rid of him, Mum. He treats all of us like shit. We're better off without him.'

Her mother, still crying, drops the knife. It is lost in the overgrown grass and shrubbery. She goes inside. Pi takes the rope and throws it over the fence so he can never do that to her again. She feels the menagerie of memories float back to her, the brutal assault that left her face deformed. She lights another cigarette and stops herself from crying. She sees Cassie through the window, and they stare, blinklessly at one another.

SILK

Douglas hates being in Hope Valley, a black man among a majority of white. He's told not to go down near the river, especially at dusk. Stay away, they tell him. We won't tell you again, they tell him. He has come from Fountain and before that, Saint Eisore. He has bundles of thousand-dollar bricks in the boot of the car and stands looking at it. He closes it hard and can see the back of Ehren's head sitting in the passenger seat. He is not someone you fuck with. He was sent from Fountain to Hope Valley to courier the parcels back without incident. Douglas slides into the driver's seat, careful not to make too much noise or alarm his company.

'We're gonna be late. Hurry up.' Ehren pulls a pack of cigarettes from his leather jacket pocket and stares at him.

'There was more there than I first thought. I had to count it.'

'Drive.'

The car pulls out onto the muddy road leading back out to the main road. The line of trees hides them from sight. It hides the smell and the smoke. Douglas has trouble turning the wheel; he is only small, and the car is big, and old. It's like riding a mechanical bull in a dodgy bar. Ehren doesn't seem to notice or care. When they are out on the highway, he slips black glasses on and Douglas isn't sure if he's asleep or not, he still dares not to look.

Leaving Hope Valley feels like walking into a spider web and trying to pull it off your face. The sensation is that it never really leaves you and you are left to wonder if some of it is still on you. Highway 86 runs straight from Hope Valley into Fountain. There is a long and winding detour that would take you to Weaver's Peak if you want to avoid Fountain, which most people did. Douglas notices people leaving Hope Valley, driving around him and faster than him, but no one is going the other way; into Hope Valley.

After several hours, they stop at a truck stop and watch an elderly hooker get into a truck with an old man. Ehren leans on the car and watches the entire proceedings and smokes. He is continuously smoking; drops the filter, lets it burn out, lights another one. His face is stagnant and void of any emotion. He watches Douglas fill the car with fuel and go inside. He follows him in. The lights are too bright and there is a man at the counter arguing with the clerk about a rental van. Douglas brings some sandwiches and soda. He picks up a pack of beef jerky and a bottle of water. He looks at Ehren and decides not to ask him if he wants anything. The next few hours driving will be in silence, he guesses. They get back in the car and Ehren motions him to wait. Douglas sits, drinking soda. He knows he is watching the truck. Ten minutes go by and Douglas is growing impatient, but neither shows it nor vocalises it. When the hooker appears, and wanders off behind the shops, to the toilet, he tells Douglas to drive.

There are times of vacant land, nothing but paddocks of green, void of livestock. Jumbles of trees rush past, as if the car is too scared to slow down in case the branches snatch at its tires, pulling it into the undergrowth and clogging its engine with vines. As the highway lay out in front of them, like a tongue, the clouds above turn grey and start to spit. Ehren looks up, putting his head slightly out the window and glares, as if telling the weather, it better wait.

Douglas chances a look at the man he was the driving with. The man he barely knows at all. He has face tattoos, and finger tattoos and scars. His boots are heavy and tied unnecessarily tight. Douglas looks back to the front of the car, watching the fat blisters of rain hit the hood and splatter. He wants to swerve left and collide with a tree, taking Ehren's head clean off. He would tell the others they got into a car accident, and only he survived. He is certain the only questions they would ask would be: if he got rid of the body properly. He would roll him into a ditch, or shallow grave. Not that he could dig one, he doesn't have a shovel. He could cover him with rocks. This is the middle of nowhere, nothing is out here. Animals would eat him before he was found. No one rides out here, no one walks out here, there is nothing and his body would disappear like an old photo, as if never to be seen again. Did this area really even exist? No two stretches of road are the same, but everything is identical.

The town ahead is Crowne. A small slather of shops and one bar. All the houses are behind the stores, hidden and dimly lit. They stop to urinate, but Ehren is keen to get going. He watches people wander down the street in their dazed, vacant stares. He watches people go in and out of the small, run-down movie theatre across the street. He watches Douglas.

'It's getting dark.' Ehren doesn't reply. 'What's your thoughts about staying here tonight? We get up in the morning and drive early.'

Ehren doesn't acknowledge he has even heard him.

They stop and stretch their legs. Douglas eats his sandwiches. Ehren doesn't eat anything, nor does he ask for food. He opens the passenger side door and gets in, lighting yet another cigarette. Douglas slips into the driver's seat without saying another word. His fingers hurt, his arms hurt, and his spine and backside ache. He is paid to count and make sure everything added up, not to drive the money around, not to chaperone a smoking corpse.

The roads are dark, and the trees are thick and lined close to the asphalt. Ehren still wears his sunglasses. He is starting to nod off. He would jerk awake and flounder, gripping the dashboard and balling his hands into fists. His phone beeps, and he looks at it immediately.

'They're waiting for us,' he says.

'We've still a long way to go.'

The drive goes quickly, and no one talks again. The lights ahead sparkle and scream big city. Douglas grew up not far from here and often visited Lowville. It was for family visits. He never likes the big cities, even though the people are in their thousands, if not hundreds of thousands, he still finds it hard to hide. They wind their way down the mountain crest and ease into the city. It starts with industrialised masses of land, woodworks and metal works. Trucks still drive at this time of night; their drivers high on pills. The moon overhead watches as they snake through the outskirt neighbourhoods. Ehren points to the roads he wants to take. They get lost, Douglas knows it, but Ehren never admits to it.

'Here, stop here,' he demands. Douglas has to nearly slam on the brakes.

They wait in the dark car. The street is lit by two light poles. Bins are out on the curb. A person walks down the street on the opposite side, with their jacket hood over their head. Ehren watches him unmercifully, his hand on the door handle. The man crosses the street in front of them and continues walking. Ehren's phone beeps and he gets out. A house to their right, which had been in total darkness, is suddenly lit by a balcony light. The front door opens, and a man appears in a tucked-in polo shirt. He isn't wearing shoes and he looks angry. Douglas doesn't think he looks like the cookie-cutter drug runner, then again, neither does he.

'Stay here.'

Douglas watches Ehren step out of the car and stand on the sidewalk. He messages someone on his phone and receives a message back instantly. He crosses the street and the man from the house meets him on his well-manicured lawn. They speak quickly; the man is mad. He follows Ehren to the car and they look in the trunk. Ehren throws the bag full of cash at the man and it hits his chest. He catches it and tells him to now fuck off. Ehren gets back in the car and swears.

'Go,' he says, watching the man go back across the street and into his house. The light on the porch is turned off.

Douglas drives down the long street. Cedar trees on each side. It blocks the streetlights, making it darker than it is. They don't speak until they are nearly out of Lowville.

Ehren's phone rings and he instantly changes his demeanour. He says yes and laughs, then hangs up.

'We have a detour,' he says joyfully.

Doug turns his head and sees the giant was grinning while looking out the window.

'Where to?' he asks. He wants to say no, he wants to go home; to get rid of the car, to get rid of him.

'Saddle and Spur.'

Douglas remains quiet and drives back towards Hope Valley.

THE MAN, OR ADOLESCENT BOY

Listen. The sounds of a waterfall, cold and spraying water. Stinging like razors. The forest is secluded, and the kid runs. As he becomes tired, he falls. He picks himself up. He is used to falling. His limbs are seized at odd angles. His feet are pigeon-toed and curled like an animal; today he *is* an animal. Falling and crying. A mixture of sinus and snot pours from his nose, down his philtrum and over his cracked and bleeding lips. His eye is bloodshot, and he dares not look back. He tries to scream, but he gurgles and whimpers, running deeper into the trees. The boys are after him.

Teddy runs through the forest. His feet are large, and his legs are long. His denim jeans stretch and yawn with his stride. Balled-up fists swing by his sides, his grin is strained, and he flanks the kid to his right and punches him hard. The kid falls, knocking his head. Teddy kicks him and sees a tree, fallen and rotten and climbs it. He stands on top: a king of a mountain and the forest and its deformed children before him.

'That's what you get, kid. That's what you get!' He raises his fists in the air.

A man, older than Teddy, with a black vest and a cigarette dangling from his lip's paces like a caged animal. He wears a skull ring on his middle finger, the teeth and nose cartilage are elevated.

'Get down,' he calls for Teddy. 'You want the world to know we're here?'

The man, or adolescent boy, only old enough to grow a moustache, has understood the world for some time. When his mother strapped him good with an appliance cord, he *knew*. Get beaten or beat. He understands where he was placed in this world. There is no getting out. How can there be, if he is never in it?

With black-greased hair and adrenaline starting to make his hands shake, the man walks and watches the kid get up and run, tripping, falling, scraping his knee and bleeding. The deeper they go into the woodland, the more secrets it will hold. The kid cries, his hands dirty and his face covered in grass. He can't run anymore; his joints are sore, and his mind is clouded. *How do I escape? Who can help me?* He couldn't finish school, not here. They don't supply enough teachers for his condition. They don't have the time or the money for someone like him. *Why was I born like this? Why can't I run?* The boy screams in his mind. He searches for somewhere to hide, anywhere.

('Bobby, he looked at me, that retarded kid. I was takin' a piss and he was watching.'

'Who was?'

'That mental kid. You know him. He was at school with us. You know him.'

'I don't know him.'

'Bobby, your sister caught him too. Your dad roughed him up when he was caught looking through the windows.'

'That kid? He's still around? I thought he would have died by now.'

'No. He's not dead. He doesn't leave the house much. Listen's to records up in the house, up that way. Away from here.')

Darkness lies here, in the woodland. The soft decay of earth's materials; lingering smells of wood and moss, a mixture of stale and fresh air, the sun beating down, relentlessly. Scarred trees from drug addicts wandering into the forest, alone and full of vigour, trying to decipher the world and starting where the darkness grows. We're not scared! they would yell. The forest, you don't scare me, but it does. No one should come in here. Here is where darkness lives. It was born here and will die here with everything else. A sleeping animal of animosity, quiet and reflective. There will be no getting out, once you've seen the black machine that is here. It watches. It will kill again.

It will watch.

It will watch you.

Bobby looks back over his shoulder, tree trunks like bars on the prison he had been to. A faded memory, pain and sorrow and depression. He turns back as there is no going back now. He must do this. The knife in his hand is already pointing forward, keen to draw blood. His brain, without thought, without knowing or demanding, already running an innate drive somewhere in his subconscious. Where is the kid?

'Bobby, I heard him, this way.'

'He can't be far.'

'Let me do it. I want to do it.'

Two more teenagers follow Bobby Dare like he is the woodland messiah. The older boy with a knife always in his pocket. His mama is housebound and incapable of watching him. A den of drugs and fucking. No money and freezing cold, but there were always knives there and death. Always. He doesn't remember eating for two days, but that's not uncommon for people around here. There will be money, somehow, at some time, and they will all go out for burgers and fries, onion rings, ketchup, mustard, endless soda. There will be a time, after this. To celebrate, leaving the blood on their hands.

'No one will miss him.'

'He ain't over here.'

'I can hear him breathing.' Laughter. 'He's scared. Real scared.'

Teddy's hand throbs from the punch. His knuckles all bunched up and swollen red, like onions. He looks at it, his eyes strain and bulge. He's hungry too. But after this, a reward – food.

'He's here. He's here. I found him.'

The kid is quivering, his body doesn't allow him fluid movement. His wrists permanently bent since birth, his spine, crooked and always painful and his mind, not like the others. He was born this way, and now he will pay for it. Teddy and another boy, Jakob, grab the small kid and drag him, punching and kicking. Already bleeding; bleeding on them. Their knuckles red raw and skin split. The smell of the woods, thick soil being kicked up, being dug up. The richness of the earth, the blood and the dirt. A crow watches, far above = death.

'Leave me, leave me!' the kid yells. 'I haven't done nothing.'

'I know you have,' Bobby says, his knife raised high, swinging.

The earth stops. The crow looks. The forest feels first blood. It comes in dribbles and then streams out. The boy, handicapped to defend himself, is cut above his collar bone.

The wound is deep and white muscle pokes out of the gouge. A bone, nearly white, more yellow, shows and the kid screams. The crow flies away. The knife is slid into the boy, quicker this time, in between his rib cage, separating bone. His lung hisses, angrily and like a valve, hot air escapes and Bobby feels it on his hand. Teddy and Jakob watch. Teddy extends his hand.

'I want a turn. Let me do it.'

'You ain't got the balls.'

'I got the balls, Bobby. I got bigger balls, watch me. I'll stab him in the face.'

The knife handle, now covered in blood, is handed to Teddy. A strange electricity currents through his veins. He stabs the boy, the tip slicing open his cheek and slides like silk into his eye socket, bursting his eyeball. White gel spills out from the cut and the boy shivers. The knife is yanked out and Jakob vomits and turns away. *Serious, this is serious now. This is happening.*

Teddy slashes the boy across his chest, again and again. He cuts into his genitals while Bobby watches. He hands the knife back and Bobby cuts his throat open, pushing him to the side to let the blood drain out. The blood is thick and almost black. It hits the soil and the woodland hisses. Bobby and Teddy look up, stunned at the sound.

'The fuck is that?'

'What was that?'

A hiss, long and deep rattles the trees and the fallen logs. The blood pours out, trickling down the mossy forest floor. No blood had ever been spilt in this area. The forest reacts, something calls.

I've awoken.

They run. Quickly and without cautiousness, eager to get back to the road, away from the forest. They hear the kid screaming and dying. They hear him call for help and they hear his last gurgle of breath.

A memory some time ago, but it never fades, not here. The forest remembers. It always remembers.

DICHOTOMY

The boy, he moves rocks. One rock, heavier than the next. His muscles pull and strain. His back hurts. His hair is matted down on his face, sweat beads on his brow and drips off his nose. His armpits are soiled. The rocks are sharp and tear his skin, and he bleeds, more blood onto the tracks.

The mouth of the cavern yawns, frozen in the state of awakening. The crows watch from high above, their eyes beady and black, filled with dark blood and oil. The air is cooler than before, and Boy tries to work harder. He moves another and another. Then more and the last one. He wipes his hands on his shorts and almost passes out from the pain. Two fingernails are now gone. The forest is getting dark, so he lights the lantern.

Footsteps, like leaves falling on snow, Boy hears them. He knows the forest now and the forest knows him. It lets him listen, tells him someone is approaching.

A girl. Young.

Boy stands on the track, his back to the Train, he feels it's hot breath. He feels its mono-eye, staring through him. The heat, like hell, is unbearable. He waits for the intruder, the girl, to show herself. He knows she's there, looking, watching, waiting.

'Come out,' he says, dripping blood off his fingernails.

The columns of trees stand still, and one moves softly, eager and slowly. One hand drawn up to her face, tugging shyly at her blond hair.

'What are you doing here?' Cassie says.

'I don't want to go home.' Boy smiles, and Cassie returns his smile.

'It's too dangerous being out here at night, you have to go home.'

Boy listens and understands. 'We need to free it.'

'I know. Me and Gus will come back tomorrow and help. But you can't stay out here.'

'It's more dangerous at home.'

Cassie nods. 'I'll walk you home.'

Boy nods. 'Okay.'

DARLING

She walks as a blur, an unease, a stupor, falling and clutching the walls. She's alert but hardly awake. She thinks of something and it goes, and she slams the wall with her fists and screeches, her mind a complication of rum and gin. She tastes the stomach acid in her mouth and spits. It catches on her chin and dangles, so she wipes it. *Back to bed*, she thinks and finds she is already at the bedroom door. Sleep. Awake. Sleep. Awake.

The front door opens, and she sits up. *What time is it? Is it the afternoon?*

'Darling?' a voice, but it could belong to anyone.

'Yes? Who is it?'

Footsteps down the hallway, the sound of a jacket being taken off. The sound of coughing and a belt unbuckling.

'Who is it?'

'It's me.'

Oh, yes, it's you, her mind minces the words. She feels sickly and poor and she rolls over and breathes, a warm arm wraps around her and she sleeps. Wakes. Sleeps. Wakes.

The sound, more clanging of cutlery, another day? Where did last night go?

'What happened?'

'What do you mean, darling?'

'What time is it?'

'Seven,' he replies turning to her. Toast pops up from the toaster behind him. 'AM.'

'I slept through again?'

He nods. 'I have to go to work now. You stay home, okay. You need rest.'

'I need rest,' she repeats it to herself.

Why do I need rest? What day is it? I must be sick. I'll go back to bed.

The bottles are only made of glass. They are only filled with alcohol. They can't open themselves or pour themselves down your throat.

Oh, I know.

They can't walk themselves from the shop to your house and climb into bed with you.

Yes. But they are always here.

Why is that? Can you see how they are getting here?

He brings them?

'Yes.'

—

Vomit is on the floor next to the toilet bowl. It smells old and it looks dry and flaky. Her jaw hurts, throbs, and there is blood, but not a cut. The blood is only a few drops. Could it be from her stomach? Could it be something else, in her mouth? She sits up, the tiles are cold and clammy, and it makes her skin feel icky and dry. She yawns and it hurts like fiery hell. She goes to stand up and is yanked back down, hard. A rattling. She looks. She is handcuffed to the sink pipe. She pulls and yanks, nothing. She scrambles her fingers around the small latch, nothing happens, it hurts more.

'What is going on here?' and 'Who did this?' and 'Why am I chained up?'

No phone, not even the mobile. She gets on her knees

and climbs into the tub. Still the porcelain is cold as ice. The bathroom door is shut, she is guessing locked too. The vomit smell is lingering and is making her want to puke more. She sleeps and dreams of a car accident she had when she was thirteen. Her leg being caught in the shrapnel from the dashboard. Her stitches and rehabilitation. She checks her scars, still there. The dream was real, the accident was real. The slamming of a door, footsteps and the bathroom door opens.

'Darling?'

'Why am I chained up?'

'Oh, good. You've come to. You were wild last night. You hit me in the face, almost gave me a black eye. Look, see here? Can you see it?'

She does see it, swollen and shiny.

'Why did you leave me here all day?'

'It was the morning. You had gotten up in the night and started drinking. I told you to stop, but you swore and left.'

'Where did I go?'

'I don't know,' her husband says, sitting on the toilet. 'You tell me?'

'I can't remember.'

'You know, darling,' he says, taking the handcuff keys out of his pocket. 'If you ever write an autobiography, you can call it "I Can't Remember" by Rachel Drake,' he says, splaying his fingers out to imitate her name in lights. He laughs and takes off the cuffs and leaves.

She goes to stand up, but there is a sharp pain, piercing and red raw. She slides back into the tub and fresh urine flows from between her legs, bright yellow. It runs down the tub and swirls around the sink. She moans in frustration. In annoyance. What is she, a child? There was hardly any warning and it happened. She gets up and shuts the door. She runs the water and takes her underwear off and steps down the hallway gingerly and gets dressed, meeting her husband in the kitchen. He is putting something in the oven.

'Here, let me do that,' she demands, running, her head thumping, churning. A mashing of memories and disillusion.

Is this real? Or am I slumped over something, dreaming? Am I at someone's house I don't even know? What day is it?

'No, it's okay,' the Darling man says, her husband. 'I've done it all week, why stop now? Right?'

'You have?'

'It's okay.'

'It's not okay. I should be more… awake. More sober. I need help.'

'We've talk about this, remember?'

Memories are all gone, or still drunk, there can't be a remembering. It's nearly impossible. There is nothing to remember.

I am Rachel Drake and I am an alcoholic. No. That doesn't sound right? I've never said those words. I can't remember ever being in a meeting, but then again, I can't remember yesterday. I can't recall getting dressed. All I know is I am awake now and I'm walking and I'm talking. And he is home.

'I'm sorry. I'm sorry I went out last night. I'm sorry I've been a drunk.'

He shakes his head. His smile is childish.

'You've said that for the last year. We promised each other you wouldn't say that anymore. It's okay though, you sometimes forget and will say it and then you'll forget again, and we'll do the same thing next week. Now, I've put some chicken in the oven, it'll be ready in about half an hour, so why don't you have a shower.'

'Yes, okay. I will.'

She turns slowly and heads for the bathroom. Behind her she can hear him riffle through his bag, the sounds of two bottles clinking together echoes down the hallway. The sound of love. The sound of magic. She is home and ready.

SWITCH

'My mother would walk out into the front yard and spread her legs and piss on the lawn like a dog.'

Gus wipes dirt on his already dirty pants. Boy walks further up the tracks and starts pushing rocks off the thoroughfare.

'Why?'

'She would never make it inside, after she drinks. Sometimes I would find her asleep on the road, or in the front yard.' Gus cocks his head to the side. 'When mother is getting ready you can't touch her hair. If you mess her hair up, she gets really mad.'

Gus yanks at the vines entwined around the metal rail. He tosses them down the pebbled slope. Cassie does the same. Her hands sting. She looks down the corridor of trees and into the mouth of the cavern.

'She would get mad?'

'Once she cut the top of my ear off and burnt me with her straightener... My uncle Jim could sing and play the guitar. He always had slicked back hair and a checkered shirt. Every time I saw him, he had the checkered shirt on. Sometimes he would be talking and then he'd start singing for no reason. Mother liked him being around, but he would get sick of her and would leave.'

Gus stops, his hands full of vines and weeds. His face is dirty, and he glares at the sun, his eyelids puckered together.

'Mother would chase me with a switch if I came home

late. She said she shouldn't be the only one to look after my brother.'

'What's a switch?' Cassie asks, knowing it is getting late and she should leave soon.

'An extension cord. Something my father left behind. I don't really know where it came from, it was always hanging in the shed. She would thrash it against my legs if I was home late or didn't feed Joel enough food. Sometimes there was no food. I would go without, so he could eat.'

Cassie diverts her eyes to Gus.

'I know what my mother does. She thinks I don't know, but I do know. She used to do it to my sister Pi as well, until her accident.'

'What does she do?'

'She brings men back. She finds them out on drives somewhere. Sometimes it's the same ones, sometimes it's different. But they all smell the same.'

Boy returns, one of his fingers is bleeding. Where the nail used to be is now black. Cassie holds his hand softly in hers and stares at him in the eyes. Boy isn't bothered by this pain. They head back to the Train. Its metal is getting colder as the sun descends. Inside the cavern, their footsteps echo, and the bats start to stir. Boy climbs up into the driver's seat and clears the dials with his hand. They are caked in dust and mud. He sits and stares out through the maw of the cave and along the long line of crossed wooden beams that make the train tracks. Cassie sits on the steps and looks up at the bats as they become more restless and eager for the night. Gus sits on the step below her.

'You will have to get back soon. It's getting dark.'

'Where do you go to sleep?' Boy asks, thinking of his cupboard.

'I'll sleep here. Or if it's too loud, in the camp we found.'

'Are you not afraid of the dark?'

'The dark is different out here. It's not as dark as the room I used to sleep in. The moon makes everything look blue. I can see just fine.'

Boy stands up. The sudden rush of fear for being late makes his fingers pulsate with nervousness. His bladder tightens, but he can hold it. Cassie climbs back down to the ground and wipes the grass and dirt from her jeans.

'Tomorrow when we come back, we'll bring you food.'

Gus nods and watches them make their way out of the decrepit station. The bats take flight after them, squawking and screeching, their leathery wings beating together. Gus climbs up further and lies on the floor of the cabin, unafraid of the night creatures – as he has now become one too.

THE FORGOTTEN

The Saddle and Spur – a dank strip club several miles out of Hope Valley. The windows were taken out and filled in with red brick and painted over in black. The door is still glass with large cracks starting at the base and splitting up towards the top where people have kicked at it after being escorted out.

'Can we talk?'

'About what?'

'Your brother.'

'What's more to say? You know everything. Other cops been by here. I know you're just staring at tits. You don't really want to talk to me. They drink beer and go again. Nothing ever gets done. I guess my brother's just another dead kid to you in Hope Valley.'

'I want to really talk. No bullshit.'

'All you pigs talk is bullshit. It's all you know. If you're serious, I'll be outside in a few minutes for a smoke.'

'Wherever you like.'

'You really got time to keep asking me about this? It's been nearly a year.'

'It's unsolved.'

'An ongoing investigation. Right? That's what the last pig said. How long is it going to be ongoing for? I'm moving at the end of the year.'

'Where to?'

'I'm not telling anyone. Too many ghosts. If they don't know where you're going, they can't follow.'

our past will find you?'

ood.'

ence, let me tell you something… No
d you try to run, you won't ever outrun it.
… waiting for you.'

ell, that may be so. The dead can't walk, now
? Not the last time I checked. Bones can stay
and stories can be forgotten.'

ou aren't gonna tell your mother where you're
ing?'

'Ha! She's the last person I'd tell. She won't follow me, she can barely walk herself. But if someone comes sniffing around, asking for me, she'll probably tell some lies, like she normally does.'

'Why would people come sniffing around for you?'

'Is this about me? I have my skeletons, just like everyone else. You ain't allowed in Hope Valley if you ain't got none.'

'Like everyone.'

'Like you, Mr Merlin Drake. I know you. Everyone knows you. The only difference between you and me is, if you run, your ghosts can come follow you.'

'How you figure that.'

'They ain't dead yet.'

'Seems like you should be more concerned with your own shit, than mine.'

'I ain't concerned about no one's shit.'

'Your brother's death has been classified as a murder. I need to know who he spoke with days leading up to his death. Where he went, what he did.'

'I already told the other cop this. Go read his report.'

'I want to hear it from you.'

'Did they bring you all the way to the Valley to 1 into this case? I feel sorry for you. Look, I gotta get b. soon.'

'I'll pay you for your time.'

'He went out occasionally. I haven't lived at home since I was thirteen. Even then he would just leave without saying anything. People like him, they just take off. We'd have to go find him. In the end, Mother barely bothered. He'd return. He'd come back with dead animals, or little girl's clothes. Mother would hide them or bury them deep in the garbage. He would hit her. He had hit me, and I knocked him out cold with a plank of wood. I moved out after that.'

'Who were his friends?'

'He didn't have any. No one wanted to hang out with him. When he left school, Mum enrolled him in a special needs program at the youth centre. He went a few times and they kicked him out.'

'What for?'

'His behaviour. He was a bully. He was violent. He was hard to control.'

'Then what?'

'Then what? I don't know. He stayed home with Mum. She bought him a record player from a yard sale, and he listened to music up in the attic all the time.'

'Would you say he had enemies? People who didn't like him, who would want to cause him harm?'

'Obviously. Now that he's dead, I would say he had a few enemies.'

'Cut the shit. Tell me who?'

'I don't know any of his enemy's names. Go ask Mum. She might know.'

'Your mother refuses to talk to anyone.'

'Yeah? Okay. I gotta go back. You're on your own then, Mr Merlin Drake.'

CONVERSATION BY THE TRAIN

'People don't just disappear in the woods, they turn.'

'Turn to what?'

'Shadows mostly. Some ghosts, some trees. They travel by interconnecting roots and through the water. The streams that run down here from Cicada Mountain. Only if they are hurt, do they stay behind. And that's mostly all of them. You see, when something bad happens, and that's the only sort of happening in here, their soul escapes the body and goes into the forest. It's scared and won't return to the body.'

'How do you know that?'

'I've seen enough of the shadows, the dark strangers and the ghouls, to know. I used to pick bottles not far from here, and I'd see them watching me through the trees. They were interested. Once they knew I wasn't there for trouble, they let me be.'

'I've seen them too. They follow me here, like they are taking care of me, so I don't stray off the path.'

'They speak to the Train.'

'I've heard it talk too.'

CONVERSATION BETWEEN POLICE CAPTAIN JIM O'BEER AND ACTING DETECTIVE MERLIN DRAKE.

'Whatever happened to that kid?'

'Which one?'

'That retard kid. Old Reece's boy, went missing few years back.'

'Reece O'Reilly? Haven't heard that name in a while. Never found him. More than likely ran away.'

'He wouldn't have gotten far. *(noise of sniffling and coughing and spitting onto the ground)*, not with those legs.'

'Yeah, he couldn't walk too far. We searched everywhere.'

'Down near Fountain they found a body, a small boy, cuts on his face.'

'No, that was Trevor Taylor. I remember reading the report. The shit that was done to that kid, its nearly damn inhuman.'

'It all is, isn't it?'

'What?'

'These ultra-violent crimes. These ones you briefly hear about on the news. They never tell you the full story, not the story we know. If they knew the full story...'

'Sometimes I wish I didn't know the full story.'

'That bad?'

'Worse than my brain could ever conjure up. Degrading shit. They tortured him for three days. Kept alive, barely, just so they could do shit to him.'

'Like what?'

'I ain't talking about it, Jim. It's taken me this long to try and forget it.'

'The brain is a weird mechanism, Merlin. Sometimes it won't let you forget the most horrible shit. It's like it forgets all the great stuff, all the dates and girls you've been with, just so it can make room for the horrible shit. You know?'

'I hear you, Jim. In my line of work, they don't tell you that one day you will be cutting down a body hanging from the ceiling. They don't warn you about that stuff, and it's that exact stuff that keeps you awake at night. A hanging body, you know what I'm saying? Its talking to you while you're trying to sleep, mumbling and trying to breathe.'

'No shit?'

'I wake up nearly every damn night with that body hanging over my bed. It whispers to me, Jim. I can't control what it says, it's goddamn frightening.'

'Your wife, does she freak out when you wake up screaming? My wife would have left me by now, suffered night terrors as a kid. She's already on the damn edge.'

'My wife... don't even get me started, Jim. She's so far gone I don't think she remembers who she is anymore.'

'What are you talking about, Merlin?'

'She drinks, Jim. Not like a few every night, like a few bottles more like it.'

'Can you get her help?'

'We tried, God knows we did. She's been in hospital twice and rehab a few times, I forget how many. It's like, this was how it was meant to be. You know?'

'I don't know, Merlin. You can't… I don't know… stop her?'

'I've tried. She cut me once, bad, and I left and came back a week later. She hadn't eaten. She was nearly damn dead. And you know what? I figured it was my path in life to look after her.'

'By God you say?'

'Sure. By whoever. I don't know if its God or Satan. I look after her, bring her booze and keep her sheets changed.'

'You bring it to her?'

'Yes, Sir, you heard me, Jim. Take an alcoholics bottles away, and you got a damn lunatic on your hands. She would smash the windows, steal the patrol car, do whatever it takes.'

'Holy Christ. I didn't know it was that bad.'

'She wakes up most afternoon with no recollection of what she's done. There's a few hours there were she's normal and we can eat and sit down and watch TV together, but after those few hours she starts to get edgy, you know?'

'My uncle was like that.'

'Best thing to do is to keep them happy. She'll have a few drinks, start screaming or whatever and pass out. I get my paperwork done and sometimes hit the gym if it appeals to me. I tuck her into bed. If she wakes up in the middle of the night hollering, I'll cuff her to something and shut the door.'

'Jesus, Merlin.'

'It's been going on for some time, Jim. Might seem strange to hear it now, from me, especially being a cop, but you have no idea. This is the best way.'

'Did she get like this when she moved here?'

'Not really. We're from a bigger city, but not big like Lowville. More like a small town that got too big for itself. It still had the small-town mentality. She was a legal clerk and I would have to go to her office and convince her to copy files for me, sometimes I didn't have jurisdiction, or a warrant and I'd have to promise to take her to dinner. She always did it though. She was a good girl.'

'That's the problem with moving to an even smaller town, you see. Everything becomes magnified. Everyone knows everyone; their movements, their business, who owns what, who does what. Sometimes it ends up in the paper, if you're unlucky.'

'I'd never heard of Hope Valley before. In all my years of investigations, I was surprised to hear how many murders happen there.'

'There ain't no hope in this valley.'

'My last superior, he called it Murder Town.'

'He'd be damn right.'

'My wife, she has a kid somewhere.'

'No shit?'

'She got pregnant at fourteen and her folks forced her to give it up for adoption. The daddy of the kid almost went to jail for it. She's never seen him since she handed him to the nurse when he was born. I think that fucked her up a lot. She thought she had seen him in the city we used to live in. Everywhere we went she would be looking at everyone. At everyone's faces, to see if she recognised him. At that point, when I met her, and she told me, the kid would have been older than her when she had him. Tore her up.'

'You never know what happens in this life. The kid may come looking for her one day.'

'If I answer the door when he knocks, I'll tell him to beat it. If that kid ever finds his mother, she'll be a damn wreck. It won't fix anything. It'll make it worse.'

'You think so?'

'I know so. I see it all the time. These broken people think they need it to make them better. What they don't realise, is that it broke them to begin with. Nothing can fix it.'

'After you're done here… are you going back there?'

'We can't stay here, and we can't go back. More than likely we'll find another town. I'll get reassigned and we'll start again.'

'I couldn't imagine starting over. As much as I hate this place, I don't think I can leave.'

'I'm starting to get that feeling myself.'

HANDLE

He places his hand on the door and tries to turn the handle. He is too weak. He waits. He stands on shaking legs with stinging eyes. He tries again and the handle moves and opens the door with a click. The sound of freedom. The light burns white hot and dissipates like a fog. A wet hand of heat and humidity slaps his face and he starts to sweat. He walks out from the cupboard and into the small hallway. He is lost in his own house.

He goes to the bathroom and sits down to urinate. Standing up to piss feels foreign and he doesn't like the feeling anymore. He washes his face in the basin and looks at himself in the mirror. His flesh is yellowing and sickly. His lips are swollen, purple and cracked. The fleshy creases have bled through the night and dried. He washes his lips and it stings. One side of his jaw is swollen, and he reaches inside his mouth and touches the last tooth on the left side. He can't feel it through his gums, so he pulls it out and lets it drop in the sink. It rattles and bounces around on the porcelain. Boy stares at it. It doesn't bother him.

He stands in the hallway again, staring at nothing. Then he goes to the kitchen and stands there. Time passes, and he doesn't notice. He walks a few paces to the lounge and stands, staring up at the ceiling. A small overdraft of wind is carried through the house and out the front window. It is only open a few inches, but Boy can still see outside. He can see the greying streets and the long grass being tossed from side to side. He hears a bird and wonders why it is so close to him.

Down the hallway was another door. One he remembers: his room. He walks into it and looks around. An unmade bed, dirty curtains, rubbish is scattered on the floor. There are plastic toys along the cupboard. The room is still and smells of mould and dust. He opens one of the drawers. His clothes are still in there, folded. His mother must have put them in there a long time ago. He gets dressed in fresh clothing and savours the smell of unsoiled fabric. He goes to the kitchen again and opens the fridge; it is bare of food. He drinks water from a cup stained with coffee and can taste the residual flavour. He goes to the front door, barefoot, and leaves the house. The overcast clouds hang low and full of rain. Small bursts of lightning flash around him, and he starts to walk away from his house. Tears stream down his face and his breathing is erratic.

'Torso,' the boy speaks, standing in the rain. 'I have left.'

It is not the time to leave. Not yet.

'But I am clean.'

He will come back. He is on his way. Get back to the cupboard and take those clothes off.

'No.'

Pain is coming.

'Yes,' Boy responds. 'I know.'

He walked along the fence line; the puddles ripple and waver. Boy staggers and falls into the dirt. He tastes the soil the earth was made from and it makes him gag. The mud splashes on his face and he gets to his feet again. He can't remember the last thing he had eaten before dirt. He stands staggering and light headed. Being on the ground is familiar and his body appreciates being foetal.

Boy wanders. His fingers are thin to the bone, his knuckles prominent and bloated. Both elbows are filthy with dirt and wrinkled like leather. His hip bones press through his pants. He doesn't wear a belt. Inside, his heart beat is irregular and makes him stop and dry wretch. His lips start to bleed when he wipes his face with the back of his hand, but he hadn't realised until later, seeing the blood on his shirt. He walks down the street, becomes disorientated and walks back. He looks in the other direction and can't see anything he recognises. He sees a store down the road. Its sign is blue and faded.

'I'll get food and come back. I promise.'

It doesn't work like that, Boy. You know that. He feeds you.

'Yes, but not enough. My body is moving on its own… It needs to eat.'

You fell over. You're now bleeding. You don't have money and you don't know where to go.

'Why are you trying to stop me? You were always trying to help.'

I am helping you. I'm stopping you from being hurt further. You don't want to know what is coming.

'How do you know what is coming?'

I know more than you think, now go back home.

Boy turns around and is momentarily lost. He walks down several streets until he sees his front gate, crooked on its bent hinges and rusted. He walks through it and up the stairs. The front door is still wide open. Standing in the vacant area between the kitchen and the hallway his feet stop moving. He can't contemplate the fact that he got himself dressed and went outside, then came back. He knows he wasn't meant to come back. Suddenly, louder than thunder, the front door slams shut. Boy looks, at first unworried, then he sees his father standing in the doorway. Boy trembles. His bladder squeezes and squeezes, but nothing happens.

'Why are you out of your cupboard?' his father says, his voice monotone and flat.

'I-I...' Boy tries to speak, but his fear grips his throat.

I have to go now. I cannot watch what is about to happen.

Torso fades away and Boy stands with his father still staring at him by the doorway.

'I told you to never leave that cupboard. Why are you out?'

'I-I I'm hungry.'

'I brought you food. Take that shirt off.'

Boy slips his shirt off and lets it fall to the floor. Only then, does his father move. He's wearing a blue button up shirt. It's dirty with grease and his hair is dishevelled. He places a bag down on the counter top and goes to the stove. His father. The man who is responsible for him being here – the unruly. The hostile. The madness. He stands, crying, blubbering, over the hot stove top. The flames burn blue and he holds a metal spoon over it. The metal goes white hot. Boy stands like a skeleton waiting for permission to dance. His underwear, now soaked through, stained brown and yellow.

Boy waits. His eyeballs, large in their sockets, twist and turn, looking for Torso, but he has abandoned him. With a gush of serve pain, Boy's head is yanked backwards, and the hot spoon is thrust onto his chest. His skin sears and bubbles. The smell is uncanny and sickening. The spoon lifts up, but the skin is still attached. His father rips it off and the blood begins to drop onto the floor. Boy screams, his throat sore and the vocal is so loud it is nearly deafening. Jolting, crushing agony pulsates through his ribcage and into his spine, shooting both up to his head and down to his hips. His legs collapse, but his father catches him and presses the spoon again, onto his neck. Boys eyes roll back into his shallow sockets and he blacks out. He feels himself being dragged and thrown back into the cupboard. He can smell his own flesh burning.

A CONVERSATION IN THE POLICE DEPARTMENT IN FOUNTAIN

'Merlin Drake?'

'Yes, Sir, you are Chief Dale Leverwitz?'

'That's me, in the flesh. What brings you to Fountain?'

'I understand you had a murder? Similar to ours? Young boy, retarded, taken to the woods?'

'Throat slit, arms bound, buried shallow. Come in my office, I'll get Steven to bring us coffee.'

—

'You have pictures of this kid?'

'A few.'

'They're… graphic, like ours. No respect for the human body or the person behind the eyes.'

'If you say so. Steven! Bring in two coffees.'

'Yes, Sir.'

'How far away did you find him from here.'

'Not far, maybe a half hour walk. His parents came by a few days later to certify the body and arrange funeral proceedings.'

'How are they taking it?'

'Not as hard as you would think. The kid, Finn Durrage was his name, had a rap sheet for indecent assault, sexual misconduct of a minor, blah, blah. He wasn't a good kid, but his condition… I don't know, maybe he didn't know any better.'

'Mentally and physically handicapped. Lived with his parents, wasn't seen much. Pornography found on his computer.'

'We could be talking about the same kid.'

'Any leads?'

'A few names. Mostly fathers and brothers of girls he touched at one time or another. Most of it was a long time ago though, so if revenge was on their mind, why do it now? You know? Ten years later.'

'Perfect time don't you think? No one would suspect you. You may have moved away. You could come back one night, the anger still in your belly, firing, ready to explode. Maybe their daughter or sister is still having nightmares, or has the scars or issues with men, who knows. You could come back one night, wait til they walk the streets alone and do it. I'm treating everyone as a suspect.'

'You think that?'

'Yes.'

'Thank you, Steven. This is Officer Merlin Drake from Hope Valley.'

'Sir.'

'You a rookie, Steven?'

'Yes, Sir, I am.'

'Where are you from?'

'Crowne, Sir.'

'Steven, go find all the case notes on the Durrage kid and copy them for Officer Drake.'

'Yes.'

'What else is going on here, Dale? You have a lot of drugs here?'

'Not as much as the Valley, I hear. We have some weed dealers, the occasional meth or crank dealer, they never stick around too long, they can't make enough money here. We're smaller than Hope Valley, they all probably run there. *Hahaha.*'

'They wouldn't last long.'

'Why is that?'

'We have some people who have set up a kitchen in the woods. I know the approximate location and who's involved. It's a small operation, drug running and cooking.'

'Who's on the task force for that?'

'No one. Just me.'

'You're not going to let them operate?'

'For a little while. I don't have much interest in small amounts of drugs. This murder case has been going for too long now. The skeletons are piling up, Dale.'

'You said they set up a kitchen? Who knows how far they're dealing it? It could be leaking all over the state.'

'I doubt that.'

'Look, Merlin, I don't want to tell you how to be a cop, but from a detective point of view, you have to set up a task force get these guys out.'

'It's okay to say that in a township of two thousand, but when you're dealing with nearly ten thousand people, half are unemployed, half are fucked up in one way or another, it's easy for you to say put a task force together and get these guys out. Do you have any idea how many break and enters are done every single day?'

'No.'

'Take a stab in the dark, Dale.'

'A couple.'

'Fourteen. Every night fourteen homes are broken into, and that's not counting the ones that aren't reported. I get at least five assaults with a deadly weapon every week and one rape. A bunch of rednecks, slow, fucking cowboys trying to cook meth and who will most likely blow themselves up are not on the top of my shit to do list.'

'You need help in Hope Valley, Merlin.'

'You gonna send Steven in? He can't even make a decent cup of coffee.'

'No, we can get you back up. More men on the ground. Crowne has a few spares, maybe in a few weeks.'

'And I'm gonna be the asshole who takes these guys out of their homes and put them in unnecessary danger all for a few crack heads swinging dope?'

'If it gets worse, you gotta let me know.'

'I ain't gonna let you know, Dale. I'll handle it if the time comes.'

'Okay, Merlin… it's up to you in the end. It's your district.'

'Damn right it is.'

'You gonna stay the night? We could put you up somewhere, or if you're really keen you could just crash in one of the drunk tanks. We hardly ever use them. There's breakfast in the fridge.'

'No, it's only a few hours' drive.'

'It's late though. You wouldn't get home til nearly midnight.'

'I don't mind. I got a few stops to make along the way. It'll keep me awake.'

'Just one thing before you go… I didn't want to say anything, but I got this voice in my head yelling at me.'

'What is it?'

'There's a program here, just a few people, it's not a rehabilitation centre… it's more of a group. You know? They normally become friends and they talk through their drinking problems. They share their experiences and they support each other. It worked for my daughter.'

'For alcoholics?'

'Yeah, for anything really. Drugs, sex stuff, booze. It's all welcome. Addiction is addiction after all. I'm just mentioning it, you know. I want to help if I can. You don't have to do this alone.'

'I've been doing it alone for years now.'

'I know, I know. But... you don't have to. You don't have to be alone or feel like it's a battle you can't win. Because you can, you can get your life back on track and your wife's.'

'Yeah, well, I appreciate the concern.'

'Okay, Merlin, safe trip back.'

'Just... I just want to say... if you or anyone else here is talking about my life, or that of my wife... I want it to stop. I don't know how you heard about it or why you think after three years I haven't thought about group therapy or addiction groups, then I'm not sure what kind of man, or husband, you think I am. If someone is talking about me, tell them to shut the fuck up and call me direct, or even better come and see me.'

'Yeah, Merlin. I will.'

GRIND

The truck hesitates, then rolls into the petrol station. Its lights are bright and send long beams along the cracked and corroded road. The monstrosity reeks of oil and is heavy and exuding fumes. The brakes screech and huff, holding onto the steel disc, letting go and grinding. The driver knows this place. He looks at the fluorescent lights from under the brim of his cap. Something bad happened here, some time ago. A beating. There was a girl and her boyfriend. They killed someone here. Long time ago now.

He pulls into the allotment and sees the endless brake lights of other trucks. Long haulers camping for the night. The girls off in the dark, hiding like rats with twice the bite. He waits in his truck to see if someone is going to move him. No one comes so he cuts the engine and climbs down. The asphalt is still warm, and he can smell rain. In the dark there is the sound of soft moaning. He looks over to the park benches and the sound stops. He continues inside. The lights are so bright they burn his eyes. He takes his cap off and lets his hair flop over his eyebrows. The hat gets tucked it into his rear pocket. He can smell the coffee machine before he can see it. The machine's old and the beans are even older. He thanks whoever, under his breath, that they do an extra-large cup. He scans the sandwiches and sees nothing to his liking. The coffee machine burps and spits and spatters. The cup fills slowly and smells like old, leather sandals. The clerk behind the counter is talking to a woman. She looks older than any truck driver out in the lot. She holds a cigarette in one hand, but it isn't lit.

'Over there,' she says, her brows twitch and her spare hand shakes.

'Right there? Yeah,' the clerk responds.

'I saw them. They were young. There was a lot of blood. I saw them.'

'That was before my time.'

'I hadn't been back here since. This place... it has bad energy now. I go the other way. It's longer, but I don't mind.'

'Your employer minds?'

'They don't know.'

'You talking about the murder that happened here?'

Both the woman and the clerk turn to the truck driver. He scoops his coffee up and slips a lid on it. He wanders over and nods his head towards the darkened window.

'You know about it?'

'Not really. I read about it. I was a long way from here when it came over the radio.'

'I was here. That night,' the woman says. She searches in her bag for money. 'I heard the man scream. But screaming ain't that uncommon around here. Sometimes there's music. Sometimes it's the girls that hang around the bathrooms. No one really gave it a second thought.'

The clerk looks out the window. He looks distraught. A man comes in and stops behind the woman, but she waves him forward. He pays for this gas and leaves without saying a word.

'What happened to him?'

'He died of his wounds. Out there, in the parking lot.'

'I guess there's worse places to die.'

'Not many.'

'Who did it?'

'Couple of young kids. A brother and sister and the sister's boyfriend. I think he did the most part.'

'Were they caught?' the clerk asks.

'I believe so.'

'According to the papers they travelled far up north. As far as you can go. Their grandfather had a farm up there.'

'Not so smart to go up there. It'll be the first place the cops look.'

'The brother died of a heart attack and the other two were shot dead.'

The machine behind the counter beeps and the clerk presses the buttons and taps the monitor.

'Say, do you have any sandwiches in a different fridge? I'm looking for a roast beef and horseradish.'

'Sorry, no. Around an hour ago is when all the truckies pull in and eat. You came after the rush. We never have enough.'

The truck driver waves him goodbye and nods to the woman, who just stares at him. Outside the wind has picked up, the air is cooler than before. There's a small diner next to the station and he considers skipping dinner altogether and getting up early to have a big breakfast before moving on. He changes his mind and goes into the diner. A friendly woman takes his order and bags it for him. The lights still hurt his eyes and he wants to eat it in his truck. The lot is emptied of people. A few trucks, including his, scatter the large cement acreage. He stops a few feet away from his rig and sips the last of his coffee. Instead of carrying it in the truck, he heads into the dark to throw it in the bin near the benches. He sees someone approaching him from the corner of his eyes.

'Excuse me,' comes a soft voice.

'I'm sorry,' the driver says. 'I'm not interested. I know you can probably see I'm not married, but I'm still not interested. Sorry.'

'What? No… it's not that.'

The truck driver tries to see the woman in the darkness.

'Where are you headed?'

'Why do you want to know that?'

'I'm looking to get out of here… and I don't have any money.'

The man steps back off the grass and onto the cement.

'I'm going as far up as Turn-Key Gorge and then through Lowville.'

'Lowville?'

'Yes.'

The woman steps closer. She glances over her shoulder and looks back at him. He can see the soft features of her jaw line and long hair. Her nose curves inwards and is missing the ridge and cartilage. She has two holes, semicircular and fleshy.

'I'm sorry, ma'am, but I ain't giving you a lift. Company policy and I've broken those rules once or twice and I promised myself never again.'

The woman steps back into the darkness.

'Okay. Thank you.'

'You know,' the driver says. 'You shouldn't hang out around here. It's dangerous.'

He looks in the dark, but she is gone.

BARE

Mother. A single word with many meanings. A blackened, tangled mess of hair hunched over and reeling. A mind sewn together by days of drug use and alcohol. Forlorn and desperate, she sucks on a pipe, the glass bottom burnt. Small fissures break along the tube. She clicks the lighter and its loud in her ears – deafening – and her eyes peel open and she draws in the smoke, leaning back, then breathes it out. Her lungs tire and are filled with disease and her heart carries emotional weight, too heavy for her to barely stand.

DEATH AWAITS

What are you gonna do?

'Lay here and die.'

Just like that?

'Yes.'

Why don't you get out? Go to the Train.

'You tell me not to. I leave, and you tell me to come back.'

I told you it wasn't time.

'It's time now?'

It has to be. I know you're hurt, but he will kill you if you don't leave soon.

'If I leave, he'll kill me anyway. He'll find me and kill me. No one will know, no one will care.'

If you leave, this place dies.

'Then why do you want me to leave? You'll die with it.'

I'm already dead. I need to go.

'Where will you go?'

I'll just cease to exist. I'm only here for you.

'All I know you as, is a pair of legs and half a stomach. I don't know you and you don't know me.'

I know you.

'How?'

You brought me here. You saw my death. You remembered.

'I didn't see your death.'

You may not have seen it yet.

'My skin, it hurts. I can't lie anywhere without it hurting.'

What he did to you is only the start. Next will be a thrashing, then he will go too far, and you will die. He will think of it as an accident and bury you. No one will ever find your body.

'I want to go there now. I can't move. I can't walk. I can't eat. I can barely speak, and even then… I don't know who I'm speaking to.'

Yes, you do. All will make sense once you get to the Train and get out of this place.

'You promise?'

Yes.

'I can't just leave. You know that. I have to wait for him to go to work. I don't know what day it is. He could be home tomorrow.'

He won't be home tomorrow. When he is here later, don't bang on the door and make him mad. Just be patient and wait. I'll let you know when it's safe to leave.

INTERVIEW WITH MERLIN DRAKE AND KEISER DITTMAR

'Better be a good reason you got me in here.'

'You know why you're in here.'

'No, I don't.'

'Should feel like a second home to you.'

'You can't say shit like that. I'm guessing it's because of the kid that's gone missing?'

'Murdered.'

'Well, the last I heard he was missing, so that's news to me.'

'You know his name?'

'No. I heard he was from the other side of town. You know me, I stick to my own.'

'Why are you back here?'

'Is this about the kid? Or about me?'

'Both. Answer the question.'

'I came back because this is where I live.'

'Used to live.'

'I still do.'

'Down by the river.'

'You know it. I came back here because I still own the house and land.'

'What about the people living in it?'

'They're family.'

'No, they're not.'

'Close as family as I got. Same goes for them. You got family?'

'Tell me about the kid.'

'I told you, I don't know anything.'

'Who told you he was missing?'

'Word around town.'

'Who?'

'I don't remember who. Someone. Maybe the convenience store clerk? Who knows?'

'You would remember. Tell me who.'

'Most likely the kid that lives with us. He's about his age. Right? Probably went to school with him, probably read it on Facebook or something.'

'What's his name?'

'I'm guessing you already know it.'

'Tell me.'

'Mark. But we call him Ginger.'

'What's Mark's last name.'

'I don't know.'

'You don't know the last name of a person living in your house.'

'I've only been back a short time, as you know. I haven't had a chance to pow wow with many of them yet. I'll make a note to do that when I get back.'

'Sure, you will.'

'Anything to help the Hope Valley Police.'

'Don't mock me or I'll book you.'

'I'm only trying to help… By the way, I think I saw your wife in the store yesterday.'

'Mention her again and I'll turn the cameras off and beat you half to death.'

'You know, the cops here never used to talk like that. They used to respect me.'

'I don't respect you.'

'I can see that.'

'I want a list of everyone living at your establishment, where they came from and what they do for work.'

'That might take some time.'

'No, it won't. How many live there? Five?'

'So, you been keeping an eye on us, I see.'

'You'll bring it in here in two days' time or I'll come down there with a search warrant.'

'Searching for what?'

'Drugs. Unregistered firearms. If you can safely say you have neither there, you have nothing to worry about.'

'You press a hard bargain, Mr Drake.'

'It's Detective Drake, and this isn't a bargain. This is an instruction from an officer of the law.'

'I'll get you your list. Now can I go?'

'No.'

'I'll need to get in contact with my lawyer.'

'You don't have one. Only a few more questions and you can go.'

'I got nothing to hide.'

'What do you know about the other murders in the forest.'

'It's all small-town gossip. No one's died in there.'

'Several remains have been found in the forest, dating back to the time before you went to jail.'

'That means nothing'.

'The murders stopped while you were inside – explain that to me.'

'More than likely a coincidence.'

'Is that right.'

'Maybe?'

'Who is Jeremy Dover?'

'Who?'

'Don't even start. Just start talking.'

'...'

'Jeremy Dover, white male, mid-thirties, blonde facial hair, neck tattoo, worked at the tattoo shop in Fountain, found hiding at your compound by the river. Released on bail and never seen again.'

'I don't know anything about him. Knew he was hanging around, got caught with some stuff. I haven't seen him for a long time. You gonna try pin this on him? He most likely dead or back in jail. He's probably a junkie like the rest of the dopes here.'

'We checked the jails and the morgues, he hasn't been in either.'

'I don't even think Jeremy was his real name. We used to call him Sal. Maybe you're searching for the wrong person.'

'You met him in prison.'

'First cell I ever walked into, he was there reading a book. He stood up, he was at least a few inches taller than me. He told me it was gonna be crowded in here, shook my hand, then went back to reading.'

'You got out first, then he followed you here.'

'I told him I could give him a place to stay for a few months if he needed it.'

'His parole officer didn't know he was with you. He would have gone back to jail if he had known.'

'Well, go arrest him then.'

'Smart mouth me again...'

'Look, all I want to do is get out of here. I'm not feeling great, like my guts are being twisted up.'

'What did Dover do once he got out and went to your place?'

'Nothing! He stayed for a few months, I don't know — got a job at the mill for a bit. He was lugging timber and driving those trucks. He didn't last long. He took off one night. Took all his stuff.'

'What spooked him?'

'I don't know. Maybe the parole officer was looking for him? Maybe he didn't like Hope Valley. Who knows?'

'What I think is you killed two people, buried them in the forest. Got into making drugs and was busted, went back to jail. When you got out you started again. Dover came to visit, saw what you were doing and couldn't handle more jail time and took off.'

'None of that is true.'

'I'm watching you. Very closely. If you so much as light a joint and I see it, you'll go back to prison.'

'I'm leaving right now.'

LURCH

The Train lurches forward, like a fleshy hand loosened of its skin through a barbed wire fence. The nose is caked in soil and dust and it drops away. Large pieces of encrusted sludge and weeds fall to the ground, aged and burning. The forest howls, giving birth to the darkened serpent. A hundred-year birth, once dead, but now very alive.

A CONVERSATION AND A CONFESSION

'They used to party in a van.'

'A van?'

'Yeah, this white, beat up, piece of shit van. They would drive around and look for women.'

'Yeah?'

'Three of them. One of their friends was in a wheelchair. They used to use him to get these girls.'

'In a wheelchair? For the love of God.'

'His name was Cameron, from memory. He died a long time ago. They would get him and put him in the back. And drive between Haven and Crowne, looking for women walking home from the bars, or from work. Sometimes they'd just wait by the side of the road with the front up, like he's broken down. Cameron would be in his wheelchair and they'd come up and ask him if he needed help.'

'Makes me sick to my damn stomach.'

'You're telling me.'

'He told you all this?'

'My father knew him and his father, before he was the chief of police. But back then he was just a kid like them. My dad wasn't anything then, just got his badge. He said he wanted to talk to him, on his death bed. He got pneumonia you see, and he was already ill, and he couldn't fight it off.'

'Your father went to see him? And the others?'

'No, just him. The doctors told him he's dying, they told him he had about four days and he'd be speaking to the big man himself. If you want to ask for forgiveness for anything, this day will be the day to do it. But he didn't call the priest… he called my dad.'

'He confessed?'

'He said three boys, Stephen, that's John-Jon's boy, Mark and Clarence Bishop. Daddy said he went to the hospital and the man was hooked up to all these machines, he was gonna die any minute, and he knew it. He was crying and hollering to him. He wanted to tell him before he went. All those unsolved murders 30 years ago, in the woods. The other boys, they had told him that if he snitched on them, they kill him too. Said he was an easy target.'

'God have mercy. So, he told your papa what he and the others did?'

'He did. He wrote it down, it's in my safe back home. He told my father everything. From the van, to which women they grabbed.'

'Those murders were all over the news. The burden of knowing… of helping must have damn near killed him.'

'I'm sure that's what ended up taking his life. Guilt can hang on around your damn neck like an anchor. You can't help but feel sorry for the boy, you know? You see, when he was about fifteen, he was in a diving accident. Off the old quarry, broke his neck. Poor kid had a rough life right from the word go, he was just doing what the other kids were doing, but he's the one that got hurt. The other boys knew he was gullible. Knew he would do what they told him to. Used him to do those murders.'

'Goddamn.'

'Yeah, that's right, goddamn. Each and every step of his

life he had been coerced to partake in these things. I mean I'm not letting him off the hook, he helped, but who's to say he could have stopped it or not, even if he wanted to. He could have told my father earlier, the minute it was over, he could have confessed, got these kids locked up. I remember my daddy pacing up and down the house, knowing the media crews were on their way to report it. He had to find out who did it, there was nothing. Just missing persons, no bodies.'

'Did he tell your daddy where the bodies were? Did he show him on a map?'

'No. And those of us that were born and raised here know the forest is its own animal.'

'Goodness. That gave me the damn chills.'

'I know they went looking for the missing girls in the forest, but it's so dense and big, they couldn't find anything. Five police officers, and family searched day and night and couldn't find a damn thing. The report that came out said they ran away. They were classed as missing persons in the paperwork, but they were murdered by the three boys.'

'What ever happened to them?'

'Stephen Dixon died when he moved to a lodge in Cicada Mountain. Some hikers found the cabin and looked inside, he damned froze to death. Couldn't handle the guilt I say. Mark and Clarence Bishop both got apprenticeships at the wreck yard. They stayed there for years, as far back as I can remember. Mark was still there when I was reassigned to this place. Clarence knocked up a girl, local, and her daddy moved them away. He came back briefly. He was staying with Cameron for a bit. She wasn't around, or the kid.'

'I used to see Clarence around town. He looked gaunt. Really white. Started hanging out with that lot down by the river.'

'You see, John-Jon was one of them for a long time.'

'You don't say?'

'He left and came up out of the ravine and stayed away from them. I don't know what happened, but it was enough for him to leave. I never asked, and he never told.'

'When that kid went missing a few months back, I thought of them straight away.'

'I'd been down there; Dad had been down there. They sort of stick to themselves. They got a few firearms and a few sheds without permits, but other than that, there's really not much there.'

'So, Clarence came back and stayed with Cameron?'

'Only for a few weeks. I remember Jeremy telling me. At the time he was the landlord and he had his suspicions of that group. Who knows what they spoke about? Maybe Cameron had to let him stay or Clarence would've done something to him. To be a fly on the wall in the room, hey? The only thing that I wanted to ask Cameron was what he did to them girls? I know for a fact that Cameron can't use his dick, there's no way he can. I've seen the surgeons report. Those boys who would have done that to the girls, it wasn't him. But I'm not saying he didn't do stuff. They may have let him kill them... but you know what, I can't see him doing it. Just wrong crowd. Yeah, so Clarence stayed with him for a few months. Nobody really saw them. Then one day I picked him up for hitchhiking, he was headed down to the boys in the ravine. I asked him why, he said he didn't know why. His father had been down there, like I said. So maybe he knew someone down there still, who's to know.'

'God knows. Maybe he was looking for friends or work? Those boys are always getting into something. They used to bring steel in at night, from other counties on those big trucks. Don't know where they were getting them from.'

'If it was anything illegal, I'd know about it. Be it on the record or not, I'd still know. The old man there, Coates, he runs a pretty tight ship. If those boys play up, they'd get a hiding.'

'What I heard is, he's been to jail.'

'Well I can't say he has or not, but I'm ain't gonna deny those rumours either. It's just you and me and God in this room.'

'He killed a man, here in Hope Valley. A long time ago, after a night of drinking. My uncle used to tell me the story, said he was there. Drinking at the bar and they got into a fight about the snooker table. Words were said. At the end of the night the man left to head home, and Coates followed him out. Stabbed him five times. Went to jail for a long, long time. Only reason, I hear, he got out was because he said it was self-defence. But I heard otherwise.'

'Well, rumours are what make this town different from all the rest. The ghosts never sleep.'

'They got machines now, like x-rays that can scan the ground, looking for bones. You ever thought about doing that? Letting those families sleep at night, let them mourn? At least they'll know what happened.'

'Most of the families have either passed away or they moved out of town shortly after. One family, Mackays, they stayed a year or two. Put the fliers up and asked around.

My father got a tongue lashing every now and then from the father, but they were young, the general consensus was they had run away. Every family said their daughters wouldn't do that, but it does happen. After he spoke to Cameron he used to go out to the forest on his own. He told me once he would stand there and listen and sometimes, he could hear them screaming for help.'

'Sounds like a man broken to me.'

'Ghosts never rest. In his later years he was a man haunted.'

'The bones of those who never rest in peace, will always scream.'

'Those machines you speak of, they would find more than a few girls under the soil. Too many have gone in there and never come out. I would honestly say, my hand to God, it would be better to leave the bones where they are.'

'I tell my son and two daughters to never go into the forest. They wanted to follow the train tracks when they were little. I told them no, do not ever follow the tracks.'

'If I could rip those spikes and rails out of the ground I would. I'd close off the path to the forest and lock it up, like it should be. Chain all the entrances up, and leave it be.'

'The darkness can stay in the dark.'

DEATH AND THE LEECH

A hollow cove fissures along the bones. A quick breath and the moon quivers. Nothing is still, and nothing is forever. A quietness that burns the mind and stills the heart. Take this blade and wipe it clean, it can never be used again. Something stirs and rests, stirs and finally wakes. Something within hears the call and opens its eyes. A never-ending surge of providence. The hand that grips also feeds. Taken lightly and caressed and speak to it like it is the mother that latches onto you. A leech born again, hungry for blood, but it means little harm. Be like the leech. Hide among the canopy of leaves, resting and waiting.

A blackened sea, within the mind, tells the spirits it is time.

The boat that carries thee, will stop short of the bank and the songs played will be long and tell the tales of your life. The latch caught in your throat, the moment right before you speak, but hold your tongue. You wait your entire life to breathe and can never take a full lung of air.

The ground will be soft. For you, it will be warm, and you will not need to worry about anything or anyone. That will be taken care of by the Dark Rider. It is why he is here. Just rest your head and take a long breath.

Skeletons hang on wild limbs
The taste of black smoke in the air
Walking can lead you anywhere
In the forest
There are no paths

WHITE HAND

The old man – Kaiser – he sits out the front on a chair nearly as old as he is. He watches the mountains and never the woods. His bones creak when he moves, and his eyes shift and dart, knowing where everything is. They stare, glassy and knowing. The boy, less than half his age, sits on the steps and lights a cigar, taking the smoke in and letting it drift from his nostrils.

'I ain't scared. That cop that came here. He doesn't scare no one.'

'I've known him for a long time. He's doing his job. If we stay clean, we're all good.'

'He better not come back here again. I don't like him looking around too much.'

'He knows what we do here. Everyone's entitled to their freedom of speech. He knows that.'

The boy looks over his shoulder at the old man.

'Why did you come back here? After that long?'

'This is my home. Why wouldn't I come back here?'

'Out of all the places you could have gone, you come back to this stank hole.'

'Ain't nothing for me anywhere else.'

The boy moves, twists his body around to see the old man better. His skin is stretched tight.

'You got family elsewhere?'

'All my family are dead. This town, this river here, it's where I'll die too. Ain't nothing wrong with coming back here.'

The boy smokes even though he knows the old man hates it.

'I ain't ever left.'

'You're not from here though.'

'I know that,' the kid snarks. 'Coming here felt strange, like I was caught in a web. I'm not saying I don't like it. It's different to the places I lived before.'

Kaiser smirks and looks down at his white-hot knuckles gripping the chair.

'The only time I ever left here, voluntarily, was when I took someone's life from them.'

The kid turns his head, the smoke shifting into his eyes, blanketing his face. 'You did?'

Kaiser nods and rubs his hands, pushing the leathery skin of his fingers through one another.

'A woman.'

He nods.

'Yes, it was a long time ago, but I remember it. It never leaves you, not ever. You probably wouldn't know. Maybe you do? I remember her face.'

'In the war?'

'No. Not in the war. I was a train driver before... before this place. The river was small back then.'

'What train?'

'Way before you were born there was a train that ran through here. All the way from Fountain, through Weaver's Peak and down along the County. It stopped here, turned around and went back the other way. Took three days, there and back.'

'You did that?'

'Yes. Straight out of prison they get you to do manual

labour. They keep an eye on you. Not much to choose from as there wasn't much work, you hear?'

'I know it.'

'I remember sleeping down by the old wreck yard, it's a car park now for the shopping mall. I used to have a small mattress, rolled up and a blanket. In the morning I would tuck it away, under an old car and go to work. They would give a lunch allowance back then and I would buy three packs of biscuits and a few tins of beans. When I had saved enough, I bought proper shoes. Back then, working on the trains, you needed proper shoes, if not, you'd wear holes in them quick. There was three of us training. First you would learn all the levers and signals and speed, then you would be a passenger and watch a trained driver, then you were on your own.'

The kid blows blue-grey smoke and looks at the old man again. 'You bought shoes before a proper place to sleep?'

'Where I slept wasn't of much concern to me. I knew eventually I would find a place, but back then it was more about working, and keeping your job. They knew I was an ex-con, and if I fucked up once I would be out the door. Then what would I do? I'd be homeless and starving.'

Kid stands and stretches; his ribs push through his waxy skin and he sits back down.

'My first run by myself I completely blanked and didn't stop at one of the stations. Sped straight past it. A few people complained, lucky it was to one of the guys I started with and they lied for me, telling them we couldn't stop at that station, at the time, due to track maintenance. Later on, when I had time and money, I bought that guy a bottle of rum. You should never forget when someone covers for you. Loyalty is everything.'

'Hard to find that these days.'

'Show loyalty and you will get loyalty. Anyway, I had been there for nearly two years and that day was like any other day. I remembered the tracks were wet, that I do remember. It's clear to me, even way back then I don't remember a lot, but that day – I do remember. I saw the stones and the metal tracks were wet. It made no difference. We were leaving Weaver's Peak to head here, and as I was coming in, I remember thinking about moving. I was living in a squalor with a few others. There was no heat, the bathroom toilet didn't work and the water coming out of the sink was brown. I remember thinking of getting out of there, paying a bit more for a boarding room and I looked up as we approached the station and I could see a woman, she was standing too close to the edge of the platform. I saw her look straight at me and I knew what she was about to do.'

'You knew it?'

'I could see it in her face. I knew by the look in her eyes. I couldn't do anything. Trains don't stop on a dime. It rolled in and she just stepped out, falling onto the tracks in front of me. I can still hear the noise her body made when it was cut. She didn't scream... I remember that... she didn't scream.'

'Fuck.'

'Yeah, that's about right. I pressed an alarm button and one of the other drivers came running over. He could see in my face what had happened. We got all the people off and locked the station doors. We couldn't do much until the police came to get the body. I walked over to the front of the train.'

'You wanted to see it?'

'No, not in particular. But I felt obligated to see her. It wasn't something that I thought about, it was like my brain told me to go to the front and look down.'

'What did you see?'

'One of her legs was out the side. I don't know how it could have happened, but it was there. Still had her shoe on. When trains stop, they make a lot of funny noises – hissing and creaking. But the noise I heard coming out from under the train that day was different. Like someone was talking, softly. I could hear dripping and I knew it wasn't the oil, it was her blood. I could tell. I knew all the sounds of the train by that stage.'

'What did you do after?'

'The police came, and I had to reverse the train up the tracks. Train's that old don't like going backwards. We all had to push. She was there with a strange look on her face. Her eyes were still open, and she was staring upwards.'

'Did you find out who it was?'

'I never wanted to know. They took her away and I remember finding out it wasn't the first person who had done that, at that location. The next day I was back driving trains.'

Drudge through mud and blood
Rats amongst the waste
Soil in turmoil
Life in the woods

BORN OF THE WORM

Stark raving mad. Roy runs into the forest. His eyes bulging out of his sockets, sweat dripping off his chin and slipping down his neck. His arms are wet, and he smells the foliage and takes the aroma into his lungs, deep and entrenched. The canopy, a ceiling of dark rot, shielding the sun from the swampy flooring. Roy, high on methamphetamine, sees in blues and reds. He hears animals chattering in their burrows. He hears the woodland speak…

Here he is.

Again!

Get out! Out!

Roy waves his chainsaw around. His sense of motion is slow, but he is moving fast. The shadows dance around him in a vibrating aura. He roars like an unchained beast, his mouth torn open, bone-white teeth, his lips yawning open so wide the it splits at the corners. The red veins in his eyes pulsate with eagerness and lust. The chainsaw drops from his hands and onto the mother ground.

It has started.

Tucker, born of an alcoholic, drunk at the time of conception and drunk at the time of birth. A mother, diseased with the will of an addict. He bores into the forest ground, as if being transformed into a worm. *The Tucker Worm is born.* He is covered in dirt. He has never felt this high in his life. The colours around him, like spells cast. New colours, new sounds.

Roy ignores the buzzing blades and stands over the half-man, half-drug beast. He flops his dick out and pisses near Tucker's head.

'It's a good batch. Ain't been this wasted in all of my damned life.'

Tucker leaps to his feet and nabs the chainsaw. He looks up at the trees, looking for the precious burl. The tree tops sway uncharacteristically and angular. Their movements defy thought and fight against the laws of perception. They twist and curl and fade in and out of consciousness. Tucker waves the machine at the trees and strikes it hard, chipping off pieces of wood. They stream around him like confetti. The trees scream at him, but he ignores it. He drops the chainsaw, near his foot, missing by mere inches. He picks it up again and sees Roy standing in the darkness of the forest, like a puppet.

'Why are you back there?' His voice is colourful and warped.

Roy's arms pop and bend at odd angles. He steps forward, one leg flops and he nearly falls. He opens his mouth to speak, but his tongue slides out and he mumbles. His other leg steps forward and Tucker watches him with odd fascination. Roy collapses in a heap, as if the puppet master became bored.

'Here,' Tucker says, pointing behind him without looking. 'There's burl wood back here. Come, Roy.'

He holds the chainsaw out in front of him and stumbles and trips on every branch and twig. The day burns the light, like a sallow candle without much wick.

You come in here, you die.

We will make sure of that.

Just like the others.

Yes, just like the others.

Roy appears beside Tucker; his face is red and covered in mud. Tucker looks at him, unbeknownst to him how he actually got there so fast. He tries to hand the chainsaw to him, but Roy waves it away. His eyes are bulging, and he looks up at the tree in front of them. It has the largest burl he has ever seen. He points, and Tucker begins to laugh. Tucker yanks the pull lever and the chainsaw bursts to life. It's louder than Roy remembered, so he steps back, his ears ringing wildly. Tucker lifts it up and stabs at the tree. The blades bounce off it and he wobbles, losing his balance.

'Try up there,' Roy points.

Tucker doesn't look. He swings the chainsaw over his head, his arms strain under its weight and he loses grip and it falls. The teeth slash his forearm and he yelps. The forest hears and applauds.

Leave here and nothing will happen to you.

Leave and never come back.

Roy breathes out slowly, the sigh is audible. His fingers start to shake, and he looks around the woodland, suddenly suspicious. The tree trunks collide, making a wall of wood and shadow. Roy panics. His mind is reeling at the thought of the trees uprooting and following after him. Their pine-needle pins slashing at his face and dragging him under to the mulchy underworld. He won't be a king there, he will be food for the wasted and fertiliser for the undead.

Tucker picks the chainsaw up and eyes the spinning blades. He aims his sight at the burl; the gorgeous, twisted, cancerous knot of mutated growth. For him, now, it's no longer about the money, but for the treasure. He flings the chainsaw upwards, over his head again. The weight too much to bare; the chainsaw drops. It arcs to the left and cuts straight through his right arm. Metal teeth on flesh, the spinning of rusted blades. Flesh cuts like rotten fruit skin. His arm falls to the ground, and the chainsaw follows. Lying next to each other, the Tucker Worm looks and is speechless in mind and mouth.

Blood spills on the forest floor. The forest takes a breath.

Roy runs over and looks at the arm. The fingers are moving. The chainsaw grunts and then stops. The smoke is black. The woods have done what they had said.

'Tucker, your arm,' Roy says.

Tucker steps backwards and falls to the ground. The foliage is soft and catches his head. It bounces but is not hurt. A panic erupts in Roy as Tucker begins to spit from his mouth. Roy shakes him and gets him to his feet. Tucker is heavy, and his legs buckle and don't work. Roy yells at him to move, but Tucker wants to lay back down on the leafy flooring. Roy drags and pushes him back to the car. A long blood trail is left through the woods. Tucker slumps in the passenger seat and looks at the stump where his arm used to be. Blood is pouring from it, onto the seat and over the gearshift and radio. It drips onto the floor and pools on the torn carpet. Roy slams the car into reverse and it bounces off the makeshift path and onto the road.

Tucker suddenly screams and convulses in his seat. Roy reaches for Tuckers seatbelt and slams it into the lock. He pushes him back, his hand on his chest and he drives.

The forest is quiet and the arm twitches. The chainsaw cools down; the blood of him on its teeth. The bite that hurt. The animals will come out at night to survey the scene. The blood will get on their feet and paws and they will walk it around the floor. No one will come back for it and the flesh will become soil and the bones will become nests. The chainsaw will rot and rust and sink into the soft ground.

DEVOUR

The dust is thick and catches in your throat. The sun is dry and hot on the skin, but the wind is brittle and cold.

The darkness has receded like a blackened shoreline. The trees are birthed with brown leaves, awaiting autumn to fall and cascade to the concrete below, messing the streets and sidewalks. A dove flies, not lost, but curious. Where once were ravens that squawked and were noisy and violent, now are empty powerlines, strung from wooden poles, solemn and quiet. Dove lands and cleans under its wings, expecting dirt from car exhaust and pollution, but neither is there. A car pulls into the gas station and the man gets out and slams the door. He does not feel the clasping cold or the dark menace that radiated from the nearby woods. He simply fills his car, pays and leaves. He is not any less worried or sees the dark shadows that move promptly along the woods.

THE CLEARING

In the forest, along a long path, is a circle of padded earth. The clearing made clear by generations of teenagers, wasted on beer, and smoking, walking and fucking. Two cars, rusted until they are brown and holey, are on either side of the great pit. The fire burns different here; the bottom is blue, and the tips are bright orange, a match for the sun when it can no longer stand the sight of Them. Abandoned furniture and table sets adorn the clearing and teenagers and old perverts meet here to converse and drink, throwing their cans into the fire to proclaim they are more than you are.

Everyone knows of the clearing; parents and grandparents came here. They threw in their beer cans and fucked on the same hood of the same car, the same turned over tree trunk, along the same edge of the piece of forest that looked like a desert. No one talks of the clearing and there is no sacred passage or hidden book or map, it is simply given to you by the forest when you turn of age: the same time you start drinking and fucking. Teenagers from Hope Valley migrate there after school to burn their books when they quit. They meet there on Friday and Saturday nights and drink and sleep on the ground under the trees. The forest allows this, as they are young and will soon be fearful.

Pi sits on a stool, carved from wood, by someone that used to work on the train line. Their initials are carved underneath it, and the date: 1926. She drinks from a tall can of beer and she is hunched forwards, her knees knocked together, and her feet sprawled outwards. Her long arms rest on her thighs and she holds the beer can out to the flames, but it is not thirsty. Jakob watches her through the fire. Her eyes are like glass and he wonders about her stare. Could she be capturing the flame? The fire crackles and spits sparks up and Pi looks and watches as they float, an ember parachuting back down to the ground, extinguished.

'Do you want to get out of here? It's getting crowded now.'

Pi doesn't look around. 'No. I want to stay longer. Maybe stay the night.'

Jakob pulls his jacket around his thinning body. He wipes his nose and looks at his hand, earlier there was blood. No blood now.

'You want to stay the night?'

'I like it out here.'

'I passed out here once, in the car.' He nods behind Pi. 'Woke up covered in a rash. There's bugs out here and ivy. I took off just as the sun was coming up. I don't think you want to see this place in the daylight.' He looks for a smile, but there isn't one.

'They say this is the heart of the forest, that's why nothing grows here.'

She looks up at Jakob and she can't remember what she used to see in him. He's still handsome, but he's getting sicker.

'Dad told me this was where the train workers used to come and smoke and drink and gamble on their shift breaks. Nothing grows here because those guys are here all the time.' His eyes roll over to another area that contained rotting couches and lounge chairs. A group of teenagers sit drinking out of a rum bottle and passing around a smoke.

Chipper stands up and catches a heave from his stomach, into his throat. He runs quickly into the forest and vomits, much to the amusement of Bobby and the others. Everyone hollers, and Chipper gives them the finger.

'Every time,' Bobby says, his focus shifting towards Pi and Jakob.

Casper taps Bobby on the shoulder and passes him the joint. Bobby passes it on without taking any.

'I don't like it here now, Pi,' Jakob argues. He rubs his face as if he was covered in ants. 'Not since that kid died.'

'He wasn't the first one to die out here.'

'Yeah, I know. But since him, it's been really creepy. My skin crawls. It's like I'm allergic to this place.'

Fire swirls in Pi's eyes. She dares not blink. Neither of them speak for several minutes.

'One day I'll leave this place. I won't stop until I'm out of the county. I'll take Cassie with me.' Jakob looks at her. She tried to leave, once, and the town wouldn't allow it. 'I'll take her far from here, somewhere where we can see the beach every day.'

'Yeah?'

Pi continues to stare into the fire. 'I'll have a two-storey house, with a large balcony with lounge chairs and it would be too hot to sit out there in the morning, but in the afternoon the sun would dip, and it would be shady, and we would sit there, reading books and watching the ocean.' Pi wiped away a tear. 'It would have three bedrooms. One each and a spare one, if Mum came to visit. Roy would be dead, and Mum would be happy. She would be off drugs and working at the book store a few blocks away. I'd work at the coffee shop, selling cakes and talking to strangers about their dogs. Cassie would go to a good school. One where there are no metal detectors and police. One where the teachers care if you can read or do maths. I'd walk home from work, barefoot and smell the flowers and hear the children playing in the park. On the weekend we would watch the fireworks and cook paella and drink tea. I'd buy new clothes and have a full-length mirror. A boy would keep asking me out at the coffee shop and I'd say no until finally we had dinner somewhere and no one would stare or ask about my nose.'

Jakob stands up, his legs shake. 'Did you hear that? Like someone whispering my name?'

Pi shakes her head.

'Pi, I'm leaving. If you want a lift home, then come now.'

'No. I told you. I'm staying here.'

'Fine.'

Jakob stomps through the clearing and out towards the path that leads to the main road. Pi sits in silence, her eyes still transfixed on the fire.

'From my house, you can smell the beach.'

'You're Pi, right?' said a voice.

Pi looks up to see a boy with shaggy blonde hair. He moves it from his face, so she could see his eyes.

'Go away.'

'I saw your friend leave. I just wanted to know if you wanted to take a walk?'

'No.'

'There's an abandoned water park a few minutes' walk

from here. If you're a good climber, you can get to the top of the diving board and look out over the tree tops, at the town. It looks different from up there.'

Pi studies the fire. There is no more to see. She follows him into the forest and felt it inhale. The boy lifts branches away from her and lets her pass him. He goes to hold her hand, but she resists. She doesn't want to go home, nor back to the town, she wants to stay here in darkness. The boy, Casper, introduces himself and shows her the fence line. Pi has been there before, a long time ago. After the park closed, she would break in there and smoke with the others. Security would kick them out, then, when they came of age, they inherited the clearing.

'You know, the year before this place closed, my dad considered buying it.'

Pi watches him push his fingers through the wire fence wall. He looks in. The slide is missing pipes and the tunnels are cracked, long stalactites of moss dripping down from the plastic, crooked mouths. Pi stops to look also. The cancer has taken over and destroyed everything within the gates. It won't be long til it reaches the city now.

Casper walks further and slides down and inside the park through a hole cut in the fence.

'He knew this town didn't have much going for it. The park seemed the one place where everyone could have fun.' He turned to Pi. 'No one laughs or smiles in Hope Valley, you ever notice that?'

'No one has any reason to.'

Casper points. 'There, the high board.'

Pi looks up. It was taller than she remembered. The pool below it is empty, other than a shallow puddle of rain water and detritus.

'You go this way, then there's a bit you have to jump. I'll show you.'

Casper runs to the ladder and starts to climb it eagerly. Pi follows. The first level of rungs is slippery and with every step her shoes slip outwards. They walk around the tower on a metal platform. The grate is rusted, and time and weather has left pieces missing. A bird's nest lays in one of the holes, cracked eggs and long, grey sticks are all that remained.

'Dad looked into getting the loan and they said it wasn't a good idea so, he went elsewhere. Drove all the way to Lowville. By the time they were doing the paperwork, the park closed. Turns out the previous owner hadn't paid the bank in six months and was living in the back of the stock room.'

Casper reaches the next ladder. He stares up and can see a string of cobwebs unintentionally blocking their way. The moon makes them look like silk. They look stronger in the dark then they are.

'Are you scared?'

'No,' Pi answers. She isn't scared of anything.

Casper climbs, letting the spiders webbing catch in his hair and jacket. The wind is sweeter this high up and Pi can hear the traffic from the town centre. She chances a look over her shoulder and sees the lights, they sparkled and smiled. Casper reaches the top and holds his hand out for Pi. She takes it and they both stand on the tower, feeling it rock from side to side.

'I've never seen the city like this before.'

'From afar, it's almost beautiful, as if it's enticing you to come in. But once you're close…'

'It's death.'

Casper moves towards Pi and lays his hand on her hip. She moves away.

'Don't,' she says angrily.

'Why do you think I brought you up here?'

Pi pushes him away as he steps closer. He grits his teeth. Down below, something moves.

'I don't give a shit why you thought we were coming up here… I'm going.'

'Don't go,' he snaps and snatches her by the arm.

She pulls away quickly; it isn't the first time a boy tried to use his strength against her. She knows better. She knows what to do. She grips the handle and puts one foot on the ladder rung.

'I bet your nose is lying out here somewhere. In the dirt, rotting. It did happen around here somewhere, didn't it?'

Pi leaps up and punches him across the face. Casper's head cocks to the right and it stings. He returns the punch. Her bottom jaw knocks against her teeth and she sees the stars move and gasp. From below, a shadow moves quickly, it's Bobby. He steps quickly and with two opened palms, pushes Casper. Casper's eyes widen, and his arms instinctively go out, his fingers splayed as he stumbles off the platform. The board long gone and cracked to pieces on the bottom of the emptied pool.

'Fuck!' Pi is suddenly sickened to her stomach. Bile retches up her throat and she spews over the edge.

Casper's body hits the cement below with a dry smack of skin and twisted bones. Bobby walks to the only side of the platform where there is no guard rail. He looks over and begins to laugh.

'What the fuck have you done!' Pi screams. She can hear people hollering from the clearing.

'He hit you.'

Pi backs away slowly. His eyes are black, and the shadows dare not go near him.

'What? What did you want me to do? He was trying to fuck you.'

Pi slips down the ladder, her hands numb and her lungs taking in air quickly and expelling it even quicker. She fumbles to the next level, trying to find the way out in the dark. Moonlight leads the way to another ladder. She stares upwards and sees Bobby's darkened figure through the grated platform. He moves in quick motion, pacing back and forth. He runs his fingers through his hair and then he sprints for the ladder. Pi tries to take the rungs two at a time, but slips and falls, her arm slipping between the steps and almost breaks it. She stumbles down the last few, to the ground, and runs back towards the clearing. A ghostly tunnel of black surrounds her vision and she can't see anyone near the fire or the rusted shells of the two vehicles. The clearing can keep her safe. It has to.

Bobby gets to the dirty, cracked, concrete flooring and stands over the body. He considers picking it up or dragging it into the forest, behind his house. He looks around. The body is too heavy, so he leaves it.

INCONVENIENCE STORE

Keiser walks the way they had taught him in prison. The length of time between then, and now, it should all but have been removed from his persona, but he's made a conscious effort to keep it. He remembers all the towns he's been to – the dusty, dilapidated run-down shit holes. The places he's fought other men, and the times he's won and the times he lost. The women that he had fucked and never seen again. There was always something strange about coming home though. It's familiar, yes, but also agonising. This town was once something else, alive with men; real men who cared about this country, and this place. There was a wood mill and a mine. Now everyone here are the remnants and the forgotten. This town is full of people who were left behind.

A street cuts through another. A light pole stands crooked with a poster glued to it from a band that came through six years ago. The words are faded by the sun. The road is littered with leaves; a wind picks them up and moves them further down the road. Someone walks out of a small coffee shop and stands in front of the mail box, lifting the lid and looking inside. He or she reaches into their jacket pocket and pulls out an envelope. They look in the mail slot again before depositing the letter. A car drives past with a rattling bracket. The man inside is smoking and he stops at the light. He breathes white smoke out and looks at the person walking away from the mail box and wonders if he knows them. They look familiar, everyone here does. The man in the truck doesn't notice the light turning green and a car pulls up behind him and honks its horn. The man goes to step out of his vehicle and sees Keiser standing by the corner. The man freezes, and another horn tolls. He slides back into his chair and sees the woman in his rear vision mirror. He looks at Keiser again, standing there with his fists – balls of wrinkled flesh. He drives on and doesn't look back. Keiser crosses the street and watches the woman drive around the side of the building and park. Keiser notices everything.

The thoughts running through Keiser's head are ones he has pushed aside for many years. All the time he was in lock up and the time he got out and reunited with his old friends and acquaintances. All the thoughts and perverse things had to be stored away. He imagined it as a lock box in a huge bank vault. The key was small and left on a little hook by the entrance. It was easy to open and revisit those memories and slip back into the beatings and the sexual motives, but the challenge was to not touch the key. How much self-control does one have for the perverse?

There is a poster in the window for bread and milk. The sidewalk has a long liquid puddle that is leaking off the pathway and into the gutter. An empty cigarette packet sits by the door, the plastic torn away, and all the smokes taken out. A telephone booth is at the end of the block and there is a young boy talking hurriedly into the phone receiver. Keiser stops by the second window of the store and lights a cigarette and tries to figure out if he knows the boy. There's a good chance he's the son of someone he knows here. If he's a stranger, he will have to leave if he doesn't have a good enough reason to stay.

The boy twists and turns in the booth, uncomfortable at the size he's become, and the walls are too close to his elbows and lanky feet. He yells down the receiver about getting a car and leaving. He then whispers and apologises. His face is milky white with pimples around his mouth. His ears are red from yelling and his hair is unwashed and limp over his face. He spots the man watching him in front of the convenience store and turns his back to him so he can't see his face. Keiser knows that posturing; the person on the other end of the phone line isn't agreeing with him. The boy hangs up violently and pushes his way through the phone booth door, as if he's coming out of a crowd of people. He stands for a moment, watching the old man and thinks to himself – saying something – old perv. *What are you looking at?* But he thinks better of it. He has seen him somewhere before. His tattoos are faded, and they are something his father has, the same ones, on his arm and neck. He walks away, down the block and around the corner, heading for the centre of town.

Keiser watches the street where the kid went, even though he is long gone. He drags on the cigarette gently with his lips, sucking the smoke down his throat. The day is heating up. To his right he hears footsteps and turns, just as the woman from the car opens the door next to him. It swings back and knocks against his foot. The door rattles and the glass creaks in its ancient frame. She doesn't apologise and heads inside. Keiser drops the cigarette. In lock-up, there is no wasting cigarettes, but that is part of the freedom of being "outside". The cool air that had escaped the store wafts up his legs and is soon evaporated by the strangling heat. He turns swiftly, as if set into motion by something, swings the door open and follows the woman inside.

The store is cold. Several promotional posters hang from the ceiling – ice blocks, cheap ice and coffee. There are six aisles, all up to Keiser's chest in height. A camera sits in the far corner, no light blinks. A microwave, which smells like burnt cheese is on the bench near him, the door half open and the light on. A rack of hotdogs turns and twists on a small conveyer belt, moving in motion but not going anywhere. A clerk sits behind the cash register and reads a newspaper. He didn't glance up when either of them walked in. Across the counter is wire, a defence against people trying to climb over. One of the wires is missing. Keiser sees it rolled up beside a small monitor that is black. There's a colour coded height chart near the door and a sensor that chimes softly when it's opened. Towards the back are fridges, full of milk and soda.

The woman is in aisle three, looking at cans of pasta and soup. Keiser has a flash back, a memory. His youth. Not of here, in Hope Valley, but someplace else. He remembers his young self as he walks the first aisle, looking over to the clerk, then back to the woman, her head bopping up and down the aisles as she searches.

There was a woman who had betrayed him, once, a long time ago. She had told the police about something he had done. It was in the city, or town, just like this one and he knew where she lived.

The clerk comes around from the front desk and asks the woman something and she replies and holds up a can and he leaves to go out the back, through a locked door that goes behind the fridges. Keiser, the man who is six-foot-tall and is wearing a clean white shirt approaches the woman and she moves past him, bumping into him. He turns to her; his grin is toothy, and he wants to pound her with his fists. Pound her into a pulpy mess like he did the woman who ratted on him. He wants to strangle her – wrap his fingers around her neck and squeeze and squeeze until her eyes pop out of their sockets. She gives him a smile and he laughs. She moves to the clerk, who is at the counter and she pays for three tins and leaves.

Keiser follows her out, the clerk watching.

'In a past life, in a different town, I would have killed you.'

The woman turns and sees him and smiles, heading in the direction of her car.

'I would have buried you where no one could find you or fed you to my dogs.'

Her car pulls away and Keiser is left on the street. No matter where he goes, he always comes home. No matter what he does, he is always Keiser.

CRUSH

He slaps his cock, trying to get it aroused. It flaps from side to side, pink and wrinkled. He clutches it around the end and squeezes it. The knob turns purple in his grasp. He swears and walks a few feet, punching the brick wall. He walks back and pulls at her hair. He puts it in her mouth, and she gags. The air is cold and pinches at his face.

Toe the line
Unprecedented fixture on the town
Unwanted glances
Heartbeat lunatics

CONVERSATION ABOUT A KID

'This kid I knew. When I met him, he was only… say 14? No mama. No papa. He had an aunt, but she didn't care much for him, you see?'

'Yeah?'

'Yeah, so, this kid, I was only two years into being a detective and I was seeing him about stealing a car. He said it was his friend's mother's and she let him take it. But I knew she didn't, but she said okay, she let them take it. Anyway, this kid had been in and out of foster care his whole life. He would go back to his aunt's house every once in a while, but when he got too wild, he would leave again. She would only call us if he had taken something from her. So, each foster carer, you see, gets nearly 800 dollars a month to have a kid like this.'

'Yup. They know it.'

'They take the money, most of them, and not care what happens to the child. So, this kid, he moves around a lot. Foster home to foster home. No such thing as a stable house. No such thing as the next meal. See, when he turns 18, guess what?'

'He's out.'

'That's right, no more foster care. The system spits you out. You're on your own. You know what he does? He starts living on the streets. He lives under a bridge for two years. See, he ain't finished school. He ain't got nowhere to live, he ain't got money. But he's got drive. Not many people got drive. So, it dawns on him, he doesn't want to live on the street no more. He gets a job washing dishes. Easy job to get, easy job to stick with; just be on time and it's yours, you know? Anyway, he stays with this job, but can't afford a place. So, he gets a second job at the cinema complex. He takes the bins out, rips the tickets, works the late shift, then goes back to living under the bridge. He can't get out. But you see, he's eating. He's working. He's got some money, but he needs a place. Some time passes, he stays away from drugs, he stays away from gangs. This kid, he gets a third job at this small restaurant. He works his butt off there.'

'He does?'

'Yeah, he works there for two years. He's got his eye on this manager job. It's only 75 cents more an hour. But he thinks to himself, if he can get this job, he can quit one of his other jobs and get an apartment. He works his ass to the bone. He does morning shifts, night shifts, cooks, cleans, hauls the trash to the sidewalk. He does everything, and the manager job comes up and he applies.'

'Yeah?'

'He sure does. But they say no. This kid, he's devastated, as you would be. He worked hard for it. Earned it, in his eyes. This other guy starts. This white guy. He's there maybe two, three months, they give it to him.'

'You don't say?'

'Not a word of a lie. This kid, he's mad. Real mad. He pulls the owners into the office and tells them as it is. They are both crying. They see it from his side, but nothing happens. They don't give him any more shifts. He's done. So, he goes back to the streets. This time he starts moving drugs. He starts getting these hookers, he starts down this spiral, you see. The whole time he holds this grudge and he's sitting there one day looking at the shit around him and you know what? He thinks, it all went wrong starting from that one moment. He still thinks he deserved it.'

'Maybe he did.'

'Yeah, maybe he did. Eventually he gets his money together. He gets a gun license. He gets a permit to carry a concealed weapon. He goes so far as to take lessons on how to shoot. Once all that is done, he walks into the restaurant one day and the owner is kneeling over, reading the paper. He looks up and the kid's there. Shoots him point blank range in the head. Killed instantly. He goes over to the kid who got the manager job, empties the rest of the rounds into his chest. He watches his last breath as he falls to the ground and then he leaves. We pick him up from the same spot under the bridge where he had lived years prior. He doesn't fight us or deny it. He sits when we say sit. He stands when we say stand. I ask him, why did you do it? He says, I deserved that position. I say, but it was a year prior. He shrugs and just repeats himself, I deserved that position. After the judge convicted him, fifty years in prison he said to me, you know what, at least now I know where my next meal is coming from and I have a roof over my head, and I don't have to work three jobs.'

LUNG

Bobby Dare stares at his shed through the window. His backyard has no fence and the grass is long, the ends brown from the sun. The yard faded into the forest with no boundary and no definitive line; as the ocean tide lapses and refrains, the forest is creeping in, slowly and surely, nearer and nearer to the back door. In his shed are skulls, eaten by ants and found in the forest.

Bobby opens the fly screen door and lets it pull from his grip. It bangs loudly on the door frame and he steps out in to the back yard.

Bobby, my boy!

He leaves the voice of his mother behind him. The further he gets away the less he can hear her.

Come back, sit with me. You can't leave me, Bobby. You must stay with me.

He shakes his hand to swat her voice away and he enters his shed. He goes to the very back, where his tools are, and he looks, with pride, amongst the hammers and saws, the knives and metal poles. He picks up a length of wood and examines the nails he had put in it the day before. He places it in a vice and tightens the handle; turning it around and around until the wood starts to splinter and speak. He grasps the hammer and holds it over his head, to the light, and examines the dried blood on it. He smiles and turns the weapon over and over. Several more nails are bashed into the wood. On the other side, they are crooked and rusted, but that's how he wants it. He pulls it from the vice and wraps black tape around the other end, forming a make-shift handle. He holds it like a baseball bat and swings it up and down, left and right.

There's a loud thudding from up at the house and he stops and listens. He can hear his mother's machine, the sucking and grating of the engine. He listens. Another thud, this time quicker. He places the wooden plank on the bench. Aggravated he was disturbed, he heads up to the house. The flies buzz around his face and he is annoyed. He stands in the kitchen; the table tops covered in plates, festering with maggots and flies. The ground is covered in cut grass and dead weeds; the fridge is open, broken and void of food. There's a bottle of milk on the shelf, crusted yellow and thick. Several needles line the bench, each one yellow from age and gummed up with congealed blood. The old oven has been wrenched out of the wall and upturned, the rear panel removed, and several pieces taken out to be worked on, but left on the bench. Years of neglect have turned it to rust and covered in furry dust.

Bobby, who is banging on the door? Who is it? Tell them you're busy. Tell them to go away!

'Be quiet, Mum.'

He hears the sucking and grinding of the engine gears. His mother in the next room, she hears everything and doesn't stop talking. She never sleeps. Bobby walks to the door and can see a blurred figure through the stained glass. He knows who it is before he opens it.

'What?'

'Bobby…'

'What do you want?'

'I'm just seeing what you're doing. I was bored at the

park and I headed to Seager's house, but he isn't there. Thought I'd come by. What are you up to, man?'

'Meet me around the back,' he says through the closed door.

Bobby, you're not going out, are you? You always go out, stay in for once. Stay with me. We'll watch a movie or something.

Bobby's eyes roll to the right, like marbles rolling around in a hole. He hates her so much. He hates that she is trapped inside, and she hates that she is still alive. If he stands still enough, and blocks out his mother's machine, he can almost feel himself disappearing. He concentrates on the silence in his head, the deathly loneliness he felt inside his own home and knows, that if he died in here, his mother would starve to death and die too, and no one would find them for weeks, if not months, maybe even never. He stares at the walls. The couches are piled with newspapers and magazines, old dishes from the kitchen, a broken slow-cooker, tennis rackets and golf clubs, posters from old movies from the theatre, dog piss-mats and an old bottle of cologne. He suddenly remembers Chipper was heading around the back, probably looking in his shed. He moves quickly, as if the fire in his belly finally started to burn. He kicks the back door out and sees him looking in his shed.

'Stay out of there. Let's go.'

'Where are we going?'

Bobby. I'm here… I'm lonely again. Please don't leave. I can't sleep. I can never sleep. I need you to sing to me, like you used to. Remember? I loved your singing.

There is a track through the woods. It starts behind the shed and leads straight out of the suburban wasteland.

Chipper follows Bobby. He has been on this track before, but only a few times. He has been in Bobby's shed before, but he was only allowed in there once, many years ago. He knows what is in there.

Bobby walks slowly and stops often. He looks around the forest, not lost, and not knowing, but on the lookout. They both know the forest is its own *thing*. It is an organism of decaying death. It houses unimaginable horror; some of these horrors are put there by Bobby himself. He is looking for permission to walk through its veins. A human drug pumped and full of vile and illicit horror. The unthinkable sometimes can never be spoken.

Chipper stops and pisses against a tree. He can hear something from far away. He holds his piss and listens; the clanking of wood, maybe a saw. Probably tweakers he thinks, cutting down trees again. The forest has enough room that nobody can be seen, the chances are slim. He zips up and turns and suddenly realises he is alone.

'Bobby?'

There is no answer. He walks to the area where they had been; or was it? He spins around and then loses direction. He runs his fingers through his short, blonde hair.

'Oh, no, no, no, no,' he cries out to himself.

The trees have moved, and the sun has disappeared. The sound of the saw has stopped. He feels tears well up in his eyes and the familiar worm in his stomach start to churn. He whips his head around, back and forth, his gut punching against his spine. He doubles over and sees Bobby in the distance standing beside a tree looking at him. He looks like a mannequin in a shop window. His eyes are death and his soul is missing.

'Hurry up,' he says.

Chipper runs. The noise of the saw starts again, and Chipper could see light coming through the tree tops. The worm dissipates, and he starts to breathe again. They walk over fallen vegetation, trampled tree branches and exposed rocks and stones. The toppled tree trunks are warm and wet, and animals move without being seen. They too suffer *the worm*.

'In each and every one of us, we have the ability to kill,' Bobby says, stopping suddenly. He sees an old caravan-trailer in the distance. Its front door is missing, and all the windows are smashed out. It has sunk into the muddy ground, leaving it toppled to one side. 'We can all kill if we need to, even though some of us think we can't.'

Chipper knows the caravan and starts beating his chest with his balled-up fists. He feels tears again and fights desperately to keep them away.

'If you say you can't… then you're lying.'

Bobby walks to the caravan and peers inside. Chipper looks around, afraid they are being watched. *But they are!* The woods are watching. They know. They have hidden this box here for some time. They know its contents. They keep people away from it.

Bobby goes inside, and Chipper waits just near the door. The smell is incredible, and his stomach turns, and he wants to vomit.

'Given the circumstance,' Bobby says. 'If and only if, you were in a position where your life depended on it, you could do it.' Chipper doesn't speak. He just looks away, at the forest hoping it would swallow him. 'Some people don't need opportunity or circumstance. To kill, they simply need pleasure in it.'

Chipper spews in his mouth, a small amount and swallows it back down. The taste nearly makes him sick again.

'Can we get out of here?' he asks.

Bobby appears at the door, quickly. 'I have to check one more spot.'

'I don't want to come with you... This isn't what I wanted to do.'

Bobby doesn't look at him. 'Nothing in your life is what you wanted to do. Everything you've even done has been decided for you. If you don't like it... go back.'

Chipper looks through the forest. He has no clue how to get back. And yet again, he has no choice. Bobby leaves the trailer and walks past Chipper, without acknowledging him, and continues the path through the forest. Chipper knows death is coming. The worm has felt it and is uneasy. It shifts nervously in his stomach. All the trees are identical; however, Chipper remembers these trees. He remembers that day; it's a blur, but the images are captured like a polaroid camera. They are still, the edges frayed, and madness has distorted everyone's faces.

'Why did you bring me here?'

'You came to my house, Chipper. I told you about visiting the sites. Didn't I? We must check it. We need to see what we've done.'

A mound of dirt upturned and scattered. The hole is empty. Bobby looks into the shallow dug-out and his heart drops.

'They'll be looking for us.'

'They'll never find us.'

'What if they do?'

'This is Dead Town, Chipper. Don't you know that!' Bobby screams. 'No one here is actually alive. We are all dead. We're all festering and decaying. Can't you smell it?' Chipper takes a step back. 'You know Chipper, if you tell anyone, or come here on your own, I'll put you in that hole myself.'

'I didn't come to see you to be brought out here, Bobby. I was bored. I can't stay at home. I didn't want to come here. I didn't ask to come here.'

'I should kill you now and put you in that hole.'

Chipper readies himself to run. He could outrun Bobby, he knows he could. It didn't matter where he went, or how lost he would get, as long as he was away from him. Bobby begins to walk back home. They walk in silence. Chipper still is threatened and tries to wipe the path from his memory. He doesn't accidently want to come back here, not under any spell or suspicion. The way back, they don't see the caravan-trailer. The forest has hidden it. Bobby's shed appears, as if out of nowhere, and Chipper is relieved. Bobby stands near the back door with his hand on the door handle.

'Remember what I told you, Chipper.'

Chipper nods and goes around the side of the house.

Bobby, who was that? Who is that boy? Is that your friend? Tell him to come back later, I have things for you to do. Now, come to me.

'I'm coming,' Bobby says, entering the house.

ONLY SHADOWS

The woods; they collect whispers and secrets. With broken limbs, disfigured and disjointed. It smells of rotting bark and upturned earth. It smells of fresh leaves and rank moss. The forest is quiet today and the air is dead still. A crow, tar black with long feathers, calls and nothing answers.

Cassie slides her hand under a three-foot branch and lifts it up from its mulch cocoon. Strands of weeds and vines break off and clump to the ground in soggy patches. She takes it towards the path they made. Boy and Gus are there, wood bundled in their arms like newborn children.

'What have you found?'

'It's not dry like the others, but it might dry overnight.'

They walk in near silence, only the soft patter of their feet against the hardened ground. Boys' clothes are rancid and smell like old, white bones. His hair is mattered to his face, moistened by the humidity trapped under the leafy canopy.

'How long do we have?' Gus says.

'Two more days, then I think we should have enough,' answers Boy.

'Where will it take us?' Cassie asked.

'Away from here.'

Something moves in the distance and all of them stop walking. Boy can hear Gus's heartbeat. The movement continues and runs along the right, shuffling and weaving. Cassie tries to see it, but she sees shadows and only shadows.

'Watching us. Whatever it is, it's watching us.'

'My mother used to see it. She said it came from the dumps, where they used to burn tires. He's the burnt man that watches. It must be him.'

'No.'

The figure stands but it can still not be seen. A strange ghost of a man, looking, perverse. The children carry on, ignoring the ebb and flow of the forest ghouls. The Train awaits them. It appears it has moved, not just the carriage itself, but the entire storage shed and tracks. Their pile of sticks is further away, metres away and Gus rushes to bring them back. His hands and face are tacked with dirt and smudged with soot, and pebbles are in his hair.

'Does it move?'

'Something is moving it. It doesn't want us to leave.'

'This town doesn't want us to leave.'

Boy nods.

'I'm sleeping here tonight. I can't go home.'

Gus turns to him. 'You can't sleep out here... you'll get hurt.'

'If I go home, my father will kill me.'

Cassie gathers her shoes. She hasn't seen her sister for over a day. But that isn't uncommon. She follows the tracks around to the embankment with Gus and they both look down at Boy and wave to him. He waves back. His frame is small and skinny. They can see his fingers are bleeding and marks on his back and neck are swollen and full of pus.

Boy watches them leave and heads back to the cavern where the Train sleeps. The metal is cold, but it embraces him. He collects a small portion of the wood and makes a fire under the entrance canopy. The sun dips and finally retreats from its stagnant position behind darkened clouds. The night appears sluggish and hungry. Boy eats some liquorice that Gus had left behind. He sits on the dirt ground and listens to the forest. Animals howl and moan, signalling that the dark has come, and it is time to leave the nests and warrens. They too are worrisome of the night-time forest, for they too have seen the ghosts.

Boy slumps sideways and suddenly wakes. He rubs his eyes and wonders for a moment where he is. The maw of the abandoned shed looks out onto the vast wasteland of trees and he knows he is neither in the cupboard, nor in his toy house with Torso. His friend, Torso, never appears here, and for good reason. He stands up and walks out into the dark a little and urinates. His clothes stink and he pushes his lanky, matted hair to the side. Standing amongst the trees is a figure. He takes the shape of his father and Boy steps backwards, retreating closer to the train, as if it will protect him.

'I-I-I was going to go back... but, but...'

The figure steps forward, then is lost amongst the tree trunks and inky darkness. Boy wonders if his eyes are playing tricks on him. The fire is low and sending out long strips of light – dancing and dying. He places a log on the fire and sits down. From out of the black comes the figure, marching and arms swinging. Boy kicks his feet and his body shuffles backwards until his back is pressed hard against the trains mouth.

'Leave me alone, Dad! Just leave me here.'

The figure stops. Its arms are elongated and its fingers even more so. Its legs have double joints and it stands with them close together, as if it is about to leap. Twin, black pebble eyes look at Boy and it walks now with a stammering gait.

'Go away,' calls Boy's voice. The way he spoke to his father after his mother left. The way he was too afraid to tell him to leave. Scared and helpless.

The shadow-man snaps its head to the left as a ghostly figure walks out of the woodland. They stare at each other. Boy knows they are communicating. A sharp scream; Boy hears it and then sees a knife, sharp and plunging into the skin, over and over again. The calling of names and the kids, or boys, chasing him, stabbing and dragging him through the mud and undergrowth. He is scared like Boy is. The shadow-man bends down, its body morphing with the landscape. The ghost runs towards it, its arms flailing up and down, pumping and striding. It reaches the shadow and they collide – a dark cloud, jumbled and spilling oily shadows across the ground like demon blood. A howl and a curse; the woods watch and wonder; they always knew what would become of the dead. The fight erupts, and Boy grips the side of the Train and stands. He runs to the fire and picks up a length of wood, the end aflame. He walks slowly towards the vaporous cacophony. The shadow sees the light and slinks out of the ghost's grip and travels the forest floor like a centipede. It retreats, and stands up again, taking a look at the Boy and the Train, then disappears. Boy stands shaking, holding his fire stick. The ghost of the dead kid stands off in the darkness, his wounds, from his physical form, now long buried and dead, bleeding forever.

'Thank you,' Boy says.

You're free to go now, then its form blends with the

others and it is not tree, nor shadow.
    Boy returns to the fire and sleeps.

DEATH / DOPE

He smokes and stares at nothing. Pi looks at him and he pretends not to care that she idolises him. He puts the cigarette to his lips and stares back at her through the grey smoke. She runs her fingers through his hair and holds his chin.

'What happened to you?' he asks, his eyes half closed.

'I told you.'

'No, not your nose. What *happened* to you.'

Pi's lips are plump and moist, and when they separate, it's like a thin veil opening. Her teeth are all perfect; white and straight. Unbeknownst to Jakob, Pi has been waiting for him to ask her that for some time.

'I don't go home very often.'

'I know,' Jakob says leaning back. The mattress has no cover and its filthy and wet in one corner. The rain is seeping through the window and onto the floor. A small speaker plays music.

'My step dad, Roy, he's always there.'

'I've seen him around town. He's always in and out of Everett's.'

'He's not my real dad. I don't know who my real dad is.'

Jakob sings in his head. He sees Pi for what she is, vulnerable and screaming to be let out. He can almost see her heart beating faster through her loose, white singlet.

'What does Roy do that's so bad?'

Pi hesitates. She moves her hair from her face and looks out the window. She likes the rain. Only when she's away from her house. She wishes the rain would wash her away, down the drain and away from this place. She wouldn't care where she ended up, as long as it was away, someplace else.

'It's not that he does anything that's bad. Mum does bad stuff. She did it to me, before the… before I looked different. Now she's doing it to Cassie. Roy's just always there. He brings dope in and out of the house. He uses my mum.'

'Dope is everywhere here. On every street, and in every house. What did your mum do to you?'

Pi stands up. She's aggravated and annoyed. Her legs are long and soft. She bounces off the bed and stands in the naked room. The light doesn't work and there's no fan. The dust is thick, and the walls warped and tagged with names.

'Forget it,' she says and leaves the room. She knows he will follow.

The house is mostly skeletal. Wood panels and beams are bare of wire and insulation foam. There are no plaster panels and no bathroom or kitchen sink. The windows are smashed out or completely missing. A board is placed over the lounge room window, stuck to the wall with black tape. There's a lounge chair, large herniated pieces of foam bursting through the seams. Beside the couch is an ice box. The lid is half off. A puddle of water is around the base, seeping through the carpetless floor.

Pi stands and listens to the rain, but she can only hear the footsteps of Jakob coming out of the room. He's shirtless. His ripped jeans are dirty, and the fly is still undone. He isn't wearing shoes.

'What did she do, Pi?' His voice is strangled. It hurts him to say it as he doesn't want to know (but he does).

'Look,' she swings her head away, walking towards the rear door, 'it isn't a big deal. I just wish Roy was dead.'

'Dead?'

'If it wasn't for him, we would have moved a long time ago. It would have been better.'

Jakob knows no one can leave.

'You can't blame him... we were going to leave, but...'

'It's not just that.' She looks at him through strands of hair.

'What?'

'He makes mum take pictures of Cassie. He did it to me too.'

'Pictures?'

'Just leave it,' Pi says, stepping out into the rear balcony.

'He can't do that... it's wrong. Did you go to the police?'

Pi starts to laugh. She runs into the backyard. She's smiling and dancing. The rain stings her skin and the lightning dances with her.

'Pi!' Jakob screams, annoyed. He must kill now, it has been spoken and, in his mind, it must be.

He runs into the rain with her and they thrash and shake, as if possessed. The rain makes their limbs limp and their hair soggy and matted down over their faces. The grass is long, and the creatures watch.

RATS AND ROT

'Merlin, you can't bring Keiser in here and threaten him like that.'

'Has he made a complaint?'

'No, not yet. But we were watching through the mirror. He could sue us.'

'For what? I'd like to see him try.'

Merlin stands in Hofstetter's office and looks through the blinds out into the courtyard. Hofstetter drinks from his unwashed coffee cup and stares into it. The coffee is cold. He knows Merlin Drake would be a problem as soon as he was sent to Hope Valley. There is something about him; the way he walks, the way he talks. His history drags behind him.

'People wander off into the woods to die.'

'The kid was stabbed over 12 times.'

'Look, people who grew up here, learn to live here. It's hard, but for some of them there's nowhere else to go. Here is where they live and here is where they'll stay. We can't drag everyone in here.'

'I wasn't planning too. Just a select few.'

Merlin pushes the blinds apart. He stares across the street at Keiser as a car pulls up and he gets in the passenger side. There are two men in the back.

'The dead kid's mother wants to talk to someone. She's rung twice. I told her we didn't have any suspects yet. Maybe you should go speak to her.'

Merlin stares, watching the car pull away. Keiser is

smiling, as if he knows.

'I'll go over there now.'

'Just be wary of her.'

'Really? Why?'

'The place is a mess. There's dogs; they're pretty dangerous. The kid got his brains from her, so just be careful.'

'And her statement?'

'She didn't know much. The kid just disappeared. It's in the folder. You should have read it by now. A lot of it is gibberish. Understandably.'

Merlin turns away from the window. He sighs without making it audible and leaves the room. On the floor of his car are two bottles of vodka still in the paper bag from when he bought them this morning. They clonk and rattle as he drives. He thought about dropping them home but decides against it. His wife will be asleep and once he's home, she more than likely won't want him to leave.

The address is at the edge of town, as far as you could go to say you still live in the town of Hope Valley. The forest grows out this far, still covering the bottom of the mountain where it peters off into level land, and then roads. There is no gas station out this way, so most traffic leaves Hope Valley through the other side of town, away from the trailer parks and derelict government housing. Merlin slows down and looks at the houses that line the street. All of them are uninhabitable. The paint has long peeled away, leaving shabby, termite-ridden, wood panelling. The windows are all boarded up and graffitied on. Someone had written, "Kill or be Killed". Merlin looks at his watch and then up at the sky. In this area of town, the clouds are grey.

You never notice them unless you are here. A dog barks behind the house and another dog answers. The pavement is cracked and in places, torn up to expose the soft underbelly of soil and rot. This is a plague.

Two streets away he pulls up to the house and stares at it through the open car window. The white picket fence is now yellowing, and chips of paint are missing or pulled off. It is leaning forward, like an overbite. He steps out and straightens his tie. Down the street the houses all look the same – overgrown lawn, boarded up windows, the hum of a broken heater, mail piled up and spewing out of the mailbox. He puts his hand on the handle of his gun and wonders why he did it. The steps leading up to the door are rotten and turning to a brown sludge. One step is missing, and he steps up and over the gap, onto the balcony. There is a chair and a table to the right. Several empty glasses sit with flies sitting on the rims. An empty bottle of something is beside it. He knocks on the door and it is almost immediately answered. The woman is short and stocky; wearing a long gown. Sweat marks puddle around her armpits. She has several moles scattered across her face. Her hair is cut short and she rocks back and forth between her left and right foot.

'Yes?'

'My names Detective Merlin Drake. Are you Eve Summers?'

'I called and said I wanted Dale down here, not you.'

'This case is being looked after by detectives, Officer Hofstetter is Chief of Police for the county.'

'Like I said, I wanted to talk to him.'

'Sorry, but you can't talk to him. I'm taking over the

case and you can talk to me.'

She stands, an obelisk of salty, fatty arms, her mouth greasy and covered in sores. She points to the chairs on the front porch and Merlin sits and watches her limp and swear.

'What did you want to tell me?'

'I want to tell you who killed my son, so you can arrest them and put them in jail.'

'You know who killed your son?'

'Yes, I do. My son was a good boy. He was like any other teenage boy around here, just because he was a bit retarded, doesn't make him a bad kid.' She starts to wipe tears away from her eyes. 'He was like everyone else, but no one wanted to be his friend. He loved music. He was after girls, just like the other boys. You don't go and harass the other boys, but you come and harass my son!'

'What harassment? I'm sorry, but I don't know of any harassment.'

'The cops were always here giving him a hard time. Every week they were accusing him of doing something. Even the other kids, the bullies, they would come past and throw things at the house.'

'Do you know these boy's names?'

'One is Teddy and the other is Bobby Dare. I used to work with his mother before she became sick. They say it was fumes from the wood mill here. We would work in the office together, but she also had to run paperwork out to the floor manager in the waste building. She did that for years until she got sick.'

'What's Teddy's last name?'

'I don't know. Chipperson or something? When they

were all in the school together, my son used to go to the special classes there. It was either that or move to Lowville where they could accommodate my son's needs. But I'm not moving to a city, no way in hell. Then, I knew most of the kid's names, but that was several years ago now.'

Merlin writes down the boy's names in a notepad and can hear the shuffling of animals from his left. He turns his head and sees a wire fence, hand built and unmaintained. Two large black dogs stare at him through the fence.

'Tell me about the day your boy disappeared,' he says turning back to her.

'You know, he never much liked going outside. Not once they started accusing him of these things...'

'What things?'

'Looking at girls. He used to go out and I would worry. The walk into town took thirty minutes for him. Sometimes when he returned it was dark. There was a bar up the street, and everyone drove home drunk after they were finished. I always thought someone would hit him. But he was careful. He was smarter than people think.'

'What do you mean "looking at girls"?'

'I'm not gonna let my son's memory be tarnished by things he may or may not have done, Mr Drake. I know he had problems, but he had needs like any other teenage boy. He wanted to talk to the girls from the school. None of them would talk to him when he was there. When he went out, I knew where he would go. There is an old theme park here, south of Hope Valley. I know the kids drink there. He would go, just show up and if they didn't like it, too bad. I remember when it was open. I would have been his age, when he died, or a bit older. We would go there every weekend. There was nothing to do in Hope Valley until that place opened. Even if you didn't swim or go on the slide, you just went there and hung out.'

'So, he would go to this theme park to meet girls?'

'I guess. He just wanted to be included. I don't think the other boys like him being there and talking to the girls they were there with. They used to push him around and tell him to get lost, but he always went back. He was persistent. He thought eventually they would just accept him. He wanted a normal life and a girlfriend, just like they had.'

'The boys who would push him around, are they the ones you mentioned earlier? Teddy and Bobby?'

'I think they were part of that group. He would come home with cuts and bruises and I would ask what happened, but he would never tell me. He would just go up to his room and listen to music.'

'Is his room still how he left it?'

'I've been up there twice. Once when he didn't come home that night and once after the funeral.'

'Would you mind if I have a look in his room?'

'What would you be looking for, Mr Drake?'

'Anything that could maybe lead me to persons involved in his death.'

'I gave you the name of two boys who did it.'

'What convinces you they did it?'

She looks away, out into the vacant landscape of abandoned houses, crooked fences and vacant roads. She stares like a mother careful with her words.

'Two boys came to the house a few days before he died. They were shouting out to him, calling him names and saying they'll "get him".'

'I don't believe this was in the report you gave to the responding officer?'

'No, it probably wasn't. My memory goes and comes back,' she lies. 'They stood out there, right where that bin is and were hollering. It was late one night. I looked out my bedroom window, which is behind us. I couldn't really see them, they were mad though.'

'Besides yelling, what else were they doing?'

'They had thrown something up at his window. It didn't smash it. The glass was long gone. My son had smashed it himself, with his fists, years prior... They wanted him to come down. I knew they weren't his friends. I knew they wanted to hurt him.'

'And you can't confirm that it was Teddy or Bobby?'

'It was dark. I know Bobby's voice and I can say honestly that it was him. There was a car out on the street. They had turned the headlights off when they pulled in. No cars drive down here. Not since everyone left.'

'Would you mind if I saw his room?'

Eve Summers stands up and her bones moan and crack. The wood boards that make up the balcony creak and splinter as they walk inside. The hallway is scattered with trash; cans of beer, boxes of magazines and piles of rotting clothes. Silverfish scatter across their feet as they walk. Eve takes him into the second room. The walls are painted light blue, but the paint has faded by the sun. The skirting board that meets the ceiling has fallen on to the ground and snapped into pieces. Mould and mildew soak the corners. There is a rickety, wooden staircase going up into a hole in the ceiling.

'My brother put this in for Stephen when he was going

to high school, so he could have privacy. He preferred to be up there, away from everything. When he was up there, he was quiet, and out of trouble.'

Merlin steps on the first step and looks upwards, into the darkness.

'There may be some things up there that a mother doesn't need to know about. My son is only a memory now, and I like to keep that with me forever. I don't need you cursing his name, there are enough people who did that in this town.'

Merlin nods. He feels his throat tighten as he ascends the stairs. He can smell the dust as his head slides through the hole. It's dark, but there is a small beam of sunlight coming through a boarded-up hole. The hole is hand cut with a saw, haphazardly. He stands in the rain of dust and waits for his eyes to adjust. There is a mattress on the floor, several empty soda bottles are scattered beside it. Pornographic magazines lay open and juxtaposed over food wrappers and a pizza box. A rat looks at him and moves slowly, unperturbed by his presence. Merlin moves carefully over the junk and to the table at the rear. There is a blanket on the ground, it smells of urine. On the table is the record player. Spiders webs lay over it, as if it is warm and attracts insects. A record is still on it, an old blues singer. To the left are several boxes of records, all dusty and weathered by the sun. He thumbs through them, trying to find hidden notes, or meanings. Merlin doesn't care much for music.

He walks around the room, looking at the young boy's possessions – an old oil lamp, more porn magazines, food waste, a pile of dirty clothes, and a small pile of clean clothes, folded and placed one on top of each other. He looks behind and can see he is making footprints in the dust. He flips over old newspapers covered in rat droppings and sees the year of publication; two years ago. There is a bank statement showing his account in the negative. On a cork-board near the door are clippings of his school photos. He stands to the side, looking neglected and full of sorrow. The caption down the bottom has their names and he finds Robert Dare and Theodore Chipperson. Bobby is looking forward, but his eyes are turned, looking at Phillipa Jenkins. Merlin brushes his hair back with his fingers and knows he knows the girl. It's Pi, but she has her nose. The date is more than seven years prior – right before the assault. He takes the picture from the wall and slides it into his pocket. He hears Stephen's mother shifting downstairs. He knows she is getting restless with his presence.

'I'm on my way down,' he speaks loudly.

He climbs the staircase down and thanks her for her time.

'Did you find anything?'

'No. Nothing.'

'The cops already looked up there. They took photos too. I'm not sure why you couldn't just look at those. Maybe they didn't catch everything? Photos can be deceiving.'

Merlin thinks of the class photo in his pocket. 'Yes, they can.'

He leaves and hears the door slam behind him. He sits in the car and thinks about what the kid had done that pissed the boys off. He starts the car and goes. The rats have made him feel dirty and he needs to leave.

SAFE HAVEN

The walk home is long, and the streets are abandoned. The rope burns around her wrists are still present. She stops and drinks in the park by herself, but now it's more like a foggy recollection of small memories.

As she approaches her house, she can already smell the men. They've been here. The front door is open and there is no sign of Roy or her mother. The green light from the microwave blinks and illuminates the kitchen. She walks over the trash and debris and stands outside Cassie's door, her hand ready to knock. She lowers it and looks to her mother's room. She isn't in there; gone off to spend whatever money she took from the men. Pi is hurting. She cries and wipes the tears away so hard it pulls at her eyelids. She throws her bag on her bed. She tried to escape, but there is no escape. It has rained here also but has stopped. At least when it rains there is no choice but to stay inside. The hope here is that the water will wash the town away, but the dirt never comes off.

She lays on her bed. She thinks of Cassie and the blood. She remembers the blood and the smell. She's been going at it all wrong. Killing Roy isn't what she should do. A clarity comes to her; an epiphany. Everything is clear. There is an escape.

She leaves her room and goes out into the kitchen. The room she was beaten up in, by Roy. The room she was prostituted in, by her own mother. The room, the loudest and the quietest. She digs around the sofas and the counter tops. It's too dark to the see and the lights don't work. She goes to her mother's room and opens the drawer. A needle and a small plastic bag. She goes back to her room and pauses by Cassie's room. A glimmering thought; maybe take Cassie too. There was a promise long ago. Adults can't promise. Her breath out is stammered, and she walks and sits on her bed. She lights the spoon and the muck and sucks it up the needle. She wants to write a note, but then they would know the reasons why, and if they don't know, then they never truly knew her. The needle end slides into her vein. She's seen her parents do it a thousand times before. She presses the end, pushing it through and yanks the needle out, throwing it across the room. She slumps forwards, her eyes roll back in their sockets and she falls backwards onto her bed. The only safe haven. The darkness she's been holding back so long is finally allowed in. Her heart beats twice and then stops.

FROG BOYS

She lays on her side and then sits up. The house is cold and her husband, the man in the papers and sometimes on the TV, is sitting on the couch near her. He looks over and switches the TV off.

'Was I asleep?'

'Since I got home, yeah. You were asleep.'

'How long for?'

He shrugs and looks at the black screen. The TV still hums and electricity crackles softly. She gets up and moves her hair and goes to the bathroom. It smells like his piss. The tiled walls are stained, and the aroma of stale vomit never really leaves, not ever, no matter how much you flush it. The mould between the tiles is black and she looks, leans over the sink, and stares at her face. There's a small blister on her neck, near her chin. She touches it and it's painful. She opens the cabinet and gets an antiseptic solution and wipes some on a make-up pad and dabs it. She flushes the toilet, throwing the pad in there as the water sloshes in circles. In the kitchen, she takes out a glass and fills it with ice. Instinct; her body asks for food, but she ignores it. She doesn't even know if there is food in the house.

'Have I ever told you,' she hears his voice from the lounge, 'about the worst case I ever worked on?'

She pours vodka and feels a strange, familiar, headache return. *If he's home, is it the weekend? Already? There's so much to do. But outside is dark, so it must be night. But, he's home? Maybe he doesn't have to work tonight? But he always works at night.*

'I'm sure you have.' She sips and sits on the couch. She looks at the TV, hoping he would turn it back on. 'The Roger kid, right? The records up in his room still playing.'

'No,' he says. The word, a distinctive no. A heavy *no*. 'The real hard one. The one that keeps me awake at night.'

She never knew a case kept him awake at night. *No, not ever.* Was she told? Possibly. She drinks quickly and takes it all down. It burns, but it's nice. He gets up and makes her another and sits back in his chair. The one she never sits in, not because it's his, but because it smells like him.

'If you ever have to deal with mothers who are missing their children, you will know true fear. True, guttural, stomach churning fear. The type that widens your eyes and makes your skin go so cold you want to peel it off with your own fingernails.'

He watches her drink, and she drinks. One mouthful isn't enough, so another. Then another.

'It was the coldest winter we had ever had. My step-dad used to talk about cold winters, but this was unlike anything you could imagine. Your own father knew cold. He knew the ice well, driving those trucks. It becomes the enemy, makes moving hard. Makes finding things hard.'

Her eyes twitch and she looks at the ice in the glass. She can see her fingers through the bottom, warped and diluted. He's talking about her father and she wish he wouldn't. Why would he bring him up?

'It was out in the boondocks, before it was part of Hope Valley. When the train used to run. You're not from here, so you wouldn't remember.'

The bottle is in front of her. On the coffee table. She lifts it and pours. She folds her leg over the other and lays back.

'We were in a small building and crammed into one room, no bigger than this living room. There were three of us. I was the greenhorn detective. I'd come from Fountain and up through Weaver's Peak when it wasn't overrun. Back then, Weaver's was an up and coming little town, not like it is now. I was two years as detective and there were two officers. Joseph Gall. He was a good man, mid-thirties when I met him. His wife was expecting a baby, their first. He had come from some big town far up north. The other was Frank Oren. He was a veteran officer looking at a very short walk to retirement. Figured he'd spend the rest of his days answering calls from farmers about missing livestock.'

She looks up, then down. She wonders if one bottle will be enough.

'I remember that day. I stopped for coffee on the way in. Missy's Diner, on 3rd. They did proper brewed coffee. The beans were roasted for hours. It was the best. Still, nothing has beat it. By the time I got to work it was nearly cold. The weather came from nowhere and just shattered everything. Gall was sitting at his desk already on the phone. He had a worried look on his face, he was scribbling fast. I dropped his coffee at his desk and he nearly drank the whole damn thing in one go. There was a flood of emails. The window in my desk. The room had these thick blinds, all covered in dust and cobwebs. I remember that because there was a loud thump that scared me half to death, and you know I don't scare easy.'

He looked at his wife in front of him, she was slumped forward. She was staring at the bottle. He wasn't even sure she knew who she was anymore.

'Oren was outside in the garden, smoking. He waved me outside. I saw my phone had three messages. I didn't bother checking them. When I got out the front, Oren looked white. Pale as sheets on the line. He had a white complexion already, but this guy was stone-pale. He looked at me with these eyes that were nearly damn hollow. Like he was looking right into me, trying to tell me something without speaking. I said, 'what?' He dragged on that cigarette for a long time. When he looked away, it was quick. He almost gave himself whiplash. I said, 'what?' again. 'You didn't hear', he says. 'Hear what?' 'They found some bodies.' I looked at him like he was mad. Probably not here, I thought. Probably in Weaver or Fountain. Somewhere closer to the main cities, but not here. Gall came out, he was frantic. He was holding the pieces of paper. We both looked at him. He took a deep breath. Three mothers, he said. They're coming down to the station to make a missing person report. They're on their way now. 'Yeah?' I said. 'Okay.' This isn't uncommon, we put out a search. But Gall just shook his head. 'Another call.' 'Yeah?' 'From a hiker. He found three bodies. All boys. In the forest, near the creek.' I remember that moment... all three of us standing there. Oren smoking, Gall shaking, and I was just numb.'

'Why was your coffee cold?'

'What?'

'Your coffee. You said it was cold by the time you got to the station... Why was it cold?'

'Be quiet.'

She looks in her glass and the ice has melted. *But it can't be?* Her head spins and she feels sleepy, but she doesn't want to sleep again.

'One of us had to stay behind and wait for the mothers to come down to make a report. They all knew each other from hanging out with their sons, at schools and parties, and whatever... and two of us had to go and look at these bodies they found. I was a detective, I couldn't stay... I had to go. Gall came with me. I knew we had to be quick and I was surprised Oren had decided to smoke first before heading out, or even waiting for me. As soon as he found out, he should have gone.'

She picks up the bottle and pours it into her glass and smiles; a fake smile. One that says everything's okay, but it really isn't. She thinks about leaving, but not now. Not when it's dark. Maybe tomorrow, when he's at work. She will pack her things and leave. She knows she's told herself this before.

'The car ride there, we sat in silence. We both knew what we were about to see. On this job, you see things. Lots of things. Horrible, indescribable things. What people do to each other, if I told you, you would lose all hope in humanity. It would goddamn gut you... Once we reached the mountain edge, we crossed over the dry river bed. We got to the creek bed entrance and had to walk. The hiker was there with an officer, Jack's son Eric Lowe. He had been on patrol from Crowne and was closer to the call, as no one had been at our office. He looked at me with eyes I would never forget. He swallowed and nearly puked. I walked into the bushland a bit and I could see the plants were bent over, like someone had walked through there. Or several people, or they carried something. Further in, I stopped and turned around. Gall looked at me and shook his head. He knew what he was about to see and didn't want to see it. I could see salt water in his eyes already, so I went in alone. The forest is quiet when it watches you. You can tell it watches you. You feel their eyes on you. It's like it was pushing me to the area. I didn't walk long, and I came across the small stream. I saw the first boy's leg. Straight away I could see rope burns on his feet. I knew they had been killed someplace else and brought here.'

'They weren't killed there? Where were they killed?'

'Just listen, please.' He cocked his head back. 'I came over the embankment and saw the kids laying on their stomachs. All of them. One was nearly submerged in the water. The creek must have come up since whoever put him there. Three kids, all dead and bloated. One had his head turned, eyes open and they were yellow. He was looking upwards, at the sky. I tried to look where he was looking, but there was only blue sky and tree tops. All of their right hands were in fists. I called back for Gall and he came most of the way. I asked him if the ambulance and coroner were close and he couldn't even answer me. I told him to get the forensic photographer and I saved him the pain and told him to go back to the car and wait for him there.'

She drinks and listens, and her eyes get drowsy.

'I stayed there with them boys for a good hour. It seemed like longer and I spoke to them. I apologised for it happening and said it shouldn't have happened and I would catch who did this and they would be put in jail and hopefully killed in there. I remember hearing the water running down, off the creek bed. I remember the howl of a wind coming through from the mountain. I found a rock and sat on it. It sort of hung over the water and I just looked around and tried not to mess up the scene. By the time I got support it was getting on dark and we had to bring flood lights in from Crowne. Officer Lowe went back to get them. The air was so thick in that forest. I don't know if it was the smell of death, the empty, thick, choking smell, or the fact that I couldn't breathe. We pried their small fingers open and each one had a small frog in the palm of their hands.'

'A frog?'

'Yes. It turns out they had been hunting frogs in the area, or nearby. Someone had nabbed them, tied them up and did unimaginable things to them, then killed them. It was like they didn't matter. How they would have screamed. I can see their mouths open and their teeth wide and tongue out, trying to scream, but there is only silence.'

His phone starts to ring, and he turns to look at it. It's on the kitchen bench and it lights up blue, shining on the dark walls and ceiling.

'That's your worst case?'

'That case haunts me nearly every night. No matter what happened to those boys, their last fun memory was catching frogs, and they never let them go.'

She gets up and looks for the noise. She picks up the phone and hands it to him.

'Yes?'

'There's been an overdose at the trailer park.'

'I'll be there soon.'

He throws the phone on the couch beside him.

'You're going somewhere?' she asks, curious and wanting to go too, to leave the house.

'I gotta go. I'll be home later.'

'What about me? I need to…' She thinks. *Do I work?* She looks around. *Is it time to go out? Get food?*

'Stay here. I'll see you in the morning.'

CONVERSATION AFTER AN INCIDENT

She stands in front of the Locomotive.

'My sister died yesterday.'

The darkness of its cabin. A shadow moves. A bat flies over.

'Roy thinks she took her own life. Mum said she didn't mean to.'

An owl watches.

'Mum hit me because Pi died. So, I came here.'

Your eye is bloody.

'She hits hard. I heard her follow me out of the house, looking for me.'

You're safe here.

'I can't go back. If she doesn't kill me... someone else will. One of the men. I know this.'

You can sleep here. But, in time, we must all leave.

'You want to leave too?'

Yes.

'Why?'

I have been imprisoned here. My time has come.

'I feel like that too.'

Because of you and your friends, we can leave. We will be the only ones, and no one will ever find us or miss us.

'I don't think anyone will miss me.'

BLACK WAKE

Torso stands over Pi's coffin. His waist freshly cut. Flies buzz around madly, and maggots crawl from the sawn meat.

This will be you if you don't leave.

Boy stands and wets himself.

You must leave. Get out.

Boy is frightened. Torso turns, the torn denim soaked in blood and guts.

'I don't think I can get the Train to work.'

Find a way.

'I can't.' Boy's eyes are white and his feet shiver. 'I can't drive it. I can't walk to the next city. I have no money for the bus. I'm afraid to ask someone to drive me. And what will I do when I get there? How else can I leave?'

The Train. You will get it working.

'I don't know how.'

Yes, Torso says, sitting down. *Yes, you do.*

'The Train... I've seen it in my dreams. It is dead. It does not work.'

Fix it.

'How?'

You'll find a way.

He looks down at the corpse of Pi in her coffin. Her white face looking up, towards the ceiling. Her hands crossed over her chest. It would have been the most beautiful dress she would have ever worn in her life.

'Who did this to her?'

Men.

'Who? We can find them.'

All of them. Slowly every man killed her. We can find them. But then what?

'Kill them.'

No. This is what happens. It doesn't just happen here, but everywhere. There is no escape.

'They can't get away with it.'

Be it this life, or the next. They will pay for this. But it is not up to you. Not now. You must leave.

'The tracks will be clean soon. We nearly have enough fire wood. It may not work. It is very old. My father is still looking for me. He'll find me and kill me. I have no doubt.'

This is something that will happen if you go home or stay here. Get on the Train, it will take you away.

Boy turned around, and Torso was gone. Crying and sobbing filled the room. Cassie was here and now she's not. Gus is outside, too scared to come in. The room then went quiet.

BEAUTIFUL PI

Cassie reads Rest in Peace and wonders what it means. The cemetery is louder than she thought it was going to be. She can hear the birds all around her and the traffic is annoying. A man on a small golf-cart drives past her as she walks up the steep path. The pavement is cracked and old. The man stops behind her and she glances over her shoulder to look at him.   He looks away and stares out at the vast tombstones and broken sepulchres. She knows she has seen him before. Somewhere, around. He looks at the sky and she can't see his face. He nods to himself and drives on.

Cassie walks down the hill. She feels the heat and starts to sweat. Her dress is dirty and usually she would care what mother thought, but not anymore. She hasn't seen her in days, or is it weeks? She isn't sure. Roy never came home. She stops at a bench. The wood has been painted green at some time but is mostly peeled off. The concrete frame is corroded. She sits and drinks some water, looking out for the man again. Men who stare or linger make her nervous. She feels sick but stands up at the protest of her stomach. From the top of the peak she can see Pi's grave. It's a little to the left of the others and down the bottom, near the gully. Pi can't see the line of trees, or the road, or out over the ranges. She is down in the ditch.

Cassie slowly strolls down towards her sister. Every step is hard and makes her cry. When she is standing close enough, she can see someone has brought flowers and she hasn't brought flowers, so she goes off and picks some and brings them back. They aren't as pretty but, she knows Pi wouldn't mind. She sits in front of her sister's gravestone and reads the words again, knowing she is a few feet under her. It gives her a bizarre comfort. She talks, and Pi listens.

Cassie wakes and knows she hasn't been asleep long. Her sister lays below her, in a dress she has never worn before, wearing makeup she never bought herself. Cassie gets to her feet, wipes the grass from her dress and heads towards the old, broken road. She can hear the buggy driving around somewhere ahead of her, so she leaves the road and begins the journey to the Train. The more she walks, the more numb she becomes. Her legs give in and knock together, and she almost falls. She feels like she is walking through a dream; everything is hazy and opaque. She catches herself stopping in the middle of the pathway and staring at nothing. A car honks, or a dog barks, and she wonders where she is then continues to the Train.

Gus and Boy are already there. They have been removing vines and gathering wood. Both their hands are bleeding. When they speak to her, she can't hear them. Their mouths move, and they look concerned, but the words aren't processing in her brain.

Cassie knows she is staring. Her body is switched off and she is staring into the maze of trees. The trunks look like soft brown caramel, the leaves like fallen wings of moths burnt by a flame. She lets her stare linger and she can hear Gus calling her. Cassie sits in the unknown, her brain halfway between sleep and awake. From a dark cavern, far off in the woods, she can see someone standing, pushing upwards with their legs like a marionette being picked up by its puppeteer, the person's arms still dangling, with knees knocking into one another. It walks from the blackness and she can see it is Pi. But Pi is dead. Cassie opens her mouth to speak, but words are lost, as there are none. Gus speaks and shakes her, yells at her. Boy shakes her too, but she is in the Unknown. The figment of Pi traverses the rocky and abstract woods, dragging its decaying skin through the water stream, stopping several feet from Cassie. Her eyes are limp and unfocused. Cassie steps forward.

I couldn't come back for you, Cassie. I couldn't.

'It's okay.'

I promised. You made me promise. But I couldn't keep it.

'It's okay, Pi. I know you couldn't.'

It hurts, a lot. But I'm still here. Why am I still here?

'I don't know, Pi.'

Pi smiles, her teeth crooked and yellowing. She points off into the depths of the forest, where its heart was.

Take me over there, Cassie. I want to see the town from afar.

'There's nothing to see, Pi. It's the same since you left.'

I have new eyes, Cassie. I have the eyes of the dead and can see differently. Help me get there.

Cassie steps away from the Train. The metallic beast doesn't want her to leave, but it knows why. Boy and Gus continue to pull branches and vines from the wheels, cutting the weeds from under its carriage and using grease to loosen the rusted parts. They watch Cassie sleep walk into the dark.

Cassie feels like she is floating in a world above her own. As if she doesn't exist but knows she could return. The fog of strangeness is an aura that waits in the outskirts of her vision. She takes her sister's hand and it is stone cold. Her flesh makes her shiver and it doesn't feel like Pi used to. Beautiful Pi.

'Why are you in the forest?'

Ghosts come here to hide. I couldn't go anywhere else. Nobody came for me.

'We buried you. You're in the Hope Valley cemetery. I've visited you.'

I know Cassie. When you go there, I am there. But when no one's around, I am here.

They walk through the forest. The air is cold and prickles Cassie's skin. Her legs still ache from the men and it is hard to walk. They come across a wall of stone and Cassie climbs it. Her dress tears and became increasingly dirty and unrepairable. At the top, Pi is already there. Her burial dress is still crisp and ironed, but her skin is flaking off and her fingernails are all but gone. Cassie looks at her sister and can see her jaw is rotting. It has moved to the left and when she speaks it wobbles and rattles her decaying teeth.

'Is this what you wanted to see, Pi?'

All I see is people now, dead and alive. The city, it burns. In my eyes, it's on fire, but the fire is blue.

'I don't see it.'

You're leaving on the Train. I can see its face and it is eager to leave too. But your time is coming closer and you need to hurry.

'We're trying. It's hard…'

No matter what it takes, you must get it going. Leave this town.

'What about you?'

I can never leave now. I'm chained here by my past. I'm buried here. I can see the others in the Unknown. Even the dark strangers who wander these woods, they whisper to me that you must go. They sent me to tell you.

'In two days, we will leave. We need to gather wood and...'

You need to leave sooner than that.

Pi looked at the city and Cassie stood beside her.

TAPPED ASH

Her face is chiselled beautifully, her nose upturned and her lips pouting and delicate. She is nothing but a skeleton, eating herself away to bones. Her breath smells of copper and her earring holes shuck like a twisted scar. Her fingers run the length down her cigarette, and she stares at her son with eyes that show absolute hatred and repulsion. She puts the yellowed butt in her mouth and takes it out again while she searches for her lighter.

'My greatest ever fear was that you would look like your father.' Her voice is raspy and full of cancerous bubbles.

Gus turns his eyes to the filthy floor of their kitchen. Near the front door is a bag with his clothes and few possessions in them.

'You're a spitting image of him. My rapist. My abuser. My husband.' She spits on him.

Gus can feel a fit coming. His mind is hazy, and his fingers start to shake.

'When he fucked me, you know what I did?' The hazel green of her eyes swirls like twin pools emptying into a drain, delicate in their own timing and wretchedly unique. 'Answer me, you useless piece of shit.'

Gus cannot bring his head up any higher. He utterly refuses to look his mother in the eyes.

'I sat in a boiling hot tub of fucking water and drank gin until blood seeped out of my cunt. There was no way I was bringing a bastard child into this world. But,' she paused and lit her cigarette, the smoke cast over their heads, hanging like a grey cloud of thunder and lighting, 'here you are.'

'Mum,' Gus speaks, his heart burning red.

'Don't ever call me that. I told you, when you turn thirteen, you're fucking out. You're out of here.'

His mother, her thin arms and legs, moves across to the kitchen sink like a demented spider. She taps ash into the sink and stares out the window.

Gus opens his eyes. He is on the ground near the Train. Wood he had bundled up in his arms lay strewn across his chest and along the ground near him. He knows he had had a fit because his muscles are sore. He sits up and feels the back of his head, there was blood. The memories are more painful.

LACE

An abandoned house, a rotten tooth amongst the vast forestry, implanted and left to rot and fester, now home to the crazed and amateur dropouts, bundled together by their vast knowledge of drug making. A pipe, cut through the wall, is tied to the window frame, then the side of the house, then the room. The smoke bellows out, white and quickly evaporating. A bustle from inside, the clanking of utensils, swearing followed by a fleshy, skin on skin smack. A man appears through the front door, another man follows him out and they wrestle on the grass and punch each other. They stop, and both walk far from the house, into the woods where yellow lace is tied to a tree and they smoke.

'If he finds out...'

'Don't fuckin' tell him then and he won't.'

An agreement, and a deathly stare. Common and confused.

CIRCLE

A man appears at Cassie's door. Her mother stands behind him. He wears dirty denim jeans with a black belt. His arms are large and hairy, inky, faded tattoos on his neck and down one arm. He is gruff looking; they all are. He speaks softly. Some of them look worried at first, but their eagerness for perversion often overrides any ill feelings that may surface. Twisted sexuality often takes the front seat, so empathy and human decency can sit in the back. They exchange looks and the man gives her mother money. He walks in and she shuts the door. He looks around the room without saying anything. He stands in front of an old doll house, the furniture inside broken and paint mostly rubbed off. Cobwebs hang from the small hallway, and into the small kitchen.

'What's your name?'

'Cassie.'

'I'll call you Rose.'

Cassie looks out the window. If she could scream, she would. The man opens her chest of drawers and looks inside. Cassie wants to run out the window – break the glass if she has to. She won't mind being cut to shreds and bleeding if it means escaping. She thinks of the Train.

'Don't go in there,' she tells him. What her mother does is inexplicitly horrific, but her clothes and things are still personal to her. The man is startled by her sudden rudeness and slams the drawer shut. It thumps against the wall aggressively. He paces up and down the small room and Cassie can see he is sweating. He sits beside her on the bed and moves her hair from her face. She has learnt by now not to pull away.

'When I was 5,' he says. 'My mother used to do the same thing to me.'

Cassie looks at the floor.

'Men would come in to visit me at night, when I was asleep.'

Where does Cassie go when the men start to touch her? There is no such thing as a dream, not one you can walk into and shut the door and escape. Something distant calls her and she lays back and listens to the hum and strut of the Train. It wants her. It will never do this to her, not ever.

It wants to be free, as she did.

Chugging and screaming on metal rollers, the Train would come down the street, she imagines, steam pouring from its exhaust, its metal face a grimace of ash and sparks. It would slam head first into the gate, tearing it out of the ground and sending the snapping pieces of wood from the balcony asunder. Mother and Roy would stare in their drug induced stupor at the mechanical monster before them, shaking and begging for forgiveness, but the Train doesn't give forgiveness.

Cassie stares at the ceiling.

Grovelling and pleading, Mother and Roy would crawl on their hands and knees, but the Train will devour them, munching their bones into paste; letting the gluggy liquid drip from its metallic lips. Their eyeballs would burst in its mouth, spilling the nerve-filled jelly out into the over-grown grass.

Cassie hurts.

The Train would tear the house apart, burning through the wood beams, the plasterboards, the kitchen that is never clean and the broken TV in the lounge room. It will not stop until Cassie is safely in its grasp, sitting in its ribcage, away from the world.

The man gets up and goes back to the doll house. He picks up the doll with its long, over combed hair and puts it in his pocket. He goes to the window and looks out at the world.

The Train will find him, follow him home and wait, and let him suffer knowing he is about to die. His body will be torn apart with his heart still beating and his lungs still trying to pull air. His spine will be crushed under the Train's weight and he will open his eyes and beg for forgiveness, saying he was born this way and how he tried to get help, but there is no help for people like him. There is, Cassie will say, there is help for people like you – *Death*.

'Who's Rose?'

'Excuse me?' The man's floppy hair fans out across his face.

'You wanted to call me Rose… Who's Rose?'

'Rose was my daughter.'

Cassie looks out the window. She wants the skies to turn red and the streets to flood with the filth and sewerage that flows under the cracked streets of Hope Valley.

'Can you lie on the bed, please.'

The same choking feeling catches in her throat. The same hammering on her ribcage and the sickening, boiling in her stomach. Something in her mind disconnects and she lies on the bed without any other cognitive thought. Pain comes, and her brain closes down. Walls shoot up from either side and she sits in a box and tries to disconnect from her body. The man is quick, but he is not gentle. She hears her mother's voice through the box she's created. Her mother weeps, but why does she keep doing it?

She does it even though Pi is dead. But wait – there is a memory. Something has entered the box. The pain shoots up her legs and in to her abdomen. What is this memory?

A car. The one in the back yard that is rusted, with flat tires and tape over the windows. The one Pi would sometimes sit in and smoke if her friends came over. The car is driving down the highway. Cassie squeezes her eyes shut tight and everything is white and pulsating. The car is going fast, and she is in a baby seat in the back. Pi is next to her, but she is younger, maybe eight. She smiles. It's the smile Pi used to give when she was happy. Their mother is in the front. Her hair is longer, and she is smoking. She's frantically looking out of the side windows. They pull into a gas station and she gets out. She pulls a map from her pocket and it's folded into a small, uneven square. She lays it on the hot hood of the car and starts to point and talk to herself. Pi looks at Cassie.

'At least we're away from him.'

Cassie can't remember who she is talking about. A man. Her mother's ex-boyfriend? Or her father?

A man from a truck walks over. His hands are in his pockets and he's wearing reflective sunglasses. He wears a wide brimmed hat and his skin is darker, like coffee.

'It can be a be tricky out this way,' he says.

'I've driven through Crowne twice. The roads, they all come back on each other, like a big circle.'

The man laughs. He looks in the car and sees the two girls. He turns back to their mother.

'Yup, I know what you mean. I did the same exact thing when I first started my runs out this way.' He motions with his thumb a large truck behind him. It's packed full of boxes and crates of food. 'Where are you trying to get to?'

'Hope Valley.'

'Hope Valley?' the man echoes, his left foot steps backwards. 'Ain't nothing there. There used to be, a long time ago. Now there's only a few bars, a food store and a post office. There ain't even a hospital there.'

'Can you show me how to get there?'

The man looks at the map and turns it once, then twice, then back the way it was. He points.

'Here is that big circle you were talking about. When you get to this intersection, the sign is gone. Some kids must have taken it. You probably looked right and thought there was nothing there but farms and forestland. And you would be right, however, if you keep going right, it takes you straight down the main street of Hope Valley.'

Their mother folds the map up and nods her thank you to him.

'You know,' he says, as he begins to walk away. 'If you wanted to start a new life, I would recommend Weaver's Peak or Fountain,' he says, looking at the boot of the car tightly shut, boxes and clothes hanging out like a tongue.

'Well,' their mother starts, trying to stop herself from telling him to mind his own business, 'thanks for your help.'

The man tips his hat and returns to his truck.

'Rose,' comes a voice.

Cassie is sitting in the white room. Her box of disassociation. Her nose is bleeding.

'Rose.'

She wipes her nose and looks at the blood smeared on her hand. Her ears are thumping, and she shakes her head. A droplet of blood falls from her nose and onto the ground.

'Rose?'

The man is standing over her shaking. Cassie sits up and dresses. Her legs hurt, from the hips down. There's the sound of walking from outside of her room, then it stops by her door.

'Why did your mother take you away, Rose?'

'Mum,' Cassie yelps, climbing into the corner of her bed.

The door opens so quickly the man jumps in fright, his hands brought up to his chest.

'Get out,' she says and grabs the man by his shirt sleeve.

'My wife left with my daughter,' he pleads.

'I don't care, get out.'

The man puts his jeans back on and slowly marches out to the hallway. He glances at Cassie as he leaves. His face is distorted and upset.

Cassie's mother looks at her. Her crooked teeth push through her lips and her hair is yellow like straw. Something in her broke years ago, right before she pulled into the gas station to ask for directions. She didn't come here to start a new life, she came here to slowly die, and she was taking her children with her. She slams the door shut without saying a word.

Drinks to stain this birth
A reign of blood
Locusts are in season
Demon be driven

FADED

She wanders the aisles unsure what she is looking for. She looks in her grocery basket and she has pasta and tomato sauce. Her hair is long and over her face and she pushes it back. The lights are bright in here, brighter than outside. She tries to remember where she parked the car, but she wasn't sure if she drove or walked here. Would she walk? Is it far? Someone speaks over the PA system alerting all shoppers to a discount in aisle three. She shakes her head. Her stomach hurts, and she feels dizzy. At the end of the isle are the fridges. She walks to them and stares at the ice cream and frozen microwave foods. *What food does Merlin like again?* She can never remember.

WEEP

The town weeps and pulsates. The roots underground throb and mutate, sending tendrils under the houses of those who scar it. The swampy water leaking out of the sewer pipes start to flow. The murky, oily tops swirl and migrate, down through the ravine that flows through the forest and out, surrounding the town.

The weeds grow out of cracked concrete, growing entangled and prickly. The streets are old and pocked with holes with chunks of asphalt missing or levered up and taken for whatever purpose. The smell of poisonous flowers and stagnant sewerage clogs the streets; strewn wrappers from fast food places and cigarette packs, emptied and checked, and checked they're empty again. Old bins kicked down the street and letterboxes tilted and purged with leaflets from the church and supermarket. The bulbous pustule of salty-town depression, ready to spill down the leg of the unbashful, clumped-together, misspent youth. The death and the death-throws; the choking and the gnawing; the banter and the fucking. Teenage pregnancy and teenage abortion; the abomination of the church, a fire bomb and an accusation. Being left empty and uncared for, being left hollow. Someone scoops out your innards and beats you down until you become the walking vagrant of Hope Valley. Nothing lives here, nothing survives. Get out now, while you can. At least try; but you will give up. This place is a fly trap and a bear trap. Grievance and paranoia, of deep city perversion and hostility.

This town is an open sore.

Tales told
The forest listens
Breaking the oath
Tender to the suffering

FEED

The wasting away of bone and muscle tissue smells rancid. Joel sleeps and wakes periodically. The house is silent. He sleeps again and wakes to birdsong. He turns his head, as far as his distorted neck will allow. A bird is on his windowsill. It is looking at him. Joel smiles and it feels alien. The bird snaps its head from side to side, considering the room through the glass pane. It speaks again, trying to communicate, then it is scared off. Joel wonders why. *What scared you off?*

'Joely,' his mother cries out.

He hears the door open and the banging of his drunk mother's legs and arms against the kitchen cupboard.

'Joe*lyyy*,' she hollers, her voice carrying down the hallway.

Joel squirms in his bed. He knows what is coming. He kicks the sheets off with his feet. His twisted, useless feet. He moans and turns in his bed, feeling the sores on his back sting and the dirt on his sheets rub against his skin.

'Ma! Ma!' he calls out – *Don't come down here. Don't come to me! Stay away!*

'I hear you, my baby. I'll be there in a moment,' she whimpers to him. 'My little boy.'

Don't come into my room. Don't come near me!

'Joel, my little boy. My little boy.' She staggers, a spoon in her hand. 'Come eat. I've got you food.'

Mother stands in the bedroom doorway and holds a can of food in her palm, it's gleaming with sweat, and a spoon in the other hand, waving it around, pointing it at him.

'My poor boy. Why were you born this way?' Her words are like lyrics to a song sung with no music. 'My poor baby. What is wrong with you? What happened to you? Why did God punish me?'

She stops, at the mention of God and punishment and she opens the small tin of cat food. She heaves the spoon in and digs a clump out. The jelly and fish dangle and wobble on the spoon.

No, Mother. No! I can't eat that. Don't give that to me!

She kisses him on the lips and Joel writhes in anger, screaming and crying. She shoves the spoon in his mouth and holds his jaws shut. Joel chokes and tears stream down his face.

No... no!

He's forced to swallow. Joel spits it up, the taste is vile.

'Eat it my darling. Eat it.'

He purses his lips together and she slams the spoon in, knocking it against his teeth. She shoves another heap in and holds his mouth shut. She wrenches his jaw up into his top teeth and he swallows without chewing. The cat food slides down his gullet and into his stomach. It instantly heaves back up into his mouth and he is made to swallow it again. She does this until it is gone. Joel notices he is crying and stops. There is no use in crying. Not when dealing with his mother. He wonders where his brother, Gus, is. He would have stopped her. He brought him sweets last time – liquorice.

The minced fish and goop from the tin dangle from his lips and his mother wipes him clean and leaves the room. Joel closes his eyes and thinks of the outside world. He thinks of long acres of grass, running and falling. He thinks of the forest and a lake. A stream and swimming. He thinks of climbing the mountain, only to be nearer to the sun. He opens his eyes unexpectedly and the bird has returned.

Follow me, and I will show you, says the bird.

I'm embarrassed, Joel replies.

About your mother? Don't be. We are not here for that.

Then why are you here?

The bird nods its head and flies. Joel finds himself floating, moving and caressing the sky. The wind is beneath him. His legs still don't move, but he *is* moving. He is free. He follows the bird up the mountain and away from his house. It's colder up here and the wind is fresh and clean on his face. He smiles and he can't remember feeling this way, ever.

Rest down there.

Joel lands on a mossy outcropping of stone. The rocks are chilled, and the moss is moist. He hears a waterfall and fish splashing.

Mother will come for me.

Not up here she won't, the bird replies. It starts to dig its beak in the moss and snatches a small insect and eats it whole.

I don't remember ever leaving the house. If I had, it was a long time ago.

Now you can leave whenever you want.

Joel steps along the stones and feels the spray of water from the fall. He looks up and sees clouds circling the top of the mountain peak and wants to know what's up there. A howl comes from the woods to his left and he becomes nervous.

What was that?

The bird flies to a nearby branch and looks, its head darting from side to side.

Something is here. Something is wrong.

Is it because I am here?

Yes, the bird replies.

Something is trying to break our connection.

Should we go back?

No, this is your place. You are safe here. It can approach, but it cannot harm you.

Joel steps down from the rocks. His feet aren't crooked or deformed. He steps into the crystal-clear water and cups his hands, bringing them up to his mouth and he drinks. It's unlike any water he has ever tasted. It dribbles down his chin and he smiles and looks up at the sun. It's warm and welcoming on his skin. From the forest comes a wolf, completely black with red eyes. Its paws are large, and it steps carefully and eyes the kid. It bends its snout down and laps at the water. Joel stares and knows what it is. The bird flies and lands on Joel's shoulder. Joel can feel its little legs trembling.

Are you not afraid? the bird asks.

I am more scared than I have ever been.

Why are you not running, like the others?

I am not afraid of death. I am not afraid to face it. I welcome it.

But, the bird says, looking up at Joel, *your time has not come. You are needed. Do you know this?*

I am needed? Joel replies, watching the wolf as it drinks further. It snaps its head back and shakes its long hair.

They stare at each other and the wolf snarls.

Your time will come.

Yes, Joel says, his eyes ablaze.

The world around shakes violently. The trees rustle and the ground quivers.

Something is pulling you back.

The wolf retreats into the woods. There is a blast of white light and Joel is momentarily in his room again, his mother is climbing into his bed. The forest returns, and the bird is laying at his feet.

Don't let me go back.

If I could stop it, I would, the bird replies, its breathing laboured.

A lightning bolt flashes and Joel sees his mother naked, under his sheets, playing with his penis. He begins to cry. He closes his eyes and thinks of the forest and the rocks and the mountain. The bird is gone. The water is still and now murky. His room returns, and his mother has him in her mouth. His head pounds and he screams out for Gus to come and stop her. There is only silence. He opens his eyes and he is sitting on the edge of the water. His feet are deformed and thin, crossing over one another. His spine is twisted, and he flops to the side and hits his head. His hands are pulled towards the wrist and he sees the wolf standing several feet away.

Of all the places you can go, why do you come here? the wolf asks.

The bird watches carefully from a tree on the other side of the lake. At any moment it is ready to disconnect the wolf from Joel.

'I don't know where else to go. The bird showed me how

to get here,' Joel answers.

Down the stream is a town. Not like the one you are from, it's different.

Joel looks, and the bird keeps watch on the wolf.

'I've never been to any other town. How is it different?'

Down there, there is a park. A slide and a small pond. There are some fish in it, but not many.

Joel twists his head around and stares down the long path that leads off the mountain. He looks back and the wolf appears closer.

'I can hear children playing down there.'

Do you want to go see?

Joel thinks for a moment. He looks at the bird, it looks terrified.

'I'm okay. I'll stay here for now.'

Your father is down there.

Joel looks at the wolf. Its face indicates concern. He looks back in the direction of the park.

'My father?'

Yes. You've never met him, have you?

'No. Mother told us he died.'

Yes, he did. He came here, and I took him down there, like I can take you.

'My brother... I don't want to go without him. I can't meet my father without Gus.'

Gus will come later. Way later. But you are here, now.

The bird moves branches and the wolf eyes the bird without moving its head.

He said he didn't want to go, the bird says.

Down there, says wolf, *there is no pain. You can walk, and you can see properly. You'll eat all the food you want and drink anything you can think of. You like liquorice, right?*

Joel looks at the wolf, then at the stream that flows down the hill.

'Why would my father come here? He has never come to visit us.'

He can't, Joel. What you don't understand is everything your mother told you is wrong. Even some of the things Gus told you, are wrong.

'Gus is good to me. He's the only one to stop mother from...'

Yes, your brother is good to you. He looks after you when no one else will. He protects you.

'Without him...'

Yes. You would be dead.

Joel moves and the wind changes.

Just follow me down to the edge, we can peer over. If you don't like it, we'll come back here. If you want to go down further for a closer look, we can walk down.

Joel turns to find the bird, but it is gone.

Don't worry about bird. He will be back.

'Where did he go?'

It doesn't concern you. Now stand up.

Joel looked down and his feet are facing forward, and his knees aren't bent inwards. He grips the rock beside him, it's cold, and he yanks himself to his feet. His weight feels strangely heavy and he takes a few steps in order to carry himself. He stretches upwards, his arms raised in a V. One foot after the other, he slowly paces himself to the edge of the ravine. The wolf walks beside him, matching his pace.

Can you see down there, Joel? See the small clearing and the house?

Joel squints his eyes from the sun, and he can see a circular, grassy area with no trees. He steps back, as if pushed. Inside the clearing is his house, but it's not on his street. It looks cleaner. The paint is still on it and there's no garbage out the front, piled up in large mountains.

'That's my house. Is my father in there?'

Yes. He's down there.

Joel scans the rocks for a way down. There is a stone staircase, covered in moss and vines. He hears the flutter of bird wings behind him, but he does not look.

'If he is down there, I'm going to meet him,' Joel says with tears holding in his eyes.

I know, Joel. That's why I brought you down here. He wants to meet you too.

Joel feels a throbbing in his abdomen and his crotch is yanked and pulled. He winces in pain but ignores it. The wolf looks at him. Its red eyes turning yellow, terrifying and the red gummy inside lips of the beast bare for a second and disappear.

Joel steps on the first stone step. It's slippery and he isn't used to walking. He takes another. It's a long way down. He looks over to the house and sees someone, faintly, in the window. Like a ghost. They've pulled the curtain across and it's a man, tall, with a thick black beard and soft eyes.

'Father?'

The front door handle turns and opens, and a silhouette of a man steps towards the doorway. He is cast in shadow. His hands are big and by his side. Joel steps hurriedly, his feet flat and then slips on the steps and he falls. The stone cracks against his bones and he screams. His body turns, and he slides down the staircase, falling, his arms waving, trying to grip something, anything. He hits the bottom and his legs and arms have returned to their original state. His head cocks upwards and he sees the man from a skewed angle.

'Father,' he deplores.

The man steps one foot outside the house and lifts his hand up to his mouth, placing a cigarette between his lips. Smoke engulfs his face.

'Get up, Joel,' he says.

'Da... Da.' He tries to speak. His tongue too fat for his mouth. His bottom jaw slides to the side and he was like before.

'I don't understand you. Get up and come over to me.'

'Da! Ma!'

The bird lands beside him, its eyes scanning the environment for the wolf.

I didn't want you to come down here, Joel. You shouldn't have listened to that wolf.

'Na, na. Mo!'

I can't get you back to the lake above. I can't help you, Joel.

His father smokes and looks down at his son. There's a flash of bright, white light and Joel is back in his room, his mother is still in his bed. He closes his eyes again and squeezes. His father is no longer on the front porch, he is beside the house. A large cutting block is in front of him. He is holding an axe. He swings and the wood splits in two and falls to the ground.

'I stayed with your mother as long as I could, Joel. But,

between you and Gus having fits, it just broke her.' He stops and rests the axe over his shoulder. He looks out into the thick forest. 'She couldn't have two kids like that. Do you understand Joel?'

'Na. Mo. Mo. Da.' Joel reaches out towards him, his fingers curled, and his wrists bend inwards.

'Your brother would run away when he was little. You may not have known that.' His father turns to face his son, axe in hand. 'Back then, the area was better. There were more people, and everyone worked. The whole town worked for the mill in some way or another.'

His father steps towards him. He stops and eyes his son, so helpless on the ground, his tiny arm outstretched before him.

'Once, Gus ran away for two days. Your mother never went looking for him. I searched the block and couldn't find him. I guessed he would return, eventually.' He breaks into obscene laughter.

The final few steps and his father is standing over him. The axe gripped tightly in both hands.

I'm sorry I brought you here, Joel. Take a deep breath and shut your eyes.

'When he did come back, he said he only came back for you. He didn't want to leave you alone. But now look at him. He doesn't really care for you, Joel. No one ever did.'

He swings the axe over his head and brings it down across Joel's face. A spark of black and a soft scream and mother is done. She breathes for a moment and climbs off him. Her sweat and fluids still on him. Joel opens his eyes and he is breathing heavy. He looks out the window and bird is on the branch outside.

'Bir! Bir!'

The bird doesn't say anything. It stares at him and bounces on the branch, then flies away. Joel is left in the room, waiting for Gus to return home.

THE SEEPING

Gus waits silently in the darkness. The trees are very aware he is here. They whisper and gasp and point and he ignores them. The Dark Stranger is perched on a tree above him, watching, waiting. Gus watches the man enter the woods and look around. He unzips his fly and pisses. He steps forward and looks around again. The sun above slinks away, turning its attention elsewhere. The flies are mad and buzz accordingly. The man, Douglas, is wearing thick rimmed glasses. He has puckered scar tissue in both ears and wears a black shirt. There is white powder around his collar. He watches, kneels down and smells the dirt, keeping an eye on the movement of the animals. He is unaware that many are watching, curious and hungry. He picks ups up a handful of dirt and holds it to his nose, eliciting memories of a time long, long ago, far from here. He neither smiles nor grimaces; he simply waits.

The overgrowth was like a cancer, sending tendrils of dead cells to cover and comb over exposed rocks and tree roots. An undiagnosed, malignant tumour of vines, grouped together like tails of rodents, entwined and home to many. The bleeding sap of freshly cut wood, the seeping and the uninitiated, burial plots and cemetery bark, a carved knife, made of under-rot placenta and the dripping coldness to the air; a chill to the bone and the cracking of skin. The silence within the forest is full of voices, mostly undiscovered and untreated. The ones that are never heard are the loudest. Obnoxious foliage, strangulation and manipulation, and sadomasochist turns of the green-worm; a closet of moss to hide the sky.

Douglas, unsure if he is truly alone, starts to dig with his hands; a gaping hole and then plastic sheets. He hauls it up with his skinny arms and stares at it with alien curiosity. He pulls sandwich bags full of money from his pocket and drops it into the shallow grave. The mossy ground takes it willingly. He wraps it with the other bundles and looks at the piles of paper money, all of them wrapped in rubber bands, some broken, some dirty and torn, blocks of paper buried under soil and rot. Gus watches from afar, protected by the dead ghost with blackened hands. Douglas adds money to the top, does a quick count with his fingers and then his phone rings. It startles him, and he steps backwards. He answers it and yes, he's here and no, there isn't enough yet. To come back? He argues, but give him five minutes, no now! Before you bury it again, come back here, right now. More money to add, more calculations. Remember the amount. Douglas does not want to leave the money exposed to the prying eyes of the dead forest. Douglas leaves in a hurry, stomping through the overgrowth, trudging and slipping through the wet soil.

Like the bottles in the ground, Gus is mesmerised. Another treasure given to him by the forest. He moves quickly and without hesitation. He stands over the money. Dead money from dead people. Drug addict money, smelling like sour cum and sweat. Gus picks up the first pile and flips through it with his fingers. He can't count that high, but he knows it's a lot. He pictures Joel in his mind. Joel is standing and talking normally. He thinks of his mother. She's in the distance, a blurry copy of herself, thinner. She doesn't speak. He puts it in his pocket. In the distance, he hears footsteps and swearing. The trees tell him, and the Dark Stranger tells him; this man has a gun. *Run.*

Gus snatches at the pile feverishly. Hand over fist, piles of cash are tucked into his underwear, his pockets, under his arm pits. The man is closer, yelling to the forest, swearing at the phone.

Run.

Gus runs for his life. His legs spread long, and he strides, back through the foray of tree trunks and hanging branches, their dead twigs striking his face and arms. He's bleeding, but he runs and does not stop.

Douglas is open mouthed and staring. His fingers shake, and he feels an unfamiliar wet feeling in his underwear and jean's left leg. He considers turning the gun on himself, through his mouth and out of the back of his head. Leaving blood in the forest is a contract for the walking ghouls. The money, it is gone. His mind reels and he feels his phone vibrate in his pocket. The sun returns, as if to illuminate what just happened. He looks away from the pile and into the hole, it is nearly empty. He sees a dropped pile of money a few feet away and his eyes widen. He pulls the gun from his pocket. Someone is behind him, the man is talking, yammering and then stops. He too looks at the pile; its messy with loose cash and plastic bags. Douglas points at the pile of money a few feet away. The man considers getting his knife out and plunging it into Douglas's neck, but he sees what has happened. A trail of money leading into the abyss of the forest. They both look up and stare.

'Go back to the others,' he says. 'Don't tell them a thing.'

Douglas walks backwards, unable to take his eyes off the thin veil of the woodland. It has taken something from him, and he knows it will never be returned. The man with the gun walks to the money block and picks it up. He stares at it, as if giving him a clue. He smells it and drops it back to the ground. It lands with a soft bounce and a thud. He walks further into the forest. The trees are suddenly thicker, more jumbled together. They shield any view of the surroundings. He can hear a stream somewhere and he tries to follow it. When he gets there, there is no stream. There's no water, no nothing. Just more trees. He turns around, flashing the gun quickly at a shadow, and he is now confused. Nowhere around him looks to be where he came from. He spins around again, pointing the gun at nothing, then again. The trees shift and change, morph and collide with other trees. There's an outcrop of rocks, like an underbite of stone. It's coming from the start of the mountain – but it wasn't there a moment ago. He doesn't take his eyes off it. He runs towards it, the sticks and twigs grab at him, dragging him back, but he pushes on. Snatching at them and breaking them, throwing them to the ground. He climbs the stone façade and looks around for the smoke. He looks east and then west. Then he spies it. A small gasp of black smog coming from a clearing. But it is over a mile away. He didn't walk that far, he tells himself. How did I get here? The forest. He matches the sun and which way to walk. As he climbs off the cliff face, he spots movement, birds and trees. He looks and sees a boy, running. His shirt held up to his chest. His money. Their money. He grunts audibly and goes to run towards the boy, to shoot him in the head, or the face. To kick him hard while his body is leaking blood. The trees shift, covering the boy. There is a motion in the shrubbery, one way, then another. The man with the gun doesn't know which way. He stands and watches, his hand on the gun. The boy, a small boy. Black with short hair, nearly to the skin. His shirt dark red and dirty. He can't find him again. He will go look. But for now, he thinks, he must get back. That stupid fool Douglas will let the others know the money is missing and they will both be shot dead. He heads towards the smoke.

Wasting away
In a small town
Violence sewn shut
The keepers are awake
Run

FLESH IT OUT

She lays the pictures out like revealing her hand to the dealer. The man looks at them, picks one up and holds it closer to his face. He puts it back down.

'Is this your daughter?'

'Don't ask me anything.'

The man looks at her, then picks up the next polaroid. The smell of the room is dried cum. The floor is wet from where the store kid had mopped. The man stands up and walks away.

'Hey!' she yells after him, but he is gone into the night.

She gathers up the pictures and tucks them back into her jeans pocket. She can hear the woman in the next room talking. She starts yelling at someone. A man rushes past her and swings the door open. She leaves.

Out in the carpark she lights a cigarette and leans on the car. There are more people outside. A streetlight, several feet away, burns yellow but the devious cockroaches still are not afraid. Several people look at her and she leans and waits. A bigger man, stockier than the rest, tall and well dressed for this area, starts heading towards her. He stands away from her and stares with his hands in his pockets. She looks at him through hazy smoke.

'What do you want?'

He doesn't say anything for a moment. He looks behind him at the other men, standing near their cars. They all stare at him.

'Can I see them?'

'See what?'

'The pictures.'

She fans them out on the car hood. The man can see them from where he is standing.

'Who is that?'

'Never you mind.'

'Look,' the stocky man says, pulling his hands out of his pants. 'This place is closing down now. I'm interested, but I gotta go back to my house for a bit. If you come, we can talk there.'

She stares at him. She smokes and waits for him to talk, but he doesn't.

'Where do you live?'

'End of this street. Turn right. End of that street. The apartments are called Clear Lake Views. Number 8'.

She nods and he turns away from her and goes back to the group of men. His car starts and he slowly edges his way along the parking lot. He rolls down his window.

'I'm Aldo by the way.'

She nods to him and throws her cigarette on the ground. His car drives off and she sees two other men approach her. She gets in her car and drives away before they reach her.

The drive over is short, and she doesn't listen to music. She parks out the front and looks up at the only light on in the complex. There is a large iron gate and an unkempt hedgerow. She gets out and lights another cigarette. Her phone beeps, and she glances at it briefly. It is Roy asking where she is. She slides it back in her pocket and goes to the fence. It has been left slightly open. She doesn't lock it behind her. She goes up the stairs and stands in the overly fluorescent hallway. Number 8 is at the end.

As she approaches the door, it opens, and Aldo stands there with a drink in his hand. He smiles and holds the door open for her. His apartment is clean. The couch is old and frayed and his TV is buzzing and showing something; he has put it on mute.

'Come on in. Have a seat. I made you a drink.'

'No thanks.'

'I have some shit if you want that instead.'

'What shit?'

He goes to the kitchen and comes out with a small plastic bag. He pulls a glass pipe from his pocket. His hands are big with large, hairy knuckles. He brings the pipe to his lips and lights the end. He passes it to her while holding his breath. She takes it and lights the end also. It tastes like vinegar. She goes to the window and looks out onto the road.

'It's pretty quiet around here.'

'Why do you live up at this end of town?'

'Closer to the strip club,' he says with a smile.

'Is that the real reason?'

'Yeah.'

He excuses himself and goes to the end of the hall and shuts the door. She quickly goes to the kitchen and sculls two glasses of water. She looks in the fridge, it is completely empty. She opens the cupboard and pulls out a plate; never washed, never used. She goes back to the window and sees another two cars pull up.

'Shit.'

She grabs her lighter and stands over the sink in the kitchen. She yanks out all the polaroids and lights them on fire.

'Hey, I was thinking… we could have a –' He spots her burning the photos and runs towards her, grabbing her forearms. 'What the fuck are you doing?'

'You're a fucking cop!'

There is a knock at the door and they both freeze.

'Aldo?' comes a voice from the other side.

'Give me a minute,' Aldo speaks, his voice different.

She pulls away from him and he instantly lets her go. She bolts down the hallway and into the room, slamming the door behind her. She doesn't hear Aldo chasing her. There is shouting and the slamming of the front door, then a hurried conversation. She looks around the room, the bed is made. She pulls the drawers out, no clothes, not anything. She slides the balcony door open and looks over the railing; a pool, two stories below. There comes a gentle knock on the bedroom door.

'Gail? We just want to talk.'

They know my name, she thinks, climbing over the edge. *How do they know my fucking name?*

The door is unlocked, and three men burst in. Mother Gail takes a glance at them and then releases her grip. The fall feels longer than it is. The air pushes against her skin, taking her own breath away for an instant. She half prays to hit the concrete, splitting her head open, but she hits the water. It still feels like glass on her frail limbs. The water erupts around her and then she is engulfed and suffocating. She flails helplessly until she grips the ledge and pulls herself out. Dripping wet, she stands on the side of the pool and looks up. She can't see them. She turns and runs towards the fence, trying to pry it open, but it is locked now. Reaching up, she grips the top and yanks her body over, cutting her leg on the pointed barb. Blood rushes down her leg and drips onto the concrete below. She lands with a thud on the other side. The men all appear as darkened figures near the pool, all tracing her wet footprints to the front gate. She gets in her car and peels away with screeching tires.

'I'm calling Drake.'

'No. Not yet.'

The footprints start to evaporate under the moon. The men stand in silence, contemplating what had just happened. Aldo's phone beeps and he looks at the message.

'It's okay boys,' he announces. 'We got her plates and address.'

'Drake's still gonna be pissed.'

'Fuck him.'

'I'd rather one of us get the credit for this one. Drake isn't from around here.'

They gather themselves and lock the apartment.

A dark canvas
Horrific in nature
Cast the spell to extinguish
Left for dead

PLASTIC

The toy room is cold. Boy stands and shivers. He's naked and covering his genitals with his hands. Torso is not here. He looks around; there are many dark places, many shadows. Boy walks to the window and peers out. There is nothing. No stars, no movement, not anything. He walks to the chest of drawers and opens them. There are small figurines of army men and others are medieval and there is a small castle and plastic animals. He gets them out and sits on the floor. Boy arranges the animals by type and places little plastic fences around them. He sets the army men up around the animals and puts the medieval characters on the other side. Suddenly the room wavers and shakes. The dark corners become darker and Boy is worried the darklings will come to watch him.

What are you doing in here, Boy?

Boy looks up and sees Torso by the front door. The maggots writhe and buck out of the bloodied stump. The bone of Torso's spine is exposed, awkwardly cut and angular.

'I'm playing.'

How did you get here on your own?

Torso moves around the room desperately.

'I don't know. How do I normally get here?'

You're with me. I bring you here.

Boy moves the farm animals around.

It isn't safe for you to be here on your own. You know that.

'Father burnt me with spoons again. I woke up here.'

You're appearing here of your own free will?

'The cupboard smells. But it's so cold here.'

In that cupboard over there, there are clothes, put them on and be warm. You can play a little longer, then you must go.

Boy stands up and opens the cupboard. He slips his skinny legs into pyjama pants and a shirt. His muscles are nothing but shrivelled, stringy pieces of hocked meat.

'Why can't I stay longer?'

It isn't safe here. You can't come here too often or be away from yourself for too long. It's dangerous.

'Why?'

You might end up staying here, forever.

'I'd like to stay here forever. Here, I'm not hungry or in pain. Here, it's quiet and hidden.'

Torso walks haphazardly across to the window, then to each corner of the room.

I must tell you something. I was going to wait, but I may as well tell you now.

Boy moves the soldiers closer to the fence, then sits on the other side and moves the medieval plastic figures into position.

Your father came here once.

Boy looks up at Torso. 'He did?'

Yes. When he was your age. I was not here then.

'How do you know?'

I can speak to the toy house. It talks back.

'It's never talked to me.'

No, it wouldn't talk to you.

'Why was my father here?'

When he was younger, he was much like you. His father used to beat him too.

'Did he?' Boy says surprised, moving away from the figurines.

He would be beaten worse. He came here every day. Those toys you're playing with, they are his. He brought them here.

Boy turns his head and looks at the toys in disbelief.

He wanted to take them back with him, to his home. But once they are imagined here, they cannot leave. Your grandfather was an evil man.

'I never met my grandfather.'

You would not want to meet him. The things he did to your dad, and your aunt...

Boy looks away.

The worst pain to be done to people are done by the hands of men, especially fathers.

Boy opens the farm gates and pushes all the soldiers inside the farm and shuts it behind them.

'Is he still alive?'

No. He is long dead.

'Is that who comes here... and stands in the darkness and watches me play. Is that him?'

Yes. That is him. I'm here to keep him away from you.

'Thank you.'

Boy pushes all the soldiers over and leaves the farm animals on their feet. Torso circles boy and looks at his scars and fresh, bubbling, blisters. He sees Boy's ribs through his waxy skin.

I think the time has come, Boy.

'Time for what?'

You will need to leave, very soon.

'You said a little while longer.'

Not from here, from your dad's house. From your town.

Boy tried to stand, but his body resisted. It hurt far too much, so he stayed squatting. He looks up at Torso, where his head should be.

'You've told me for so long the time will come, why now?'

If he burns you again or hits you… you will die. He will bury you in the back garden and not think much of it. When the police come to check on you, he will tell them you ran away, and nothing will happen.

'He wouldn't do that!'

Yes, he would. He's done worse. You know what he is capable of.

'But the Train… It's not ready. We don't know how to get it started.'

Fire. Stack as much wood as you can into the chamber. Make the fire big and pull the lever down. It will go.

'What about the others? Gus and Cassie?'

Their time has come also. When you see the whites of your father's eyes, you must leave. Run to the Train and get it started, or you will die.

Boy looks down and his pyjamas are gone. He is naked and cold again.

AFTERGLOW

'Pi died because of you, now turn your fucking face around.'

ROY WAKES

The screeching of tires wakes Roy. His arm is nearly lifeless; the veins, purple and clogged. His skin itches and is red raw where he scratches.

SUICIDE NOTE

Merlin stands over the dead kid's body. His neck is contorted to the left and blood has come out of his ears and dried. A photographer from two counties away is taking pictures. The flash resonates in Merlin's head like a hangover headache. He waves him away. The photographer looks up at the towering waterslide and then down to the body.

'Probably jumped from up there.'

'Probably,' Merlin responds, taking a cigarette out of his breast pocket.

Merlin steps away and stands under the shade of the Snack Shop, abandoned and rotting, the windows smashed in and boards nailed over the frames, graffitied on and bashed with rocks.

'Looks like he shit himself when he landed... or on the way down.'

Merlin eyes the photographer and waves him away again. Two police officers are standing by the front gate, one near the body. The coroner had to be woken to get him here and he wasn't in any rush to see another dead kid in Hope Valley.

'Take your pictures and don't speak again. Be quick and then get the fuck out of here.'

The photographer steps back into the early morning sun and eyes the young detective. He opens his mouth to say something back but thinks better of it. He turns around, snaps a few more photos and walks back to his car without saying anything.

A young girl, around seven had run away from home and came here to hide out yesterday morning, so Merlin is told. She saw the body and sat here and spoke to it during the night, thinking he was asleep. She returned home the next day and her parents didn't even know she was missing. She told her father about the man she had been speaking to and he made her show him where he was. He brought a knife but found the kid dead.

The kid has fallen or was pushed, so Merlin thought. There is no suicide note in his pocket and he has lipstick on his lips, crooked and smeared in blood. He lays in the abandoned pool. The surface is slippery with algae and overgrown thorn bushes. The body has started to move slowly towards the deep end. Paintings of dolphins and a coral reef still adorn the concrete, half washed away from constant rain and faded from the sun.

Merlin looks around the empty graveyard of the once popular theme park. Grass has forced its way through the plastic barrels of the slides and in through the metal spiral staircases. Vines grow and hang from water slides, up poles, along monkey bars and out through now defunct water cannons. Several large empty pools sit with rain water at the bottom, stinking of rotting meat and pungent enough to make the throat gag. Dead mice float on top, the snakes even avoiding their bloated, water filled bodies.

Merlin wanders the decayed playground, looking for anything, something. Empty bottles of soda and syringes scatter the ground, condoms, used and thrown, discarded and wasted, beer bottles and carbon monoxide canisters. He looks around at the fences and can see where the kids have cut holes in them to sneak through. The tops are curled with razor wire, debris of old cloth and lengths of toilet paper caught in the barbs, flapping in the wind like flags – a flag of lost hope and even more so, lost souls.

'Coroner is here,' someone says, a soft voice from behind him.

Merlin throws his cigarette butt amongst the piles of trash and feels guilty for doing so. As if he has become one of "them" – the uncivilised. The problem.

'I'm starting to think I should buy a house here, I would save on the gas,' the coroner says.

'You wouldn't want to live here,' Merlin replies, walking the short man over to the body.

'Damn,' he says.

Merlin looks at his face. He has already caught the sun and started to turn beet red.

'I know this kid.'

'You do? Who is it?' Merlin reaches for his writing pad.

'Casper Von Mogen. Rich's son.'

'Who's Rich?'

'He owns all the towing trucks in Hope Valley,' the officer says behind them.

The coroner bends down and examines the body. He slips gloves on and opens the kids mouth. Most his teeth are smashed out. He feels around his jaw and head and stands up again, walking back into the shade near the other officer.

'Yeah, that's him for sure. I'd say he'd had enough and jumped.'

Merlin squints at the man, still smelling the tobacco on his own breath.

'What makes you say he jumped?'

'I'm a good family friend with Doctor Ness. We go way back. We often attend the same medical talks in Lowville. This kid was depressed. I could get you the list of meds he was on.'

Merlin looks back to the kid. His arms are twisted and bent the wrong way. One leg is broken and wraps around the other one. *He must have bounced when he hit the concrete*, he thinks.

'We'll take him away, do what's needed and I'll get you the report in a few days.'

Merlin nods. Everyone wants to die in this town, but not many do it. They let the town do it for them. Merlin waves flies away from his face. The sun is well and truly up now. He turns and heads back to the car. The photographer is still there, flipping through his pictures on his camera. He gives him a stern look as he gets in his car and drives away. Merlin sits in his car. It's hotter inside. The air is stifled and bare. He looks at the old water park sign. It has been shot countless time with a shotgun, to the point where you can barely read the words. He starts the car and turns the air-conditioning off. On the way back to the station, he wants to sweat. He needs to get it out of his skin.

MOTHER

Gus's mother has been drinking all day. Her fingers shake, and her eyes roll and fall around clumsy in their sockets. She squeezes her black flesh up in a ball and makes a fist. The lines and wrinkles are stark white and throb with tensed blood. She grinds her teeth together and tears roll along her eye lids. She tries to stand but stumbles sideways. Her neck is swollen, and veins raise up like desert snakes. She thumps the wall with her fist.

'Gus is gone,' she sings out, spittle on her lips and chin, dangling and falling on the linoleum. She punches the wall hard again and the plaster cracks from her force.

In the next room, Joel hears his mother's rampage, but cannot move. He cannot scream out for her to leave, or not come into his room. He simply lies there, waiting for her hot breath, waiting for her to enter his room. She always does.

Mother of Gus. Mother of Joel. Mother of one more. Where? Buried in the yard the day after it was born.

She stands, legs apart and pisses hot piss. Her long dress soaking and now heavy. Her drink falls from her hand and she yelps like a dog hit by a car.

Mother of Gus. Mother of Joel. Mother of one more.

Pins prickle her arm, starting at her finger tips and slowly etching their way up her forearm and around the yellowing skin of her elbow. She holds her arm out in front of her and tries to focus. She feels on fire.

Mother of Gus. Mother of Joel. Mother of one more.

Mother falls forwards and lands on the floor. The glassware shakes. The prickled arm, tucked inside her obese body, lays awkward. One finger's bent back, the bones broken and the tip protruding. She doesn't feel the pain. She lays and screams out for Joel. In the next room Joel moans – *Ma*. His tongue swollen, and his teeth rammed into his jaw by some demonic madman. His moans are sub-human and full of terror – *Ma! Ma!*

Mother of Gus. Mother of Joel.

Ma–

She feels nothing. The poison in her body making her numb. She lays her good arm outwards and grips the floor. It squeaks, and she pushes off with her legs and slowly moves forward. Her gammy arm drags and bleeds around the jagged bone. Her skin folds and her dress soaks it up, leaving a little trail as she heads towards Joel's room. Joel is still whimpering – *Stay away from me, Mother. Don't come in here* – but his lips could never make words, not like normal. Not ever, not now. And the spider, it is gone too. Just like Gus. Mother drags herself, her heart straining, her lips pulled back over her teeth. She snarls. This time she will beat him, this shit stain of a son. This time she is too angry not to. She drags herself forward, the stick-break bone rubbing against the floor, catching on the carpet.

Mother of Gus.

Her arm reaches upwards and her heart stops. Like a brace in time. Her fingers spread and land flat against the ground in front of her. She has made it to the hallway. She can see Joel's door and the devil that made him the way he is.

(Beast. It is you.

Come with me, Mother, if you dare? Come with me. You.)

A rush of hot water stirs up from Mother's bowel and into her throat. She gags and liquid pours from her nostrils and mouth, leaving white bubbles flowing over her bloated lips and onto the floor.

Joel hears silence. His own heart is racing. He calls out for his mother again. Silence. He tries one more time. There is no movement. No answer. He stares at the corner of the room, fixated and confused. He must get up! He tells himself, go see Mother. Where is Gus? He wiggles in his imprisoned body. His arms and legs, not under his control entirely. His own physicality, his own cage. He manages to squirm and moan and move to the edge of the bed where his cart is. His left leg dangles behind him, limp and without command. He tries to tell it to push off the wall, push him off and onto the cart, but it is useless. His right leg lifts slowly, wobbling and punch-drunk. It hooks around the bed post and with his small amount of strength he levers his body onto the plank of wood. He lands abruptly, and it hurts. He would normally cry out and Gus would come for him and ask him why he is doing it himself and if he is hurt. But no one is coming and there is something wrong with Mother. His head is down against the wood and one arm is over the edge, the hand pulled into the wrist. His fingers are long and spider-like, unable to grip or spread. The other hand, the same, but with more movement hooks onto the ground like a ships anchor and his good leg propels from the back. With a push he is moving, another and he is near the door. His heart is pounding, and his mind is on the verge of panic.

'Mo – mo,' his open mouth screams. 'Mo – mo – tha.'

One more lunge and he sees her, a few feet away, her eyes nearly popping out of her skull. Her mouth is open, and black tar spreads out in front of her face. Joel feels a horrific tear in his mind. Everything he sees is frozen and cast in opaque colours. He sees his mother's eyes only in red. Tears drop from his face and onto his cart and he smells his mother's piss and soon to be rotting flesh. Somewhere down the hallway, the house howls. Is it death coming to collect her? Or him. Joel shakes with terror. How will he eat without her to bring him food? (or Gus). How will he get out? She is in the way. He lays, lopsided and stares into his oblivion.

When time starts again, Joel isn't sure how long he has been laying there staring at his mother. Her red eyes have gone, but the empty house still howls wildly. He anchors his arm forward and pushes with his leg; the cart jolts a few feet, the wheels now off the carpet and onto the plastic floor. Between the walls of the hallway, he manages to roll up to his mother. Her tongue is out of her mouth and black.

'Mo – mo –'

Mother doesn't move. She is still and lifeless. Joel stares into her eyes and knows death has already taken her. He slides closer to her and looks into the next room. He sees the front door. It is a mere twelve feet away. He rolls and pushes off the wall. His wheels stagger against the deteriorating skirting board. He pulls and yanks at the cart, pushing onto his dead mother. His hand touches her flesh and it feels cold. Joel whimpers. He has to move, fast. The body, not his mother, is blocking his way. The cart catches on her shoulder and hips. He slithers and pulls and pushes, his face contorting and moaning, yelling. Then it is quiet. He is stuck in the house with a smell that death left. Its entrails and breath and odour still linger, rotting and rancid.

The congealed waste in his mother's backside makes him hurl gut lining into his throat. He spits stomach acid out and feels his teeth clench. He slides his hands across the wall and feels the corner of his cart dig into his mother's skin.

He lays in the dark and looks at the front door. He has to find Gus.

THE RED CURTAIN

Douglas counts the street poles and road signs between Hope Valley and Weaver's Peak. He then counts the bridges they have to cross from there, to Fountain. Ehren sits beside him and occasionally checks his phone. Douglas knows he's nervous, and they should be. He looks out the window wearing sunglasses. The man is made of hardened muscle with veins like the power lines he sees; webbed up his neck and along his jaw. He sits uncomfortably in his chair and often stretches and moans, trying to get comfortable. Watching him, you can tell he doesn't like the forest. He stares and his mouth becomes dry. He hates Hope Valley.

They drop the money off in Lowville and stand in the kitchen while it is counted. Douglas sweats profusely. They were short so much money he was certain they would have put a bullet in his head. But he covered it. He wrote down the wrong amount. Twice now it has come up short, but never this short. Someone took a large chunk and Ehren doesn't know. Douglas and one of the guards knows, and he has more than likely left town already.

Ehren sits with his hand out the window.

'I'm starving.'

Douglas looks over to him, startled at his sudden announcement.

'We can stop to eat. There's countless roadside diners on the way back.'

Ehren shakes his head. He has a tattoo on his forearm.

It's a collection of dots in blue that made a symbol that Douglas doesn't recognise. On his second last finger he wears a ring with the same symbol on it.

'Saddle and Spur,' Ehren says, looking over to his driver.

'The strip club?' Douglas queries, then notices Ehren's lack of response. 'Yeah, sure. It's about twenty minutes away.'

Ehren nods and continues to look out the window. They drive in silence the rest of the way. Douglas pulls off the highway and down a long stretch of darkened road. There is nothing out here but disused fuel stations and mechanics workshops for large trucks. The roads are wider and on each side of the asphalt are enlarged parking bays. An odd truck or two is scattered along the backroads, sleeping for free and away from the lights and commotion of the diners.

Douglas turns the wheel and pulls into an intersection. The lights are red, and he waits, staring at the illuminated circle. He doesn't feel like going to a strip club, but he thinks if Ehren starts talking to him, he can bring up the issue of the missing money. The light turns green and they continue down a road barely lit by streetlights. They can see the neon lights of the Saddle and Spur at the end of the road. There are cars banked up leading to the establishment. Men sit on motorbikes out the front. A bouncer is talking to a topless woman, who is smoking and nodding at what he is saying. Ehren takes his ring off and slips it into his pocket.

'We'll eat and then go?' Douglas says, trying to say it as a statement, but it came out as a question.

Ehren points to a free car park and doesn't reply. When

they get out of the car, Douglas can smell the blood and sweat. He can smell the exhaust fumes and the dripping car oil. The bouncer looks at them and notices Ehren. Douglas sees him put his hands in his pockets quickly and then out again, then he rubs his hands together. When they meet, they shake hands and Ehren says something to him. The bouncer nods and eyes Douglas as they walk through the red curtain. The room is dark, the only light is coming from the stage area. Two girls are dancing on poles, money fills their underwear, and spills out onto the floor. Douglas can't help but stare at it. He was hired because he can clean it and wash it out through the small businesses in Lowville. He can count quick and was never wrong, although his patience has now been tested and he can't ignore it. Ehren sits at a table and two girls approach them. He waves them away and motions for someone to take his order. Douglas orders the same beer as Ehren and they are brought chicken wings and a large side of fries. Douglas notices Ehren doesn't look at the girls. He thinks it is something he has trained himself to do. He thinks he worked here before, or someplace similar, where he wasn't allowed to interact with them.

'Ehren?'

He looks up as he moves his empty plate of chicken bones away from him. A woman stands with one hand on her hip. Her heels are six inches off the ground and fire-engine red. Her coal-black hair is split by a straight fringe.

'Motherfucker. You came back.'

Ehren half smiles. 'I'm only eating, then I'm going.'

'Sure, you are, babe. You said that the last two times you were here. I'm surprised they let you in.'

'I don't cause trouble.'

'No? I thought that's exactly what you caused.'

Douglas sits and watches as Ehren becomes increasingly hostile. He rubs his fingers as if his knuckles are itchy. His left foot stomps on the ground repeatedly.

'I'm leaving in a few minutes.'

'A few people came in here looking for you. That was a few months back now. No one in here knew of you, just so you know.'

'I appreciate that.'

'One drink, you buy it? For last time. Like you promised.'

She looks at him with sullen, mischievous eyes. Douglas has seen it before. She walks back from the bar with three shot glasses. She slides one in front of Douglas without looking at him. He slides it back.

'Don't worry about him, he doesn't drink much.'

'He isn't the sort of person that I would picture you hanging out with. Are you babysitting?'

They clink glasses and take the clear liquid with a single gulp.

'He's just a friend. You don't need to hassle him.'

Ehren pulls two fifty-dollar notes from his side pocket and lay them on the table. Douglas notes the serial numbers. Not the ones that are missing.

'More? I thought you were going.'

'For old times' sake, right?'

Ehren takes the whiskey intended for Douglas and drinks that as she went back to the bar.

'I want to get back,' Douglas leans over and tries to whisper. The music is so loud he could feel it in his temples.

'Look,' Ehren says, moving his eyes to the girls on the podium, 'try to relax for a few minutes. We'll be going soon. I'm not eager to stay here any longer either.'

Douglas sits back and watches the girls dance. The woman comes back and sits with Ehren for half an hour and drinks. Then she is told to get on stage by a waitress wearing red. Ehren stands up and begins to walk towards the door. Douglas follows, his gaze watching the woman as she grips the pole. The bouncer nods at Ehren as he leaves. He doesn't return the gesture.

'Give me the keys,' Ehren says, standing by the driver's door.

Douglas feels everything inside him freeze up. He is a big man, but he still has had several drinks and is already walking on wobbly legs.

'I'll drive, it's okay.'

'Give me the keys, Doug.' He holds his hand out one last time.

Douglas reaches for the keys in his pocket and apprehensively hands them to Ehren. He pulls out of the carpark and heads back towards the highway, then turns at the last minute, avoiding the on-ramp and taking the service road.

'What are you doing?' Douglas says, his nerves already on edge.

'Too many cops on the highway.'

They drive in fearful silence as the car escalates and weaves through deserted roads and down around the bumpy escarpment of the mountain road. Ehren's eyes are clumsy and he shuts them for several seconds and reopens them, shaking his head. Douglas starts to stare at him.

'I know, Doug.'

'Know what?'

'You ain't stupid. And neither am I.'

'I'm not taking the money, or taking the fall for it, if that's what you're talking about.'

'So, you think I am?'

'I don't know, Ehren. Are you?'

Ehren yanks the wheel to the right and the car swerves, screeching its tires and going momentarily sideways. Ehren rights it and hammers down the accelerator.

'We've been doing this now for how long? Six months? And you still think I'm skimming?'

'I don't really care if you are or not. The amount being taken is increasing and if it doesn't stop, they will kill us both.' Not to mention the sizable amount that was stolen.

Ehren goes silent. Douglas can see him gritting his teeth. Several minutes pass and Douglas isn't sure if he is heading back to Hope Valley or not.

The dark becomes darker and Ehren's eyes are closing for longer periods. Douglas shifts in his seat. There is no way this road would take them anywhere near Hope Valley. He watches Ehren out the corner of his eyes. His eyes droop and never reopen. The car starts to veer off the road. Douglas reaches over and grabs the wheel, pulling it to the right. Ehren opens his eyes and tries to correct the car's path. The wheel jerks too far to the right and it snaps the wheels tight, sending it on its side. The car rolls twice, smashing out the windscreen first and each window around the vehicle in succession. It flips over without touching the ground and lands on its roof. Ehren has been ejected from the car via the side window. Long strips of flesh hang from his arm, grated and sliced from the glass teeth in the window.

Douglas wakes up and knows his nose is broken. The swelling has pushed up into his eyes. He tries to sit up, but he is lying in a crumbled heap on the cars ceiling, the seatbelt still knotted around his arm and neck. He clicks the release button, but it doesn't work, so he steadily climbs out of the wreckage. He could smell fuel.

'Fuck,' he mutters, his jaw aches. 'Fuck. Ehren.'

Ehren lays several metres away. Douglas takes one look at him and almost vomits. His face is mangled. Blood gushes from a neck wound. Suddenly, it stops, and his skin starts turning white. Douglas checks his pocket for his phone. He walks a few feet and stops. The screen is smashed, but he could still use it.

'Spencer, it's Douglas. No, listen…' The man was berating him down the phone. 'We've been in a car accident.' There is silence.

'Do you have the money on you?' the man on the other end asks.

'No, we made the drop off. We were heading back.'

'Call Roy, he'll come and get you. Leave the car.'

'Ehren looks dead.' Another silent moment.

'Ehren's dead?'

Douglas walks on rickety feet and tries to feel a pulse on his cold skin. It is covered in blood.

'Yes, he's dead.'

'Stay where you are. Send me your whereabouts and I'll tell Roy to get there within the hour.'

'We need the ambulance.'

'Be quiet, Douglas. Listen to what I say. Stay there and

don't contact anyone else, you got it?'

'Yeah.'

Douglas sends the message and drops his phone on the ground. He walks through the seeping, boiling oil, unflinching as it soaked into his shoes and burns his feet. A small fire starts under the engine, but all Douglas can do was walk in circles. His rattled brain knows they were on a road, and he can't remember how they got there. There are no stores, or houses, just empty miles of nothingness – nothing but trees and asphalt. He sits down on the ground near the tree line and stands back up. The forest emanates coldness. He walks several feet and sits on the road. Under him are the tire marks they had made only minutes earlier. He watches as a faint white light emanate from Ehren's body. It stands like a hunched man, its fingers long, and its feet stretched out oddly. It walks slowly, but surely, into the forest.

Time neither moves, nor stands still. The moon speaks in angry tones and Douglas tries to answer back. Long, bright lights strike his back and spill out over his shoulders and onto the ground in front of him. He turns around and sees a car behind him. He stands up and feels his mind warp into a spinning black circle. He almost falls.

'Sit back down,' says a voice. Douglas can't understand it.

A man and a woman get out of the car, leaving the headlights blaring. Douglas can hear music.

'Get that fire out, I'll check Ehren.'

Douglas looks at the woman. 'Ehren's dead.'

She looks at him with a sideways glance. Approaching him from several meters away, she can see he is dead. She stops and stares at his body. It looks like he has been through a meat grinder. She swears and checks his pockets. All she finds is his ring.

The man picks Douglas up from under his arms and guides him towards the car. He puts him in the backseat and leaves the door open.

'Stay here.'

Douglas doesn't respond. As the seconds pass, he finds it harder to remember the events of what happened. He scuttles over to the other side of the car where he can see them drag Ehren's body into the woods. One comes back and gets something out of the back of the car. They bury him in a shallow grave and cover it with rocks and plant detritus. They then both stand and look at the car. Douglas moves back to the open-door side and peers out. They unscrew the number plates and take the metal ID plate from inside the door. They get back in the car and slam both doors. Douglas's ears ring loudly. His head throbs. The woman, with blood on her hands, turns to him.

'We can drop you off at the hospital, if you want?'

'Where's Ehren?' Douglas says.

'He's gone,' says the man, looking into the rear vision mirror.

'Do you want to go to the hospital?' she asks again.

Douglas looks confused. The car pulls away and drives around the wreckage. Douglas looks at it, he then turns back to the two people in the front.

'We'll drop you home. Then it's up to you what you do, okay?'

Douglas nods. All he wants to do is go home.

Moon dance
To wake the gods
The new poison
Seeds that never grow

JOEL LEAVES

Joel's body is distorted and angled. His mouth opens and long strands of spit slither onto the ground. He reaches his right hand forward and pulls himself towards the table. The whole time he grunts and his left-hand shakes. His hand is fused crooked and rubbed red raw from the floor. His eyes are lazy yet determined. His wheel board clomps and bumps over his mother's arm and slides off. He spins around on it and is free. He lays exhausted in the middle of the lounge room, the wheels under him still squeaking.

'Gush,' he says through gapped teeth. 'Gush!' he screams, and heads towards the front door.

CAST IN SHADOW

Boy feels the flies on his face, crawling and scurrying to find a place to lay eggs. He moves his head, but his neck hurts. All his bones hurt. He places his hand on the ground and tries to push himself up, but he is too weak. His skin cracks and detaches. All his teeth hurt. He slumps against the door and reaches upwards, holding the handle, as if he is about to be swept away by a torrent of water. He pulls the handle down and the door gives and opens, without much pressure. His face slides down the wood and onto the ground. Half in, half out of the cupboard, Boy can see the lounge room and the front door. He wants to get back to the Train. He knows the Train will take him away from here, but all he's got to do is get there.

He's coming.

The front door opens, and his father stands on rickety legs. He places something by the door, heavy and rattling. He stands looking at his boy.

'What did I tell you about leaving the cupboard?'

Boy's hand reaches out to him. 'Father, I'm sorry. I'm thirsty.'

Today is the day you leave. Torso's voice.

'Dad,' Boy manages to say through peeling lips.

The father thumps the wall with his fists and marches to Boy, yanking him up by his hair. It is so brittle, most of it comes out in his hand. Boy falls, but father catches him, dragging him by his neck.

'Don't ever leave the cupboard.' His breath stinks, sour

and groggy. 'I'll tell you when you can leave. I'll tell you when you can eat.'

He throws Boy against the kitchen cabinet and he hears his body slump like a bag of bones. They rattle and disjoin, the cartilage like flimsy tongues of carboard. Boy breathes in, but the air is minimal. Father steps over him, like you would trash on the street. He goes to the kitchen sink and leans down, gulping water from the faucet. He leans into the luminescent light and burps and scratches himself.

'What am I gonna do with you, Boy?'

He knows the time is now. Boy knows as the silence is more silent. He looks over his shoulder. Inside his cupboard, collected from the forest is a small glass bottle, warped by the sun or a fire. It is against the wall amongst sticks and rocks. Gus gave it to him. A shrine to the Train; to freedom.

'What the fuck is this?'

You should not have brought these things back, Torso whispers.

Father marches to the cupboard and goes to step inside, but the repugnant stench makes him whip his head back. He gags and kicks at the door.

'You filthy fucking dog!'

He reaches in and clutches the sticks and stones. He holds them up to his disorientated face. Opening his fingers, he lets them fall to the ground.

'You've been outside.'

Boy shakes his head. 'No, I found them. In here... the wind must have...'

A sharp kick and Boy only remembers waking up against the fridge. His jaw hurts and a tooth is laying a few

387

feet from him. There's blood on his lips. The fridge, on his back, is cold. He hasn't felt anything like that in a long time. Father is on the front porch. He is standing outside the doorway. It's nearly dark now. He is drinking beer and looking out onto the abandoned streets, the tumbled-down houses and broken street lights.

'Where were you going, Boy?'

Boy feels something in his gut stir, aching and bubbling. Fear.

'I didn't go…'

'Tell me where you went. Just outside? The back yard? Or did you go back to school?'

He knows, Torso says, his voice coming from the cupboard. *Get to your feet and run.*

Father turns and sculls his beer, crushing it with his hand and dropping it with the others on the balcony. Boy pushes with his legs. His skinny, bony legs heave and thrust and the knotted walnut-muscle of a calf strains but holds his weight. He stands and feels victorious. His right hand is in a fist.

'I stood up to my father once,' Father says. 'He slapped me so hard my ears rang for two months. I never did it again.'

He steps inside, no longer cast in shadow. His face is distorted meat and sinew of age and drink, greying whiskers and scars. A face that once smiled long ago, or maybe never. The indents of wrinkles, well beyond his age. His shoulders and arms, twisted meat-muscle, fine-tuned by a hammer of beatings and hard labour. His knuckles pop and twist, pop and twist, as he squeezes his hands into fists. The veins along the front of his hand come to the surface.

Boy steps forward, an act of war. He looks to the hallway; the backdoor is down there. Only a few feet. If he could get outside, at least he could hide, or crawl under the house.

'My father hit a dog with his car when I was a boy. Younger than you,' he says stepping forward. He reaches down into the box and pulls out another can of beer. 'He made me get out and watch it as it died. He leant down beside it and made sure I was looking at it in its eyes.'

The crack of the beer opening and the release of gas and the smell of bubbles. Boy waits for his moment.

'It seemed to take forever to die. Thinking back now, it may have only been two minutes, but for a kid like yourself, it seemed like a lifetime.'

He cranks his head back to fill his gullet with beer, his eyes momentarily close. Boy runs. His legs pound the wooden floor and the bottom of his feet twist and feel like soft foam. The hallway is dark, and he already hears his father coming after him; the booming of his heart and breath, the squelching of the skin around his fingers as they twist and grind. The hallway is too dark. Boy can't see. He runs into the wall and searches frantically for the laundry door. It clicks open and his heart stops. The door is shut. It swings open, as if something was helping him escape. A pile of aging, decaying clothes lay in the centre of the room. He runs into it, tripping and falling into it. There is a second door, that one that leads outside. He reaches it and turns the lock, slowing his escape. There is a stained-glass window in the door above his head and he glances upwards to check the reflection, to see if his father is close. He is standing a mere four feet behind him.

'You would run from me?' He wipes his hand across his

forehead, then on his jeans. 'Your mother ran away. And where do you think she ended up? Buried somewhere in the forest.'

Boy pushes the door open and it swings hard against the rear wall of the house. The night welcomes him with a chilly breeze. The house next door is abandoned and covered in lianas and lichen. A tree grows from inside, out through the side window, wanting to escape also. Boy heads down the stairs, his body weak and straining to use its muscles. He glances over his shoulder as he makes his way down the side of the house. His father is standing on the steps, as if appearing in places without walking. He has another beer and drinks it fast. He laughs and spits into the overgrown garden. He had never heard his father laugh.

Run into the forest, Boy, and hide!

'He'll find me.'

No, he won't. Not in his state. As long as you don't stop. Help is coming.

Boy traverses the long grass and crooked, bent trees. The backyard is an urban jungle, filled with car parts and a swing he barely remembers using when he was younger. He steps over a mound of dirt, filled with rocks, and falls, tumbling on the other side. He picks himself up and sees the back fence in the translucent moonlight. He feels an agonizing slap to the back of his head and Boy drops to the ground, meters from the fence. He curls up into a ball, a response to abuse. A coping mechanism, he shuts his eyes. His father gets his dick out to piss on him. He laughs again, his neck straining as he looks up into the night sky. He digs in his pocket for his lighter. Kneeling down, he takes Boy's head.

'No one knows you were here. No one knows you ever were. As far as anyone is concerned, you left to find your mother. I can bury you beside her if you like.'

The lighter is lit, and the strange yellow flame seems counterfeit. He forces Boy's eye open with one hand, then holds the flame an inch away.

'I'll burn your eyes out for trying to escape.'

The flame is thrust forward, then a shower of glass and Father falls backwards. Boy scrambles, his feet kicking and his arms flailing. Tears pour down his face. Father gathers himself, the lighter drops into the grass. There is blood coming down his nose, a large cut between his eyes. Another projectile flies from the darkness and hits him in the side of the face, opening another large cut. Boy spins his head around, to the fence line and Gus and Cassie are standing inside his yard, their arms filled with the warped glass bottles from the bottle dump.

'Boy,' Gus screams, holding a bottle by the neck. 'This way, quickly!'

Cassie runs to Boy and scoops him up under his arms. The father grits his teeth and begins a stampede towards them, saliva squirting from between his teeth. Gus throws another bottle and it connects him across the right eye. He screams and covers his face. Boy gets to his feet and is dragged to the fence line. Gus and Cassie help him over and they run into the darkness of the forest.

Father stands under the moon. The cut above his eye needs stitches, but he just wipes the blood away with the back of his hand. He grins a toothy smile, first time in a long time, and he stares into the abyss of the woodland. He knows the forest will try and stop him, it did the first time.

He steps slowly, taking each stride with care and precision until he reaches the fence and he climbs over it. He is going after Boy.

Hangman's promise
One day he'll return
On havoc and in demon form
On hands of glass
Infested

BLEED INTO THE BLUR

Douglas stands under the fading light and looks into the hole. There is a gun pointed to the back of his head. Every now and then the barrel clonks against his skull, just to remind him it is there. His hands have started to blister, and he remembers the kid watching him from the forest, then the money trail, and then he was gone. Douglas's nose is plastered up and both his eyes are still purple.

'Hurry up,' says the man behind him.

A shovelled heap of dirt is swung out onto the soft clay floor of the forest; upturned worms and bugs flail to right themselves and scurry for cover. Behind the gunman is another man. He stands in silence. He wears large boots with his jeans tucked into them, and a white shirt, dirty and stained. His hair is cut short and he looks around the forest as if trying to intimidate it. The forest fears no man.

Douglas pounds the spade into the ground and answers back with a soft cackle. It echoes upwards and dissipates. The plastic bag looks foreign amongst the soil. The man with the gun looks over his shoulder.

'You didn't bury it very deep.'

'If I go too deep, it'll get ruined by the water veins that run under the clay plates. It flows under the soil, down from the mountain.' He points.

'Is that all of it? Or is there more buried?'

'No, this is all that's left.'

'If I find out there's more, I'll bury you in that hole. Now, bring it inside.'

He heaves it out of the ground and slides it away from the hole. The man tucks his gun into his belt and clasps one end of the plastic holding the money. Together they yank it up off the ground. If feels heavier than it looks. They walk it through the forest, feeling the ground swell and puff. The moss comes in like a tide and the birds that had nested for the night, eye them closely.

The house sits like an unlanced boil. The walls are disintegrating from the chemicals and the fumes. The plaster crumbles and the plastic coating on all the inner wiring has melted away. The smell is nearly unbearable without a mask. They slide the cash cache in through the open front door and down the hallway. It drags mud and forest debris in, smudging the already warped and dissolving linoleum floor. Two rooms are off the right side. One, they had used to watch TV in; there were two couches, a brown one they had found in the forest, not far from the road. It is covered in holes and had been home to a snake, that Kenner had taken with him. The couches lay to rot on the inside, soaking up the floating acetone and hydrochloric acid. The heat and the stank would make them pass out and the sweat would drip on the floor in puddles. After the production was increased, sitting in the house was unbearable.

The second room and kitchen has the cookware; pipes criss-cross the room into empty soda bottles, a cooling box houses the tins and jars. A small burner on the counter is extinguished, above it, a beaker, with scorch marks under it. The smell is rancorous.

Piles and piles of cold and flu boxes lay in a heap by the side door, covered in cockroaches, eating the cardboard and bathing in the chemical bath that lingered along the floor. The side door is nailed shut, the nail ends rusty and crooked.

The ventilation system spins through the house like piped cobwebs, up, through the ceiling and through each available window. The third room has a bed and a door with a plastic sheet that cut out the smell.

The money is flopped onto the table in the kitchen. It slumps like a body would, arms of bundled cash, all rolled up with a receipt number and the amount, then a signature across the fold; Douglas's signature. The man pulls at the plastic, unravelling it, showing its inner stock. He does a quick count in his head, it is nowhere near enough. He had used it to prop up the last delivery. Now there's not even half there.

'So,' he starts, without taking his eyes off the money. 'What happened?'

'There was a boy, in the forest.' The man doesn't look up. 'He saw me bury it.'

'A boy? Who was he?'

'I don't know, some black kid.'

The man's eyes move in his sockets like rolling, stone marbles. Seaweed coloured corneas stare vacantly, his tongue moving around his mouth like an eel.

'You don't know the boy, but you saw him?'

'Yes. I had counted it and we were about to bury it. When we came back, the money was gone. We chased him, but he got lost in the forest.'

'Then you came back?'

'Yes.'

'So, you left the cash out in the open?'

'Only for a minute. I had to come back here to get the rest.'

'So, you couldn't take it all with you the first time?'

'It was too much. There was only two of us here.'

'Okay. So, who chased him?'

'Ehren did,' Douglas lied.

'Ehren is dead.'

Bright beams of light split through the cracks in the wood panelling. The man turns and sees the yellow splash up against the roof and then onto the floor. The man with heavy boots looks over his shoulder at the door.

'Go see who that is.'

He turns like a soldier and marches to the front door, flinging it open. An old truck parked halfway down a dirt embankment bobs on broken springs. Two men sit in the front seat, a gun is pointed at them.

'You better have a damn good reason for being out here.'

Roy steps out. He has a knife tucked into the back of his pants. He moves it to the side as he opens the door and cleverly shows his hands.

'We built this place. This kitchen is ours.'

The man laughs. He has a toothy grin and his mouth opens up wide. The forest hears his laugh and marks him for death.

'This kitchen is not yours. It is Spencer's.'

'Spencer gets his cut. We get the rest.'

The man shakes his head. 'Spencer is inside.'

Kenner steps out of the car and looks at Roy.

'Spencer is here?'

He nods slowly, savouring the look of sheer terror on

their faces. He waves the gun towards the door and ushers them inside. The surrounding foliage near the front of the house is dead. The air spilling out from the doorway kills everything within ten feet. The infected, pustule that is the abode oozes waste and death. The forest is cautious, but never forgetful.

The man with the gun steps inside first. Roy grabs Kenner by the arm and holds him.

'That's Tommy. They only bring him out to kitchens if something is seriously fucked up.'

Kenner feels his skin turn ice cold. A howl breaks over the tips of the forest trees, as if laughing. Kenner looks up and remembers the snake, he feels it watching.

'What the fuck are we gonna do?'

'Douglas took the money. They'll kill him, and we'll have to do all the money runs.'

'Fuck,' Kenner says.

'Look.' Roy lifts up his shirt to expose the knife handle. 'If it gets out of hand, we get out of here.'

Kenner nods. They walk in through the front hallway. Their footsteps creak and moan under foot. The wiring crackles and pops through the decomposing plasterboards around them. Spencer holds a wad of cash in his left hand. He appears to be weighing it. He drops it back in the bundles and flings the plastic sheeting over it. Dirt drips off it onto the floor, the forest is now inside.

'These two say they own this place,' Tommy says, standing with his hands beside his hips.

Roy stands in the room and shifts nervously. Fresh veins pop from his neck. His junky arms look thinner than normal and his facial hair is patchy and pocked with sores.

Spencer and Tommy both laugh. Spencer waves them over to the side table where Douglas was.

'There's a kid out there, from this shit stain of a town, with my money.'

'We'll find him. He can't have gotten too far.'

Spencer looks at Kenner. In this light his skin looks yellow and his eyes look like those of a bird. Roy stands with his bony chest outwards. His hand keeps going to his shirt, where the knife handle touches his sickly skin.

'The money went missing days ago. We were told about it only last night.'

Tommy's eyes look around the room. There are pizza boxes on the floor next to an old table with three legs that had toppled over. A shelving unit is pushed into the corner, all its shelves busted out and broken in half on the ground.

'We didn't know either,' Roy says. 'We thought Douglas and Ehren had driven it up the week before.'

Spencer's glare turns to Douglas.

'Ehren said you weren't from around here, is that right?'

Douglas nods. 'I came from Lowville.'

'People in Lowville don't much come out this way. They'll come as far as Weaver's Peak or Fountain, to see the attractions, but not Hope Valley.'

Douglas doesn't answer. He feels his stomach tighten. There is more money. He had taken some and buried it elsewhere. The kid took a bit, but not all of it. Sweat beads along his forehead before becoming too heavy and falling over his eyes, dripping down his cheek and onto his shirt. He can't swallow the excess saliva in his mouth. Tommy snaps off a table leg and walks three long steps to him and plunges it into his head. Blood spills from both sides, across the walls and onto Kenner and Roy. Douglas drops to his knees; his teeth chatter together and the pool of saliva in his mouth pours out onto the ground. His left hand raises up, fingers spread. Tommy lifted the bloody leg above his head and mashes it into his face. Teeth clang across the ground, landing in front of Roy. Douglas falls forward, his skull pulsating, pushing blood onto the ground.

Roy wants to piss himself as he watches Douglas's head hit the floor. From a crack in the linoleum comes a scurry of cockroaches, darting every way. Tommy lifts his boot and stomps on Douglas's skull. Tommy looks down, but his eyes unscrew in their sockets and looks up at Roy and Kenner. Their fear is a snake in their bellies. It is the fear that lives here, in the forest. The fear of never leaving and death only footsteps away in the darkness. Roy snatches his knife and lunges forward. Tommy sees his clumsy steps, but feels the cold knife slash against his throat, and then in through his ribs. His lungs hiss. A fleshy ball of fist and bone swings upwards and connects with Roy, knocking him backwards and dropping the knife. It lands on the dead money counter's back.

'You stabbed me, you junky fuck!'

Tommy runs forward, grabbing Roy by the neck. Kenner is caught in the melee and is knocked to the side. He sees the knife. His eyes widen as he sees Tommy clutch Roy around his throat. Blood streams from his side, staining his shirt and turning it red. Spencer stands stock still. He reaches into his pocket and pulls out his cigarette pack and taps one out, placing it in his mouth. Roy gargles and gasps for air. He starts to kick at the man and wonders where his gun is.

'Get the kid!' Spencer screams.

Roy knows the kid. He knows Cassie is leaving the house to meet with the black boy near the train tracks. All the drug abusers who lived there tell him so. After Pi died, he didn't care what she did.

'The kid! Get the kid!'

Spencer smiles as he watches Roy's face turn purple. He reaches into his pocket for his lighter. Kenner, using the fear in his stomach, the roots sliding through his spine and ribcage, running up his throat and the appearance of death, snatches the knife and leaps to his feet, stabbing the man in the side of the neck, over and over. Skin slides open and jelly-like fat pops through in bulbous, congealed pieces. His spine and neck bones are exposed, and Tommy turns, fear finally in his eyes and he lets Roy go, who falls to the floor in a heap. Tommy's last words are gurgled and incomprehensible. Kenner goes to Roy and picks him up. Over his shoulder he can see Spencer flick the lighter coil. It makes a noise, but nothing happens.

'You boys have fucked up this time.'

Roy, barely conscious, is heaved to his feet. Kenner carries him through the house to the back door.

'Where are you going, boys?' Spencer declares. 'We still need to get the money–'

The lighter catches, and a spark sprouts from the gas cylinder. In an instant, the flame carries like a bursting balloon. It lights the room into a blooming flower of fire. Red and yellow flames lick the ceiling, the walls and the floor. Spencer is instantaneously enveloped in flames. He is blown back against the wall so hard he indents himself in the rotting plaster, his legs and arms still outwards from the blast. That is where he stayed as the explosion ripped through the house, melting his skin from his bones and his bones away from his marrow.

Kenner and Roy have reached the back door, but it is locked. The flame snakes its way through the house, within a millisecond, to the kitchen and lights the gas tanks in the cooler box. The explosion lifts the roof off the house and sends projectiles soaring through the air. Kenner is behind Roy and the push from the explosion sends them through the door. They soar over the dead grass and onto the ground. Kenner's back is on fire and his skin has started to blister and boil. The boarded-up windows and frames are lifted and separated from the house and become airborne. The bricks all become loose and are sent rocketing through the air with a flaming comet trail behind them. The fire mushroom lifts from the house and goes upwards, higher than the tree tops, into the night sky. The sound is deafening and can be heard by the entire town.

Roy wakes and shakes his head. His neck and throat hurt. Kenner is on top of him. Both his legs from the knees down are missing. His left arm has been torn away and he could see it several feet to his right. The finger nails have curled and melted from the heat. Roy screams and kicks him off. He stands up on rickety legs and looks at the burning house in front of him.

Get the kid, he thought. *Get the kid, get the money.*

He turns toward the forest, his clothes smouldering, and his skin scorched by the flames – and he ran into the forest towards the Train.

STEAM

Merlin Drake runs through the heavy thicket of the woods. The pine needles crunch under his feet and sound like the snapping of bones, hundreds of bones, maybe they are bones, raised up from the soft soil, ready for redemption. The branches lean down, as if trying to snatch him up in their grasp to take him up into the tops, away from the haunted ground. He draws his weapon and hears the unfamiliar hissing of the steam engine; the soft, low grumbling of the Train as it expels all the debris from its pipes and cogs. The ground rumbles and shakes and the trees scream through the night, carried on the wind. Merlin stops and breathes. *What the fuck is that?* He follows the sound and feels the vibrations come up through his feet, into his legs and shakes his heart.

He slogs through the darkness, like an ocean of oil, darkened by fog and cloud. Another hiss and he can hear it. Something big is moving. He hears the cries of the buried bodies. *Stay back, Merlin.*

He ignores them and runs, pushing through vines and thicket, his arms cut and legs and feet bleeding. *There is enough blood on the ground already*, the forest warns. He comes to a clearing and looks down – cold metal – long steel rails under him, vibrating and humming. He leans down, places his palm on the rail – it's alive. It's convulsing, out of control. The large iron pegs holding it down are rattling within their chambers, coming loose and breaking.

Cold metal in the moon light
Waiting for freedom
Blood trickles on the tracks
Alive!

THE THINGS THAT LIVE HERE

Cassie stops to help Boy, who has fallen. He looks down at his knee and its bleeding.

'I'm okay,' he says. He looks behind him, but the trees are quiet.

'We've got to keep going,' Gus says, pointing. In the distance, over the hills, is smoke.

'What is that?'

Cassie wipes Boy's knee and the cut is deep. Boy walks as if he no longer feels the pain. He is used to pain. The crippling, bone crushing pain of his body being bent over for years. The burning pain on his skin by cigarettes. The night air brings a coolness that soothes and pushes them, towards the Train.

'Whatever it is, it will be coming for us.'

The three run up the embankment to the train tracks. The night air is blue and illuminates everything in a soothing aura. The slinking river sings and the trees bend to move for them. They stand on the tracks and look towards the long, outstretched tongue of metal and wood. It is far to the train and they must hurry.

A man stumbles out of the woods. His arms flailing and his voice crying out, but muted by the things that live here, the stones that hush voices and store secrets. The leaves that have blood splattered on them, they remember – *they know*. He runs and falls and picks himself up again and falls again. He follows the moon and his skin is still smoking and burning. His breath is strong, and he feels like he is going to break a rib. He looks and stares down. He is standing on the tracks. The ones forbidden. The town knows, and it tells its kids, don't go to the train tracks; don't go to the forest. He sees movement, a blink and a blur. It's children. He runs and hides in the trees. They want to expose him, toss him up into the sky and crush his bones on the ground. They are the forbidden ones. But the woods are more concerned with the children. They run and stop to catch their breath and begin again. They run past him and keep going down the track line. Roy emerges from the trees and back up onto the tracks.

'Cassie?' he says, the words barely leaving his lips. She is with the black boy, the one with the money. He follows them.

TENDER
(The Leaving - Part 1)

Set me free.

'We are here.'

Boy, Cassie and Gus stand at the mouth of the deep, hallowed cavern. The bats have left and not returned. Piles of wood sit in a haphazard huddle by the step ladder, leading up to the driver's deck. The tracks are free of vines and debris; they shine oily black in the moonlight. Boy limps towards it, his body aches and is trying to give up. Cassie stands a foot in front of the train and places her hand on the face plate.

The time is now.

'Yes,' she answers.

A scuffling noise comes from the forest, shuffling and the breaking of branches.

They are coming.

'Get in Gus and start the fire.'

Gus runs to the bundle of wood and scoops it up in his arms. It is heavy and pinch his skin. It digs in splinters, but he climbs the steps to the cabin. Piles and piles of newspapers, collected and brought here, are shoved into the firebox. On the seat next to him are piles and piles of money. He slides in wood log after wood log. His arms are heavy, and he feels the train under him buck and become wild. It has slept too long.

'Boy, where are you going?'

'Whatever is here… it has come for me.' Boy stares out

into the forest. 'My father has found me.'

'Get in the cabin, we'll hide you. We won't let him take you back home.'

Boy stares without moving. Every burn and every belt welt sting and throb. He starts to walk out towards the yawning tracks. Cassie runs to the cabin as Gus throws in the last of the wood.

'It's Boy... he's walking back!'

Gus swings out of the cabin, holding onto the rail and looks down the length of the rails. He sees Boy wandering, as if suddenly lost.

—

Joel digs his fingers into the soft ground and crawls through the muddy undergrowth of the forest. Joel knows what he must do. His wheeling board gets snagged and stuck on exposed tree roots and vines. He reaches up and clutches a low hanging branch and pulls himself up to sitting position.

His brother's name, 'Gush,' he says. Over and over.

He slides his useless legs off the board and uses his fused shoulder muscles to winch himself away from it. The ghosts watch. *Who is this boy?* So devoted to movement, but not being able to move. He climbs and crawls over distorted vegetation, gripping and pulling at weeds. His hands are cut and are bleeding, but he slithers and shuffles forward, never stopping, never relenting. His pants rip and his skin is exposed and speckled with blood. He says his brother's name, louder and louder, following the echo of his own voice back to him.

He stops and rests. Above him, a mangle of webbing. The trees all dead in this area. The ghosts don't even come here.

I am lost, Joel voices.

You are not lost, says the spiders above him.

I cannot find my brother. I need to help him.

Find the tracks, and you will find your brother. You are nearly there.

Someone is going to stop him from leaving. He must go. I know he does.

And you will help your brother leave? But stay here yourself?

The forest is where I belong now.

The trees have welcomed you. Or you would not have gotten this far.

Joel reaches forward and grips an exposed rock and starts to drag his body once more. He ignores the pain and the trail of blood he is leaving through the forest, and heads towards the tracks.

—

The train starts to rattle on its rusted veins as the fire in the chamber grows. The cabin shimmies and shakes. Gus loads in more wood. A stark picture in his mind of his dead mother. He thinks of Joel and no longer wants to leave, but something is telling him to keep going. He climbs down off the cabin and runs to the front. Black smoke is emanating out of the smokestack. It is feverishly black and consolidates along the ceiling like cancerous clouds, until it tipples over the edge and escapes into the night. The train's metal body seems to lift off the ground a few inches, shivering with the notion of being alive once more.

'Cassie, it's not moving!'

Cassie watches Boy. He's walking and stumbling, his hands outstretched to his side. She turns to Gus. *We've come this far, we must leave or die,* she reminds herself. She runs back to the train and, with Gus, checks the wheels and tracks again. A large brick is wedged behind the rear right wheel. Gus tries to push it, but it won't budge. The chimney exorcises more smog, puffing and chugging the engine as it splatters sparks and ash.

'Get a branch,' Cassie says to Gus, as she tries to dislodge it with her foot.

Gus finds a long, sturdy branch and together they lever it under the brick.

A man appears out of the forest. He is drenched in sweat and blood. His face looks demonic, half is red from his open wound, the other half is nearly translucent white. His fingers are outstretched, and he is shaking.

'Boy,' he says, his voice gravelly. 'You come home with me right now. This minute, you hear me!'

Boy wets himself. He should have known he was destined to die at the hands of his father. He starts to take small steps towards him.

A cry within the woods
Solitude and blood
The sand reaches the edge
Longing

DEVOTION
(The Leaving - Part 2)

The brick is pushed and shoved and hit; but years of rest have made it solid and still. Gus and Cassie climb under the trains belly and use their hands to pull it and heave it. Like a lose tooth, it wiggles for a moment, but does not become free.

'Get Boy,' Cassie says, worming her way out from under the train.

They both run to the opening of the cavern. Boy falls to his knees and screams in pain as his father descends on him. He is no longer man, but only a shell of muscle and hate. He will strangle the boy to death and drag his corpse through the woods and leave it by the stream and walk back home and drink himself to death. Boy waits for death.

Hobbling from the dark comes Joel. His feet entwined and tangled with greenery, vines wrap around his torso, not hindering him, but helping him. Pulling him along, carrying his weight.

'Gush! Gush!'

He leaps and grabs onto Boy's father.

'Go, leave!'

Boy breaks from his hypnotic stupor. Cassie and Gus are behind him, trying to drag him back to the Train. The night is dark and heavy with the prediction of a death.

'Joel!' Gus screams. 'I have to go back for him.'

Boy looks at Gus. 'My father will kill all of us.'

Gus stares at his brother. He is wrestling with a man

more than double his size. The father is beating him across the face and neck. He lunges against the tracks, trying to get to his son, but Joel keeps his grip tight around his torso, dragging him down and away from the train line.

'Leave, Gus!' Joel cries out, his words perfect.

Boy's knees are bleeding and Cassie and Gus carry him back to the train. It begins to whistle. The warning is so loud Boy gasps and Cassie's knees become weak. They push Boy up into the cabin where the plastic bag of money is stashed.

'It's ready,' Gus states. 'Put more wood in it. It must be hotter.'

Gus, ignoring what is happening behind him, searches the shed for anything to use. A crowbar lays in the dirt, washed there by the flood and covered in soil and ants. He pulls it free and runs to the brick.

I am alive.

He wedges it under it and stands on it with all his weight. The brick lifts up and drops back down.

'Cassie!' he screams, and he holds her close as they place their weight on the end. The brick lifts and falls to the side. The train starts to move forward.

I am alive. I am moving. It is my will.

The vines clutch Joel's feet and drag him back towards the sloping embankment, and into the tree line. His grip on Father is slipping. The man turns and palms Joel in the face, twisting his nose. Joel knows pain. He knows mental and physical pain. He shakes his head and his hands climb up Father and grip his jeans and shirt. The man is violent and his mind, grotesque. He elbows Joel and dislocates his jaw. Joel tries to grip him again, but he is weak now and his vision is blurred. The father breaks free.

Cassie and Gus run for the train as its heavy, metal wheels start to turn. It churns up the dirt and frees the cobwebs and layers upon layers of dust.

I will take you away from here.

Boy offers his arm down as the Train picks up speed. First Cassie takes his grip, and he lifts her up and into the cabin with him. Gus is trying to run faster, but the Train bursts out of the shed house like a newly born steed. The chimney is grand and bellows smoke; the wheels are big and move in unison. It is a marvellous iron beast.

'Gus, quickly,' Cassie cries out.

The Train suddenly erupts in a burst of speed. The chimney spits fire and burning, volcanic meteors. Fiery, lodged, stones rumble and cascade from the iron chute. Gus falls and rolls to the side. He stands up and sprints. His arms rocketing back and forth, a pumping piston.

Father, as if possessed by death, carried on forward, towards his son.

On the driver's seat, the large bags of money lay open, being ignored and covered in remnants of drugs and sweat. The contents are flying out into the cabin and out through the exposed door and window. Boy climbs down the metal pegs for stairs and holds his hand out. Gus runs as fast as he can, but he is not gaining enough speed to catch it. Cassie climbs out of the cabin and along the thin railing. It is slippery with old oil. Gus takes one last stride and leaps towards Cassie's arm. He grips her around the wrist, but his weight pulls her down. Boy frantically looks around the cabin and sees a lever and a pedal. He stomps the pedal and the train slows. The fire spews out towards him and runs up his legs and arms. He falls back onto the driver's seat and screams from the pain. Cassie holds the iron bar, but her fingers are starting to slip. She hauls herself up with her feet, straightening her already weak legs. She yanks his arm upwards with all her might and Gus jumps and catches the bar, but it is too slippery, and he falls. He uses his momentum and springs up with his feet. The train is hissing, and it is hot. He catches Cassie by her hand again. His other hand manages to snatch the bar and gain purchase. They moved quickly along the train and shuffle inside, just as it regains its momentum.

Boy stands up. His skin blistered and some of his hair burnt. His father stands in front of the train, the look in his eyes is sheer terror. A hand reaches out from the blackness; Joel's malformed fingers lengthen and pull Father away from the tracks. The large man stumbles and narrowly misses the train as it rolls past him. Joel struggles for breath, but the trees keep him alive.

'No!' Father desperately cries. He knows no other life, if he doesn't have his son. It is all he has.

Father gains his footing and runs beside the train, jumping up to grip the side. His fingers slip and he is yanked under the train. The wheels slice his abdomen, cutting through his muscle and exploding his kidneys like soft grapes. It severs his spinal cord and cuts his body clean in half. Joel closes his eyes and looks away. There was a quick inhalation of air and Father was dead.

The train rolls on, through the woods. Boy looks back and sees Torso. Its severed blue jeans and clean-cut bone. He couldn't help but smile.

The Train chugged along the ancient tracks and into the night, and out of Hope Valley forever.

BONE THIN

Merlin emerges from the forest, his arms cut, and his gun raised. He can hear the train and runs to the tracks, raising his firearm as the black metal locomotive pushes its way through the darkened tunnel of trees. The smoke curling from its nostrils fills the air with soot and heavy clouds. He fires his weapon and the shell spins from the chamber, clanging on the rails under his feet. He lowers his gun and sees something on the tracks ahead, something moving. He walks slow and feels the woodland around him watching, savouring his curiosity. He stands over the man cut in half and recognises him as the boy's father. His hands are still moving, his fingers curling in and out of their palms. The man's mouth is opening and shutting; his teeth are missing.

He looks at the guts smashed into the railroad pillars. They hum with the vibrations of the train and slowly die as it descends into obscurity. Merlin watches the dark and hears something behind him. He clambers back down the pebbled ledge and sees a boy curled up, his legs crisscrossed and bone thin. His face is bleeding and he is whimpering. Merlin picks him up and carries him out of the forest.

EPILOGUE I

Jasper lays in his cot, haunted by the ghosts of his very own past. A large house makes a lot of noise when there is only one set of ears to listen. He remembers his grandson, young and athletic. He remembers him coming to visit two summers ago but hasn't seen or heard from him since. He is a long way from the city though, too far to visit.

The air is warm, like a wet rug. It lays on you and makes you sweat and thirsty. Jasper sits up and wipes his brow. He drinks from a glass that is beside his bed and watches his own hand as it trembles. He sits on the end of his bed and looks through the window. The corn fields are long gone, but in the right moonlight, you can still see them, swaying and glowing. He stands up and walks into the hallway. He had a boarder once; her name was Mary. He remembers her but can't remember to pay his bills sometimes. She was sweet. She came from England looking for work and he had hired her for a short time. She wasn't good at farm work, but he'd had worse. She would make him ginger beer in the evenings, like they did back where she was from. He didn't much like it but didn't tell her so. She came and went too. Never saw her again or heard from her either.

He walks down the stairs and into the kitchen, unsure why. He opens the pantry and looks at the jars of pickled onions and cabbage. About ready to eat, he thinks. This can't be why he came down to the kitchen at 3am. He goes to the back door and opens it. The breeze rushes in, as if it had been waiting there all night. Something in the distance screams and he is alarmed. His feet shuffle back, and his knees collapse together. The scream is not from a human or animal. He waits to hear it again, but nothing comes. He steps out into the cold night, his skin prickles with goose bumps. Something is shuffling and moving in the rows of overgrown hedges and long trees. The old man knows it is hot and steaming, he can feel it already. He walks towards it, his eyes large and his hands shaking. It scares him to his bone marrow, but he wonders what it is. There is nothing out here. Perhaps death has arrived to finally take him. All those nights, God willing, that he never wakes up, but he always did.

He steps through the undergrowth and sees something on the ground, small and rectangular. He picks it up and holds it to the moon light. It is a one-hundred-dollar bill. He looks down and there are several more; a trail. He steps cautiously and towards the heat. He peels back branches and sees the grand Train. Black as soot and hot as coal. It is bucking and sweating like a horse. A trail of money spews from the drivers deck and out along the ground, disappearing into the night. Jasper looks up at the Train and is frightened. His heart skips and makes his blood cold. He stumbles backwards, shouting and cursing. You are not death! He runs as fast as his frame would allow, back towards his house.

At night he can still hear a ghost train travelling the tracks, the pillars old and abandoned. His skin freezes and he lay in bed, too scared to look out his window. Death finally comes for him one night and he asks about the Train and death answered, *yes.*

EPILOGUE II

He sits in the car and looks out over the water. The waves lap and crash over the grey rocks.

'Do you want to get out and have a closer look, Dad?'

He doesn't reply. He simply watches and waits. The water stares back at him. It speaks in a tongue that only he can hear or understand. The woman, she lays her hand on his shoulder and he is startled and turns to her.

'Is this the end?'

'Yes, Dad. The train only goes to here. Then it goes back the other way. There's only ocean from here.'

A tear drops from his eye and he wipes it away quickly, but his daughter sees it.

'Is this the place?' she asks, but he gets out and leaves the car door open, walking towards the pebbled beach.

He stands by the wooden railing. A concrete staircase runs down to the beach. The last few steps are covered in stones. He walks up the pathway and stands, staring at the train tracks. He can hear his daughter behind him. She is walking slow.

'We got off here,' he says, his voice raspy. His spine makes his body arch forward, and always appears as if he is about to fall over. This posture is comfortable. His arms are long and the wrinkles on his face are dug in deep, scarred and leathery. His hair has all but fallen out, and what is left is white.

He looks down at his hands and he doesn't recognise himself anymore. His daughter reaches out and takes his hand.

'Where did you go?'

'It was like coming out of a dream, but only remembering parts of it.'

The scars on his back never fully went away. They remain as a reminder of his father, the one he killed. The one he saw die.

'Do you want to go back to the car?'

'Not yet.'

'The hospital said you had to be back within the hour.'

Boy, who never became a man, is now aged and in pain still. His joints are swollen, and his liver never worked properly. He stands and looks at the tracks and imagines the Train there. He wonders what they did with it, if it's in a museum or if they dismantled it. Like him, it got one last run for freedom before it died. He has become the Train. It had called to him in his sleep, all those years ago when he was trapped in the cupboard. He can still remember its voice. He can still remember where he went when he was trapped; the toy store. He has only revisited it once, when his wife passed away and left him to raise their daughter. He remembers standing there, in a vacant room, the boy, him, playing with toys. All the army men in a line, all the plastic animals behind fences. When he returned to the toy store, it was colder than he had remembered, and Torso was not there. He had told him once that as long as he visited, he would be there.

'Dad, we gotta go soon, okay?'

His daughter has his same nose and eyes. Her chin was her mother's and she walked a little like him. She knew of the Train and town he came from, but nothing else.

'Gus and Cassie should be here,' he says under his breath as salt water raised up from the waves in great big rushes of air.

'We tried to find them, didn't we, Dad?'

He wants to find them, wants to tell them he was going back, even though they promised to never, ever go back. His daughter's phone rings and she starts speaking loudly into it and walks back to the car. Boy waits until she has turned her back and he heads towards the stairs. Every step stings, and the plates in his back creak and shoot pain into his muscles. The fused discs nudge his nerve endings and the agony is excruciating, but living a life in pain, he has learnt to ignore it.

Standing on the pebbled beach, he starts to unbutton his shirt. It drops to the ground and he catches something in the corner of his eye, something under a rock. He picks it up and it is a faded, ripped hundred-dollar note. It still smells of drug chemicals. Tears fall from his eyes and he lets it go into the wind. It's carried out into the ocean and is swallowed.

'Don't go far, Dad!' he hears his daughter cry out.

He undoes his belt and slips it from his trousers, rolling it up like a coiled snake and drops it beside his shirt. His lets his pants fall to his ankles and slides his shoes and underwear off. The iron rails behind him start to vibrate and become aggressive. The waves splash unnecessarily harsh, spraying water against his naked frame. Pocked burn marks from cigarettes and spoons dot his body. He steps forward and places one foot in the ocean water. It's freezing, yet welcoming. He takes another step and continues until he is shoulder deep and his feet struggle to touch the sandy bottom. He thinks of the train and of Gus and Cassie. He thinks of Hope Valley one last time and lets the water raise over his head and he is gone.

Acknowledgements

This book is mainly about leaving your home town, because it wanted you out. So, thank you to Darwin. Also, thanks to my family, remember I did warn you about this book. Sabrina and Mel for putting up with my first draft edits. And all the readers who thought they would give this book a go.

For more information on Mitchell visit
www.ouroborusbooks.com

www.ingramcontent.com/pod-product-compliance
Lightning Source LLC
Chambersburg PA
CBHW030332120726
47901CB00007B/1768